To Johanna —
With very best
wishes.
Sincerely,
Ruth Brown Krueh

BROOKLYN
IN MY HEART

BROOKLYN
IN MY HEART

Ruth Broun Kruh

To order additional copies of this book, contact:
Xlibris Corporation
1-888-795-4274
www.Xlibris.com
Orders@Xlibris.com
15545

Dedication

For my husband, Irving, daughter, Valerie, son, Jeffrey and his wife, Stella, my sister, Dorothy and brother, Moe, with all my love.

In memory of my mother, Anna, father, Jack, sister, Sylvia and brother, Harry.

With respect, gratitude and affection to Dr. Carol Portlock

Dr. Kalmon Post

Dr. Melvin Klein

PRAISES

"Congratulations on your manuscript *Brooklyn In My Heart*. Your life story with its small and large achievements tells a very human tale of the struggle from childhood poverty to adulthood. Your descriptions of Brooklyn during this era are evocative and convey the social history of the borough within the context of major world events such as World War II. Again, congratulations on a fascinating and compelling life history."

Sincerely, Howard Golden, President of the Borough of Brooklyn

Take a walk down memory lane with Ruth Broun Kruh, pioneer music columnist, as she takes you from the tenements of Brooklyn to the glamour of Broadway. Ruth will lead you through the Big Band Era as she regales with encounters concerning the greats and ingrates of popular music through the 1930's and 1940's. This is a true story, backed up by her authentic diaries. "Brooklyn In My Heart" is based on observances and experiences devoted to life, love, ambition and the excitement of escaping from poverty into the beautiful world of music and its not so beautiful aspects.

Joe Franklin, Memory Lane

Radio Station WOR

PROLOGUE

It was on a weekday afternoon in 1939, during the "Big Band" era, when she walked into the Roseland Ballroom on an assignment from *Orchestra World* magazine. The place was totally empty, except that on the raised stage, which was also the dance platform, she saw a young man who was up there sweeping the floor.

She went close to the platform and looked up at him. He was about her age. She was twenty-one and he might have been just a couple of years older. She noticed that he wore a crumpled white shirt, sleeves rolled up, and black pants and that he was skinny. He came to the edge of the stage and bent down to ask if he could help her. She was aware of his blue eyes and was grateful that his expression was one of respect, not like some of the arrogant people she sometimes encountered.

"I'm Miss Blick from *Orchestra World* magazine and I'd like to speak with the orchestra's arranger." She showed him her card. "I want to write about him in my "Arranger's Spotlight" column.

"I sing with the band," he said.

"May I ask your name?" she inquired.

"Frank Sinatra," he replied. Then he yelled, "Hey Harry," and another young man, also about his age, skinny, wearing a crumpled white shirt, sleeves rolled up, and black pants, appeared from backstage.

"This is Miss Blick from *Orchestra World* magazine," Frank explained. "Do you have the phone number of your arranger? She writes for the magazine." Then he added, "Miss Blick, this is Harry James, our orchestra leader."

"Let's see," said Harry, and he pulled a small address book from his pants pocket and gave her the phone number.

She admired these two very polite and obliging young men. Although she had doubted her own credibility at first, she related to them and they inspired her. Where did she get the nerve to expect to be a famous songwriter? She was Rachel Blick, short for Blickstein, a poor girl from Brooklyn, trying to succeed in this almost impossible field. They're also working on their dreams with such odds against them, she thought. That's why they probably don't think I'm crazy.

She had a fierce desire to be a songwriter. She was better at conveying her emotions in words, especially words and music, than in speaking. It brought her tremendous release. It was as if she wanted the whole world to be inspired to find love and beauty, a world in which she could share and be happy, not like her present life.

She figured out that if she could write for this top-notch music magazine, she would be in a position to meet all the famous orchestra leaders, arrangers, vocalists and publishers. She would get them to hear her songs and perhaps she would get her big break. In the meantime, it would be wonderful to be exposed to the world of beautiful music and the artists whom she admired so much.

"You can do it, you can do it; you must," she told herself, when within a very short time; Frank Sinatra and Harry James became household names. It was unbelievable. They were appearing at the Paramount Theatre on Broadway. Long lines of people formed all around the block of the theatre. Everyone was talking about

"Frankie." Even Rachel's mother, who hardly went any place, said, "For Frankie, I'll stand in line," and she accompanied Rachel to hear him. Young girls were so thrilled and excited that they screamed when Frankie, the skinny, spunky kid, sang. He had a golden voice and an innocent sort of boyish charm that evoked loving and romantic responses from the audience.

Tears came into her eyes when young Frank Sinatra came out on the stage and started to sing. The audience went wild. "He made it!" her heart cried. She would never forget her encounter with him at the Roseland Ballroom that day when he was sweeping the floor. Now as she watched him perform at the Paramount, she knew he was a winner.

As for her, she had climbed step one. People were beginning to notice her as she met them at nightclubs, backstage at theaters, at publishing companies, rehearsal halls, and jam sessions and at their homes. She wrote gossip, personal interviews and about their future bookings. They began to give her advertising for the magazine for which she earned commission, with their greetings, especially during Christmas and New Year's.

Best of all, she was getting the "right" people in the music field to hear her songs.

Frank Sinatra

CHAPTER 1

The things her mother said, the wisdom she imparted, were irritating when she said them, but were to be indelible in Rachel's mind forever.

Anna Fluger repeated her past history to her children year after year. "When I was born, I was named Ashes. How I hated that name. Things were so bad at home and that name made me feel like Cinderella cleaning the ashes in the fireplace, dressed in rags. When I got older, I kept dreaming about my prince who would come and rescue me. Finally, when I was fifteen, I got enough courage to make it known that I was never to be called Ashes again and that was the end of it. From then on everyone called me Anna."

Anna reached young womanhood amidst chaos and deprivation. She didn't know where it was worse, at home or in the hat factory where she trimmed hats all day and yearned for the sunshine which never entered the windowless loft where she worked with about two dozen other young girls. Whereas some of the others seemed to take it in stride, her spirit yearned for something better.

"Do you know, I always dreamed of becoming an actress, but my dream was doomed. I had to work to get money to live on and besides, I didn't know what to do or where to go. I was too upset to follow my dream."

Anna Fluger had a kind of striking beauty. Her Alice-blue eyes contrasted with her rich brown hair which formed a widow's peak on her forehead and was draped softly about her face, pulled upwards in back and turned into a bun. At night when she took the hairpins out and her hair fell gracefully almost to her waist, she looked like a little princess. She was rather self-conscious about her height even though she was only five feet six inches tall.

Her mother and father, Jennie and Isaac Fluger, had bought a small shingled house in Jersey City where the six Fluger children were born and raised. It would haunt her forever to remember the screaming and cursing between her parents. There was no physical abuse, just a seething hatred which pervaded and rang out into the depths of her heart and soul.

The only heat in the house came from the black coal stove in the kitchen which was used for cooking and heating. You could warm up a bit in the kitchen, but the rest of the house was brutally cold in the winter. The children were bathed in the kitchen wash tub which was next to the stove. The lone toilet was in the cellar. As a child, Anna was terrified when she had to descend the rickety wooden steps and go down into the darkness and feel for the string which controlled the hanging light bulb. Then she had to walk past the two water-stained, stinking sheds which housed the pipes and other metal items that her father gathered as he drove his horse and wagon around town, clanging the bell and calling out in his coarse, asthma-stricken voice, "Metals, junk, metals, junk."

Isaac Fluger was an old man for his sixty-eight years. He was gaunt and pale, with sunken eyes, sparse gray hair and impoverished frame. He was terribly asthmatic. When he came home from his rounds, he went to his freezing upstairs room, locked the door and lay on a single brown metal bed with its striped, sheetless mattress and coughed his lungs out into a spittoon on the floor beside it.

"Good for nothing," her mother would call out, standing at the foot of the staircase. "Don't you care that your children need shoes?" Then the curses would fly. He would never defend himself and all Ashes heard from his room was his ghastly wheezing and coughing. She wanted to run up the stairs and comfort him, but she was afraid to take sides. She felt her mother was too harsh and that her father would have provided better if he were not that ill. What was life all about? What and where was happiness? Certainly not in this house. Perhaps when she grew up she would find out.

Ashes and her three sisters and two brothers somehow survived in what she felt was a house of horrors. They grew up sickly and nervous. There was usually a lack of good food and inadequate sleeping quarters, which resulted in sleepless nights. Two of the sisters died in their thirties, one during childbirth and the other of a heart attack. They had made terrible marriages and had endured unspeakable abuse from their husbands. One brother, Hymie, also had a heart condition. His marriage too was disastrous and ended in divorce after his wife started running around with other men. The other brother, Max, the taxi driver, was a bachelor. When he was in his fifties, he was found dead in the garage next to his taxi which he drove as far back as one could remember. It was said that either he suffered a heart attack or was the victim of a criminal of some sort.

The only one untouched by the past was Etta. She was staunch, assertive, and capable and possessed good health. She demanded respect and got it from her husband, Louis and their two sons and two daughters. There was peace and cooperation in their household. Louis and Etta together ruled the roost and the results were very good. Etta was a hard-working, determined woman, and Louis supported her in the raising of their children as well as other facets of their marriage. She had met Louis when she was sixteen and he was eighteen, and within months, they were married. She was glad to get out of the Fluger household.

Etta and Louis were somehow able to purchase a small farm in Freehold, New Jersey. They took in boarders. Etta was like a farm horse. She worked from morning to nightfall, cooking, baking, cleaning, servicing the boarders, milking the cows and never seemed to be weary.

Louis thought it would be a good idea to bring his cousin Jake over from Rumania and put him to work on the farm.

"Etta, Jake is here," Louis announced in his high, rather effeminate voice. "I'm glad you're here, Jake. We need you. Get the horses into the stable. It looks like rain. Then wash the dishes in the kitchen. Etta will show you what to do."

"Those boarders sure can eat," said Etta. "Are you ready?" "Sure," Jake answered simply and he followed her into the kitchen. The dishes were piled up in big stacks.

"Here's a big basin, some soap powder and a wash rag. Water is heating on the stove. Wash the dishes, then make sure you rinse off all the soap afterwards in a basin of cold water. Never mind about the horses. Tomorrow I'll take you to the horses and show you the barn. Right now it looks like rain so I'll go out and get the horses into the barn right away."

Jake took off his jacket, rolled up his sleeves and began to tackle the job of doing the dishes. He did what he had to do although he was by no means happy about it. He was just finishing up when Etta came back. She checked to see if he had washed and rinsed the dishes well. She was pleased.

"Are you hungry?" she asked. "I am," he replied.

She set some challah and a bowl of beef stew before him and he ate hungrily.

"Do you have a glass of tea?"

She brought him a glass of tea with a piece of lemon and a slice of sponge cake which she had baked that morning.

"We don't have much money, but at least you'll have a roof over your head and food in your mouth."

"What will I do for money?"

"We'll give you $10 a month for expenses," she said without a wince.

"Sure," said Jake. He finished the tea and cake and went outside. It was so peaceful out there in the early spring evening. He sat down on the ground near a small creek, watched the water trickle down the rocks and observed that it went on endlessly. "I don't want to end up like this creek," he thought. "I have to find a way out."

CHAPTER 2

Jake was a great help. Furthermore, the boarders loved him. He was kind, had a wonderful sense of humor and never complained about anything. He had been at the farm a few weeks when Etta and Louis took him aside.

"We're going to visit my mother in Jersey City," Etta said. "We'd like you to come with us."

"Sure," said Jake.

After they had attended to the daily chores the next day, they left. When they arrived, Etta's mother, Jennie, came to the door and let them in. Jake pitied her. She was old, parched and thin, like a dried up prune, he thought. They sat in the kitchen near the stove. Although it was early Spring, there was still a chill in the air and it was rather cold in the house. Etta kept glancing at the door.

"When is Anna coming home?" she finally asked.

Soon they heard a key turning in the door. It was Anna.

"Oh, hello," she said, surprised at the unexpected visitors. "How are you, Etta, and you, Lou?"

"We're fine," they said in unison.

Anna looked at Jake and he looked at her. She blushed.

"This is Jake," said Etta. "We sent for him in Rumania to help us at the farm. He wanted to come to this country. His mother is related to Tonta Hecht. They're sisters. She lives in Brooklyn."

"Glad to meet you," Jake said. He was very nice looking, especially when he smiled. It seemed apparent that he liked her at first sight.

They stayed awhile talking about the farm and then about Max being a bachelor and Hymie being divorced. Then they kissed each other goodbye and left after Etta remarked about how late it was getting.

On the way back to the farm, Etta asked Jake, "What do you think of Anna? You're seventeen and she is sixteen; not too young to get married."

"I think she's beautiful," Jake replied.

"Then we'll see," said Etta with resolve.

When Etta made her mind up about something, she usually found a way to see it through. She had told Louis about her feelings and that is why they went to Jersey City with Jake. He was crazy about Anna from the moment he saw her. With Etta's help, it didn't take long before he and Anna were engaged.

Anna liked Jake because of his kindness, his sense of humor and the fact that he was ambitious and hard working. He was also nice looking and clean cut. She was always self-conscious about her height, although she was only five feet, six inches tall. Jake was only an inch or two taller than she was and it bothered her that he was not taller. Also, he was European and she felt it would take some time to get used to his habits.

She needed someone badly and had to escape from the house, so she accepted his offer of marriage. He bought her a salmon colored satin dress covered with black lace and a small diamond ring as an engagement gift, which was all he could afford.

They were married and Anna joined Jake at the farm. She couldn't keep up with Etta as she was frail and sensitive. Helping take care of the boarders, milking the cows and other chores proved too much for her, especially as she soon became pregnant with her first child, Danny.

Anna and Jake's Engagement

Anna

CHAPTER 3

All was quiet on the farm. The horses and cows were in the barn. The boarders were sitting on the large wooden porch chatting with each other. Dinner was over and Jake and Anna were clearing the tables.

Etta and Louis motioned to Anna and Jake to follow them into the kitchen. Anna would soon be giving birth to her first born child, but she carried beautifully and was still slim and lovely.

"You'll probably be surprised when you hear this," said Etta. She looked at Louis knowingly. "We're selling the farm and going into the fur manufacturing business in New York City with Lou's two brothers."

Anna and Jake were visibly shocked, but somewhat glad. Maybe God was beginning to make other plans for them.

"You're going to learn how to be a furrier, Jake," she said, without consulting him. Luckily, he approved. "You're going to give me a job? Anna is going to have the baby soon. We'll need the money."

"I'm sure you'll be bettering yourself," Etta remarked.

Louis nodded in agreement. "My brothers are doing very well and want to cut me in on it."

Etta laughed. "I've had enough of this place, anyway. We're buying a small house on Sutter Avenue in East New York. You two can get an apartment near us."

The next number of weeks were very hectic ones. Etta and Louis finalized the selling of the farm, the purchasing of their new house and went through the ordeal of packing and moving. Anna and Jake found a modest apartment on Dumont Avenue near Pennsylvania Avenue, also in East New York. Shortly after, Anna gave birth to a beautiful baby boy whom she named Danny.

Louis and his brothers gave Jake a job in their factory. He worked for a pittance, doing menial jobs and making himself generally useful.

The three bosses, Louis and his two brothers, called on Jake all day. So did the other nailers, operators and cutters. The first week he felt like a nobody. He was asked to pick up nails and pins from the factory floor with a large magnet that looked like a horseshoe. He swept the floor, ran errands and did any other odd job they asked him to do. He felt the hairs which flew around from the furs, piling up inside his nose and throat until he could hardly stand it. But not until he left the factory would he cough or blow his nose much, lest they would think he couldn't take it.

There were nailers, operators and cutters, the latter being the highest paid and requiring the most skill. The large boards, which were set up on wooden legs, called horses, were their working tables.

While picking up nails which the nailers had dropped, Jake took a good look at what they were doing. He watched their hands, red from the dye of the skins, as they nailed the partially finished garments to the chalk outlines on the board. The operators sat at their machines, sewing at top speed. They sewed the skins with the fur side underneath. With their thumbs they pushed any protruding fur under and away from the skin side, which was on top, so that the fur would not get caught in the seams.

The cutters were the master craftsmen. After the designer gave them a pattern, which he had made out of strong wrapping paper, they cut the skins to fit the pattern as closely as possible. They cut the skins in a rotation series to produce a design and the operators sewed the pieces together. The pattern was then traced on the board with chalk and the skins were wet and stretched to eliminate any lumps and nailed as closely to the chalk marks as possible.

When he went home in the evening, Jake described all this to Anna.

"That's not all," he said. "The next day, after the skins are dry, the nails are taken out and the cutter lays these parts out on the board again. This time he starts cutting again and makes sure everything fits 100% exactly to the chalk outline. You should see it, Anna. It then goes to the finisher who puts in buckram."

Anna listened intently. "What's buckram?"

"It's a stiff material that they sew inside the garment to strengthen and stiffen it."

"And then what?"

"I forgot to say, that before the buckram, the operators sew an edging of tape all around the garment to hold its shape. After it is all taped out, the sleeves and collar are sewn in. Then the finisher sews in the buckram and an interlining and then the regular lining."

"How about buttons?"

"That's right. They put on loops and buttons."

"Sounds good, but what good does that do us?"

"You'll see, Dolly. I'm keeping my eyes open. Tomorrow I'm telling Louis I want to be a nailer. Next I'll be an operator. After that I'll be a cutter. They make the most money."

"I hope so," she said. Then she left the room and went in to diaper the baby.

Natalie in front of 592 Dumont Ave, Tenement
where she was born.

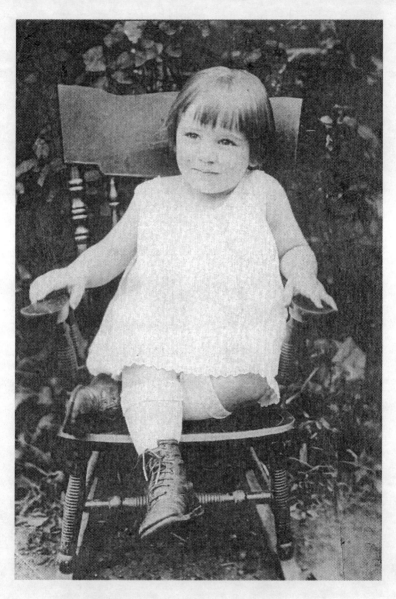

Natalie

Natalie and Debbie
In front of 592 Dumont Ave, Tenement where they were born.

CHAPTER 4

Jake got up very early and got to the factory before most of the other workers had arrived. When Louis came in, Jake approached him.

"Good morning, Louis. Can I talk to you for just a minute?"

"What can I do for you?"

"I've been watching the nailers and I know I can do what they're doing. Will you give me a chance?"

"I'll have to speak to my brothers," Louis answered. "After all, they're my partners. I'll let you know."

"Thanks, Louis. You won't be sorry. I can't be picking up nails all my life."

"I'll talk to them and let you know."

Right before the end of the day, Louis said, "Jake, it's a good idea. Tomorrow you can go to the table and nail up a coat."

That was only the beginning. In the next ten months, Jake had become a terrific operator and was on his way to becoming a skilled cutter. He was making a fairly decent salary now and just in time. A strange thing had happened to Anna. One day she experienced severe stomach pains. Not having much money, she went to the emergency room of the hospital, rather than to a private doctor. They refused to help her and she went to another hospital where, much to her surprise, they delivered a baby. She didn't know it, but she was pregnant. The doctors said this happened but only rarely. She named the baby Monroe. He was a healthy perfect specimen of a baby.

Two years later, Rachel was born. She was to be the eldest of three girls. When Rachel was six years old, Natalie was born, followed by Debbie three years after that. That made three girls and two boys. Debbie was the baby of the family.

Danny and Monroe in front of 592 Dumont Ave, Tenement where they were born.

Monroe and Danny in front of 592 Dumont Ave, Tenement
where they were born.

Danny and Monroe in front of 592 Dumont Ave, Tenement
where they were born.

1919
Clockwise: Anna, Danny, Monroe, Rachel in Anna's lap.

January 1926
Rachel—top row, 6th from left.

Natalie and Debbie, Liberty Ave. and
121 St., Richmond Hill, N.Y.

Danny

Right before Debbie was born, Jake had another plan.

"Anna, a worker can never get rich. I decided to try retailing this time. There's a store on Liberty Avenue in Richmond Hill. It's a beautiful neighborhood and the store is on a busy street."

"How will you pay the rent there? What will we live on until money comes in?"

"I figure I'll get a job in New York until things get started. It's hard to get a job as a cutter, but there are plenty of operator jobs around. Annie please help me. I'm doing this for you. While I'm working you'll have to take care of the store. I'll have to hire a finisher. She can help you too."

He pleaded and explained, "I hate schnorers who like to take from others. You'll see, we won't have to ask favors from anyone any more."

Jake found a way to get a loan, rent the store and had a grand opening. He had ink blotters printed up and got a boy to distribute them all over the neighborhood. On one side was blue blotting paper. The other side read: Canadian Fur Company, J. Blickstein, Prop. The rest of the wording included the address, telephone number and a description of merchandise and mentioned "expert repairs and custom made garments."

Anna and Mrs. Olsten, an elderly, refined woman, waited on the customers but had to hold them off on repair costs until Jake called them when he got back from work. He held his outside job as a fur operator and did all the work in the store and never complained.

Anna was miserable and exhausted. There was hardly money for clothes or other necessities and she toiled from morning to night.

There were two mannequins in the show window which she dressed every morning with the help of Mrs. Olsten. They opened the safe and took out two fur coats, one muskrat and the other seal, and put them on the mannequins. There were also two metal stands, one upon which they put a grey Persian Lamb jacket and draped it about the window's floor and likewise displayed a silver fox scarf upon the other. At night, the furs were taken out of the window and put back into the safe.

The family lived behind the store in one and a half rooms. There was a fairly large room, windowless, dark and damp, except for a small skylight. There was also a tiny bathroom which the customers used, as well as Mrs. Olsten and the family. If she had a moment to spare, Anna was always trying to disinfect the toilet. This main room had a three quarter size bed for Anna and Jake and they put up a partition with another three quarter size bed in which Rachel, Natalie and Debbie slept, or rather tossed about on each night. The mattress sagged and Natalie and Debbie slept on one side and Rachel on the other with her feet facing them since she was on the opposite side.

Beyond this room there was a little kitchen which had a door leading to the backyard. Danny and Monroe slept in the kitchen on a single size bed.

The yard was Rachel's haven. It had a grapevine which yielded purple grapes. The children loved to help Anna pluck the grapes each year. After the grapes were washed, the girls helped their mother put them into a huge barrel in the cellar. The wine was delicious and was used especially for Passover.

The little garden was like a magic island to Rachel. She loved the variety of flowers, lily of the valley, bleeding hearts, huge yellow sunflowers and others. She bought a package of radish seeds, planted them and was delighted when the radishes grew. She dug them out, washed them and sat in the sun eating them.

At the age of ten, Rachel's teacher, Miss Holland, announced that there was to be a city-wide poetry contest. Pupils from elementary to high school were invited to enter. Rachel was in class 5A at the time. The first half of the year was called "A" and the second half "B." As Rachel sat in her sanctuary, the backyard, she wrote:

Summer Time

Where the pinkest roses blow,
Where the sweetest blossoms grow,
Where the squirrels like to play,
That is where I like to stay;
Dancing in the golden sun,
Hopping, skipping,
Oh, what fun!

Little breezes here and there,
Coming from the summer air;
Little birds are flying round;
Grasshoppers hopping on the ground.
And the trees that God hath made
Give me shelter in the shade;
So that is where I like to stay,
Hop and skip the livelong day.

Rachel Blickstein, 5A1

The next day, Rachel handed the poem to Miss Holland to be entered in the poetry contest. It was the first poem she had ever written and she didn't think too much about it. She didn't even know if anyone would bother to give it a second thought. So what, it had taken her only a few minutes to write it.

CHAPTER 5

"Hands clasped," ordered the teacher, Miss Holland. Obediently, the children in her 5A class clasped their hands and placed them on their desks.

A student came in the door and handed Miss Holland a note which she quickly read. "Rachel," she called out, "you are to go to the Principal's office." Rachel was bewildered. You were usually sent to the Principal's office for discipline because of bad behavior.

She went to the Principal's office and was surprised to find her mother there talking to the Principal. Her mother had on a nice little hat and flowered dress. She always managed to look clean and pretty somehow. Rachel was so proud of her.

Why had her mother been called in? She was scared. What had she done? It couldn't be poor grades. She had excellent grades. But soon the Principal and her mother were smiling at her.

"Rachel, you've been awarded a silver medal for your poem, Summer Time," the principal beamed. It couldn't be possible. She was only ten years old, in fifth grade and the contest was open to students up to the twelfth grade. She accepted the medal which was engraved, "Poetry, 1928, Rachel Blickstein."

The poem appeared in the next issue of the school bulletin. Miss Holland urged Rachel to write more poetry, which was always published in the school bulletins. This was the beginning of her life-long desire to be a writer and poet.

One damp, windy March day, when Rachel was a studious, eager little girl of eleven, she sat down at her desk at school feeling a bit stiff at the knees. She felt even stiffer when she attempted to stand up. However, she didn't make too much of it and went home from school without so much as a word of it to her mother.

For the next three days, it was getting more and more painful to stand up from a seated position. She had to tell her mother. At the same time, Danny came home from school with the same symptoms. Anna was frantic. She had no money to call a doctor to the house, so she went to a doctor in the neighborhood, cried and pleaded with him to help her children. Luckily, he was kind and came to the house. It didn't take long for him to diagnose the illness as rheumatic fever.

The ravaging disease attacked knees, knuckles, ankles and finally the little bones at the back of the neck. All became swollen and inflamed. As instructed by the doctor, Anna kept these joints anointed with oil of wintergreen and wrapped in flannel. He also prescribed "sweating powders" which were salycilates. The slightest pressure, gentlest touch of even a sheet brushing against the affected joints, caused pain almost too sharp to endure. The danger involved was that rheumatic fever could cause damage to the heart. Anna tended to her children night and day and in a couple of months, the rheumatic fever subsided. By summer, Rachel and Danny were back to almost normal.

Anna appealed to her sister, Etta, for help. She explained that it was important that Danny got some good country air and nourishment for at least a couple of weeks as conditions behind the store would not be good for him in his recuperative state. He was old enough to go away by himself. She would do the best she could with Rachel.

Etta's house was beautiful. Louis and his brothers were doing very well and they had also moved to Richmond Hill. They bought three houses, one for each of them, on the same block. All of their children had the benefit of growing up with cousins, aunts and uncles surrounding them. They rode their bikes up and down the block. There was always an abundance of delicious food, including home baked cakes and happy holiday celebrations.

Etta and Louis were very active in the Synagogue, which they were instrumental in building, donating large sums of money on its behalf. Anna was very hurt that her sister was not more compassionate with regard to her hardships, especially that she was such a "socialite."

With a heavy heart, Anna went to her sister for help. Etta gave her a couple of dollars and said she would tell Louis to go over to Anna's house and "see what the Lodge would do." Jake belonged to that Lodge for years too, paying dues until he could no longer afford it.

That night, Louis came over with a group of men from the Lodge and said they would send Danny to a small hotel in the Catskills for two weeks. Anna and Jake were numb with humiliation, but had to bury their pride for Danny's sake. Danny, who was sixteen years old, was sent away for two weeks by himself. He sent cheerful postcards daily even though he was actually very lonely and unhappy.

The next year, again, in the month of March, Rachel, aged twelve, came down with rheumatic fever again. Anna nursed her back to health once more. However, the following March, just like clockwork, for the third year in a row, Rachel was stricken anew. This was evidently the month for coming down with this affliction. This time, however, it was very bad. Rachel's heart was badly involved and she was taken to the hospital in an ambulance.

As she was carried out on a stretcher, a small crowd of neighbors watched sadly. Since it was raining slightly, the ambulance attendant covered her face with a blanket. She heard the murmur of people, saw her mother crying and soon found herself in a ward in Kings County Hospital. March was "pneumonia month," people said. In her semi-conscious state, Rachel heard people coughing their lungs out and moaning all night all around her in the ward where they put her.

A few days later, they put her on a stretcher and wheeled her into a private room for two. Her mother had cried and begged and finally, with the good doctor's assistance, had managed to get her out of the ward. It was like night to day. The food trays were special and it was quiet. Sun streamed in from the window in back of her bed. In the other bed, there was an old woman who happened to be related to the director of the hospital. She received preferential treatment, fresh cherries for instance, which she grumpily put aside. Rachel asked her if she could have them and the woman nodded her head. The nurse brought them over to Rachel.

The nurses were very good to Rachel, for she was just a twelve year old little girl. The doctors came in clusters to study her case, drawing diagrams in ink around her heart to pinpoint where the trouble was.

For the next three months, Rachel was not permitted to even sit up on the side of the bed, no less to stand up or walk. She lay there, undaunted, reading, insisting that a tutor who was sent by the Board of Education, continue to come. There was a priest, Father Manning, who came every day, told her stories and sang songs to her. She loved his visits. In truth, she loved almost everyone, and trusted them.

A Swedish middle aged nurse with blonde hair would come into Rachel's room, pull her over to her side and change the sheet, one side at a time. She would wash Rachel, give her an alcohol rub and tell her all about wonderful books. There was so much strength in the innocence of childhood. Love and trust seemed to evoke love and trust from others. At night, a nurse came around with sleeping potions, small glasses on a tray. They didn't wait to see if she drank it, so Rachel spilled the contents under her bed. She knew enough not to want to be drugged.

Anna had to look after Debbie and Natalie, as well as manage the store and keep up with the cooking, cleaning and washing as well. She couldn't come to visit every day, but at night, after visiting hours, Jake would sneak around to the back court of the huge hospital and climb the fire escape to her second floor room. The night nurse never reported him. He would come in his own quiet way, always bringing a small paper bag containing some fruit, usually a couple of oranges or perhaps a peach and some cherries, which Anna would manage to get for her.

Oh how Rachel loved her father and his visits. One evening, Rachel felt very bad. The nurses and doctors ran down the corridor and into her room. She had a terrible feeling of weakness and her chest felt somewhat heavy. The worse thing was that she seemed to be sinking into a lethargy from which she could not come out of. She lay there half conscious, after the doctors and nurses had left. Just then, her father came with his cheerful voice and bag of fruit. She came out of her lethargic state.

The next morning, more nurses and doctors came into the room, this time carrying a huge tank-like jar of some sort. They sat her up on the side of the bed and inserted a long needle in her back. She noticed that the jar was filling up with fluid and heard the word, thoracenthesis. This procedure removed fluid from the lungs.

After that, Rachel's condition improved. Now it was June and her thirteenth birthday was June 30th. Her mother promised to take her home on her birthday. A few days before her birthday, a nurse appeared in her room with a wheelchair.

"You're going out on the terrace."

Rachel was filled with joy. She couldn't believe it. The nurse helped her sit up on the edge of the bed. Then the nurse asked her to stand up near the wheelchair. After having been so ill and in bed for three months, standing up took all the strength Rachel could summon. She felt she would pass out, but she had to do it. Then she was helped to get onto the wheelchair and was wheeled into the corridor and then on to a small terrace with a black wrought iron railing.

Rachel felt like she was coming alive again. The huge green trees, the blue sky with its small white clouds, and the birds singing, were unbelievable. She was in awe, as if she were close to God. She asked the nurse for a piece of paper and wrote a beautifully poem. It took her only a few minutes. That's how inspired she was. How wondrous, how precious and how taken for granted all this was, she thought.

On the morning of her daughter's thirteenth birthday, Anna kept her promise. She arrived fairly early and told Rachel they would have to go up to the hospital director's office to get his approval for her release. An attendant wheeled her up to his office in the wheelchair. The director was looking at Rachel's chart and she heard him tell her mother that it was inadvisable to take her home, that she would be an invalid for the rest of her life, not being able to work, to marry and certainly not to have children.

Her mother said, "But I promised her." Rachel gripped the arm of the wheelchair.

"Then you'll have to take her out on your own risk. Here, sign this release, but you're making a mistake."

Anna signed the paper.

CHAPTER 6

There was so much going on at home, which Rachel had known nothing about. For one thing, there was no more store. Anna had rented the ground floor of a frame house in Brooklyn because it had a porch where she could wheel Rachel out for fresh air and sunshine and to see people passing by.

Jake was in Cleveland. He was trying to sell furs for a manufacturer. There was hardly money for food, and Anna put Rachel out on the porch in Debbie's old stroller carriage, since she could not afford a wheelchair. She gave Rachel orange juice and an egg or cereal for breakfast, made chicken soup, even if she had money for only one quarter of a chicken. Rachel worried about her sisters and brothers and felt guilty about the food not being distributed evenly. But everyone insisted that she just work on getting well.

It was wonderful being out on the porch on sunny days. Friends and neighbors stopped by. She still got tutored, but after a few months was able to go back to school. She had kept up with her studies and hadn't fallen behind.

Jake kept promising to send money for the rent and food, but it was usually the same. The bell would ring, sometimes in the middle of the night, "Western Union for Mrs. Anna Blickstein." Anna and the children would jump out of bed and flock to the door, shocked from being woken out of their sleep and disappointed by the news. Anna would read the telegram. "Sorry, can't send money tonight. Will wire fifty dollars Wednesday, signed, Papa." But when Wednesday would come, the same thing happened and Jake would send another telegram with a false promise. The promises kept them alive, but the subsequent disappointments devastated them.

Rachel had to go to the grocery store and get some food. She would feel her face burning. "My father is working and we will get money in a few days and pay you. May I have a can of salmon, a bottle of milk, white bread, half a dozen eggs and a pound of potatoes, please?" Then she took the bag and ran out as if she were a thief, with the other customers staring after her. "Did you get it?" everyone asked nervously when she came back from the grocery. They were all starved and this was a feast for them.

Danny got a paper route and delivered groceries. He gave everything to his mother. Monroe was secretive, defiant and miserable. The stint in Cleveland failed and Jake, weary and exhausted, went to Chicago. His brother, Manny, had a flourishing retail fur business out there and Jake begged him to help him get started to open a store. Manny signed for a loan and secured merchandise on credit from people he purchased from. With Manny's help, Jake bought an old car and came home to take Monroe back with him as he needed someone to help him. Monroe was seventeen when he went to Chicago in the old car. Manny recommended a woman who would be a finisher. Jake taught Monroe how to be a furrier and both of them slept in the finisher's shabby, ill-kept apartment.

Danny, who was eighteen, stayed behind with Anna and the three girls. He became the substitute father. Anna cried on his shoulder in her wretchedness and he in turn was subjected to responsibilities far beyond his years. He was a wonderful young man, kind, thoughtful and caring. Despite being frail from his bout with rheumatic fever, he got a job as a sort of manager in a coal yard.

He had to leave the house at four a.m. to be there to open the coal yard. It was freezing there in the winter as he had to be outside a good deal to see that the trucks were loaded and dispatched.

Rachel was fourteen. She loved Danny dearly. He was never too busy to listen to her. When she won the poetry medal, he was thrilled and encouraged her to continue writing. He never wavered in his faith in her ability. He was slim and handsome, sensitive and refined. He cheerfully came home on Fridays when he got paid and gave Anna a box of chocolates and most of his salary, kissing her and patting her on the head.

When Jake advised the family to join him and Monroe in Chicago, Danny arranged everything. He found out that there was an excursion train going there which would cut the fare down drastically. He helped his mother pack their meager belongings, not much more than the clothes on their backs, and a few household items. There was no furniture worth moving.

The week before they were going to leave, Jake and Monroe came home unexpectedly. Something terrible had happened. The night before the grand opening of the store, some crooks had drilled a hole in the wall of the empty store next to theirs, had gotten in and cracked open the safes. The awful part of it was that the insurance policy had not come through yet. All was lost. Uncle Manny and his wife, Aunt Bella, who was a shrewd businesswoman and "captain of the ship" as far as her husband and children were concerned, engineered all the details of settling the catastrophe and thus another failed episode ended. Jake was back where he had started, nowhere. Monroe, being the strong one, suffered in silence.

Danny was gentle and understanding as usual, and Anna leaned heavily upon his support. Rachel was sustained by his interest and guidance. The two little girls were too young to comprehend.

Danny went back to work in the coal yard. Monroe became very bitter. He drove a cab, worked at numerous fur establishments when they could use him. The Chicago venture had affected him very badly. He became distant and angry. After all, he was only eighteen. The truth was that he could not bear to watch the suffering of the family. Once in a while he would slip his mother and the girls a few dollars. He loathed the turmoil and the poverty.

Sam Newhouse, who had a candy store down the block where their fur store had been in Richmond Hill, had always had his eye on Monroe who was an athletic, handsome young man. Sam got in touch with Monroe again when he was most vulnerable. Much to Anna's dismay, he arranged for Monroe to get into prize fighting.

Monroe and Danny concocted a small crystal set, which was one of the first radio transmitters. Rachel would sneak behind them and watch them working it. It did not operate on electricity. It was a very small piece of apparatus. There were wires attached and an earphone and it was grounded to a radiator.

"Here, listen," said Monroe as he handed the earphone to Rachel. She was excited being included in her brothers' experiment. Her eyes were wide with wonder as she put the earphone to her ear and heard a man's voice, followed by music. It was magic and unbelievable.

Danny smiled and Monroe said, "Now that's enough. And don't forget, never touch this thing." Rachel left the room in amazement. She went into the kitchen where Natalie and Debbie were watching their mother bake apple cake and cookies. Anna was bemoaning the fact that she had found out that Monroe would be in the ring that night and that the fight was being broadcast.

When everyone was asleep, Rachel smuggled the set out of the drawer where they kept it and listened in to the fight. She couldn't believe it. There was Monroe winning each round, fighting with all his might. She put the crystal set back after Monroe was proclaimed the winner and waited for him to come home, praying that he wouldn't be hurt.

The next day, Rachel looked in Monroe's room and discovered that his prize was a beautiful gold watch. Whenever she knew he would be fighting, she listened in. He always won and the next day there would be another gold watch.

Monroe loved taking part in school musicals, singing in his powerful baritone voice. He had always wanted to learn to play the saxophone. He pawned the watches he had won and bought a saxophone and started taking lessons, but he couldn't keep up with the expense, so he pawned the saxophone too. It was sad to see that he had not only lost his hard won watches, but his beloved saxophone as well. Worst of all was that his beautiful nose had been bashed in making him look like a real prize fighter.

Danny was the hero, never losing patience, loving and thoughtful, with everyone leaning on him for strength, especially Anna. It was as if he was the husband and father. Monroe became more distant. He hated the bare floors and poverty with a passion and began to hate Jake for his business escapades and Anna for her crying sessions. The turmoil and struggle for survival seemed to overwhelm Monroe, and he reacted with hostility. Once in a while he would slip Anna and the girls a few dollars.

Jake was undaunted. He had a good reputation in the fur market but jobs were scarce. He was a super speedy fur operator, but was miserable when he had to be a worker. He made constant promises to the family that one day he would pay them back for all their suffering.

"A worker can never get rich," he would say. He was going to make it big somehow. Then Anna and the family wouldn't have to struggle any more. Rachel would sit with him during the rare times that he was home and he would shake his head sadly when she related some inhumanity that befell her. "Low lives," he proclaimed. "Why don't they live and let live." Then he would try to cheer her up with a little story of some kind.

Jake couldn't stand Etta and Louis with their grandiose attitudes and condescending ways. To make it worse, Anna constantly compared him to Louis. "Louis fixes things and takes an interest in his house. Etta is lucky. Not like me. You're never around when I need you. Everything is on my head."

Anna would cry helplessly and Jake would try to hug her, but she drew away. "Dolly, let's go out for a ride. Maybe we can go out to a restaurant." Almost every Sunday it was like that. Anna would run to the bedroom, lie down and bury her head in her pillow and stay that way for hours.

"Please, Mama, why don't you go," Rachel pleaded, but to no avail. When Anna finally came out to the kitchen to serve supper, Jake said in anguish, "You'll see, Dolly. I'll make it up to you." Silently she served him something to eat. Days like these were torture to Rachel. If she grew up and got married, the man would have to be well off financially. But he would also have to be kind and peace-loving like her father, with his sense of humor, which he displayed so often despite his frustration.

Rachel was a young teenager now and subject to periods of day dreaming. She sometimes thought back to the past, when she was about six years old, how she ran after Danny and Monroe.

"Take me with you."

"Aw, go away. You're a girl." She would turn back in disappointment.

There was usually a group of kids near the stoop of their tenement house. Her mother would open their third floor window and throw down a piece of bread and butter in a paper bag. After eating it, Rachel would organize a game of "school." "Hands clasped," she said. She was always the teacher. The stoop was the class room.

After a while she changed the game. "Let's play grocery store." The children ran down the steps of the stoop with a clamor and went gleefully searching for small rocks to be sold as eggs and weeds to be sold as soup greens. They scrambled near the curb to fetch a few pieces of discarded newspaper which they used as wrapping paper for their purchases.

"I'll have two eggs," said a cute little girl, her long hanging curls gently rustling in the early summer breeze. "Two cents soup greens," said another. Tiny stones were used as money to pay for their purchases.

"I have to go up," said Rachel. She ran up the three flights of stairs. It was Friday and she would never forget the sight of her mother preparing for the Sabbath, or the scent of chicken soup, fresh baked apple cake, Mondel bread and the twisted Challah, just out of the oven.

When she came in, her mother was slicing the noodle dough. Chop, chop, chop went the knife remarkably fast. The kitchen floor had been washed and newspapers were spread out lest the children trampled on it before it was fully dry.

Anna's hair was still wet, wrapped in a towel and she had on a fresh housedress that she had washed by hand and starched and ironed. Glorious, glorious Sabbath; Rachel did not know all the connotations, but she knew she would always love and remember those Fridays and Saturdays.

She heard her mother praying, "Boruch A-Toh Ado-Noi, Blessed are You, God our Lord, King of the universe who has hallowed us through His commandments and has commanded us to kindle the lights of the holy Shabbos." Her head was covered with a scarf, and as she lit the candles, the warm glow made Rachel feel at peace.

Her brothers came in. "Danny, Monroe, wash your hands. I'm putting supper on the table. Rachel, wash your hands, too." The three children washed their hands, then scrambled in one by one and took seats at the table, nudging each other playfully.

"When's papa coming home?" asked Rachel.

"He's working late. I don't know." There was something defiant, yet sad about the woman. She seemed defeated, resigned to the facts, as she waited on the children.

One night there was a thunderstorm. Rachel ran into her parents' bedroom and into their bed and covered her face with the blanket. She trembled at the awesome flashes of lightning and the tremendous blasts of thunder which followed. Jake awoke and calmed her. "You mustn't be afraid. Cherries and plums will grow." Anna awoke too and said, "God is riding in his chariot. You mustn't be afraid of God."

"I'm not. I can't help it, I guess. It's scary."

Jake laughed gently. "Let me tell you a funny story." He soon had her giggling. Then he added, "Who do you love most, your mother or me?" She answered, "Both." He laughed and pretended not to understand. "A boat? You like a boat?" Being a child, she found this amusing. She returned to her bed and fell asleep before she knew it.

"Wake up," said Anna. She raised the window shade and the sunlight came in. "You have to get ready for school." This was to be her first day at school. Oh that day, wondrous of days. Her brothers ate their breakfast and left for school. She went with her mother who took her to the line, wished her good luck and waved to her as the line began to move. She felt lost, but didn't cry. She had to be brave.

CHAPTER 7

Rachel loved going to school. She was content being with her schoolmates and learning all sorts of things about people, the world, reading, writing and arithmetic. She eagerly took to this quest for knowledge.

First of all, it was an escape from the unhappiness at home. She excelled in all she attempted and her grades were always excellent. Her low self esteem was partially remedied by her teacher's praises. Also, as far back as she could remember, everyone complimented her on her talent for writing.

It began when she won the silver medal for poetry when she was only ten. Her poems appeared in almost all of the school bulletins after that. Everyone praised her work. She was thus given the attention she lacked at home.

However, Rachel was still ill at ease. She had missed some of the best years of growing up because of her recurring attacks of rheumatic fever. It seemed as if she had missed a good deal of her youth and was suddenly becoming a woman.

She knew she needed a bra, but not only was she embarrassed to speak of it to her mother, but she was afraid there might not be money to buy one. Secretly, she found an old piece of brocaded fabric in the house left over from something and she proceeded to make a bra. The material was rather thick, but it was just what she wanted. She hemmed it around and put hooks in the back, no straps, and made sure it was tight enough to take her in so that her budding breasts would not be obvious.

Rachel worked on the bra on and off for a few days, whenever no one was around, and felt relieved when she finally put it on and wore it. Now she felt more secure, hiding her blossoming womanhood.

Other girls wore sweaters and were more heavily endowed, but they seemed to flaunt it. They flirted with the boys in the class and hung out at the corners or at the ice cream parlor with them. Rachel felt like an outsider. She wondered if boys would ever look at her. Although she was slim, with pleasant features, flawless skin and a sweet smile, she never felt pretty. She hardly had any nice clothes to wear. They were mostly hand-me-downs and too large for her. Another thing, she hated her straight hair.

It was 1933, the year of the Chicago World's Fair. Jake was determined to try again in Chicago. His brother, Manny, and wife, Bella, were running a very successful retail fur business there. They had built up a wonderful reputation. Jake appealed to them for help in opening up a store in another part of Chicago, his own independent enterprise. He was not discouraged by the failure of the first try in Chicago because, after all, there had been the robbery and the place had closed before it opened.

Jake took Monroe to Chicago with him again and they worked night and day to get the place started. They slept behind the store on the fur boards. Monroe was now just nineteen, a time when he should have been enjoying himself with young people like himself. Jake and Monroe suffered in Chicago and back home in Brooklyn, Anna, Danny and the girls suffered too. The promises kept coming, but not the money.

After a few months, Jake advised Anna to come to Chicago with the rest of the family. He said he had deposits on purchases and repairs and that he would get an apartment and some furniture. Danny took over again. He found another excursion train and they left for Chicago.

Rachel loved the idea of this new adventure. She looked out of the window of the moving train and her imagination ran wild. In the dark of night, they passed different towns, farms and houses. She had never been outside of Brooklyn and Richmond Hill and sometimes, Jersey City to visit her grandmother.

The chug, chug of the train soothed her. She wondered who lived in those houses and on those farms and what lives they led. Some day, she promised herself, she would meet lots of people and write about them.

A phiz-like noise startled her. The lights had blown out for some unknown reason and remained off for the rest of the night. It was more conducive to sleeping, but she was too excited to sleep. Dawn came, the afternoon passed and just before sunset, the conductor shouted, "All aboard, Chicago." They all scrambled off the train.

Jake and Monroe were waiting on the platform. Jake had some bad news. The customers had not taken their garments out so he could not rent an apartment or get furniture. They were to go to the finisher's apartment in the meanwhile. It was devastating. Monroe looked like he would die. Danny, as usual, tried to calm everyone and Anna was in shock.

The finisher's place was filthy. She was a widow with a teenage daughter, a heavy set friendly girl who had some kind of foul body odor which made it obnoxious to be near her. To make matters worse, the accommodations were an old bedspring, covered with some old blankets and a sheet, which was to be their sleeping quarters. It was on the floor in a corner of the living room. This was for Anna and the girls. Danny, Monroe and Jake slept behind the store on the fur boards.

Nights were the most miserable of all. It was unbearable trying to get some sleep, cramped together on the bedspring. For the rest of his life, Monroe bitterly referred to this as our "Spring Outfit."

No wonder that after two weeks of this, Natalie and Debbie became very ill, running high fevers. Anna had done the best she could. The sheet and pillow cases smelled horribly and the day after their arrival, she had washed them out by hand and put up a makeshift clothesline and hung them up to dry. Evidently the finisher had not changed the bedclothes, which apparently had been used before, maybe by the daughter with the body odor.

Anna, as she frequently had done before, pawned her tiny diamond engagement ring to get money to call a doctor and get some medicine. The girls had come down with scarlet fever. Natalie was ten and Debbie was seven. They finally recovered and went back to school where they had registered when they first got to Chicago.

Rachel had lost her high school transcript, probably on the train. She told the admissions people at Hyde Park High School that she had studied French for two years and they placed her in third year French. What they failed to derive was that she had studied that French in Junior High School, which was not nearly as advanced as High School French. She loved studying and got the highest grades, so she thought she could master it. Her first day in class was a tense one. She didn't know what was going on. It was lucky that she met Lucille Friend that week.

Lucille lived at a residence club for girls, The Beatrice House. She was twenty-one and had no parents or family. She and Rachel became very close friends. The residence provided sitting rooms where the residents could entertain their friends. Rachel felt so grown up when she went there. She imagined what being on her own would be.

Lucille was rather homely, with acne skin, but she was caring and sincere. She coached Rachel in her French studies and brought her through the crisis of catching up with the class.

After two months of agony, the family finally moved into an apartment on Drexel Boulevard. It was a big, six room "railroad flat," that is, the rooms went in one long direction. The two front rooms were extremely cold, since it was winter and there was insufficient heat to heat the whole apartment. The last and largest room, which faced the front of the building was devoid of any furniture and was closed off by sliding doors. Rachel loved to go in there since it was so quiet and private. It had a fireplace which was never used, but it fascinated her somehow as she had never seen a fireplace. It was also a good hiding place for her diary which she kept in it.

When she looked out the front window of this room, she faced the campus of the University of Chicago. She watched the students walking with their books in their arms and wished that someday she would go to college and live on such a campus. She would major in Journalism and become a great writer and be rich and famous.

One day, Anna took the girls to the World's Fair. It was unbelievable. They saw Sally Rand, who appeared on a stage with two huge white swan-like fans. She skillfully manipulated these fans in a sort of strip-tease act, all in a magical setting of blue lights and romantic music, while she danced gracefully, weaving her fans about her. Then there was the Belgium Village with cobblestones, houses and all, just like in Belgium. There was so much more, but these were to remain in Rachel's memory of the 1933 World's Fair.

The best part of this Chicago episode was going to Aunt Bella and Uncle Manny's house. Rachel loved being with her cousins, Fern and Edith, who were close to her age, and their little brother, Harry. Aunt Bella and Uncle Manny were always busy at their store, and Rachel spent a good deal of time at their house.

It was beautiful, the baby grand piano, the white bear rug in the upstairs bedroom, the paintings, furniture, the wonderful large and bright kitchen. Then there was the phonograph and great records. Fern and Edith would put on the records and teach Rachel how to dance. There was the lilting tango, "Orchids Fade in the Moonlight," which she would never forget. They took their shoes off and danced their hearts out on the plush living room carpet, taking turns with each other.

Fern and Edith had to practice their violins each day for they performed at the World's Fair. Aunt Bella sewed lovely costumes for them to wear at their performances. There was a scrap book with newspaper clippings about the "Blick Sisters." Little Harry would sit quietly in a corner and watch them dance. He was hardly noticed.

When Aunt Bella came home from the store in the late afternoon, she always made her three children go to their rooms, lock their doors, do their homework and study. If the Queen of Sheba was there, she would have bade her leave. Nothing must disturb her children's studies. They did not resent this, but took it as a matter of course, kissed cousin Rachel goodbye and went to their rooms. Aunt Bella was so organized, so efficient. She was very nice to Rachel, but knew what she wanted for her family and herself. She was to be admired for her achievements.

How exciting it was when Fern and Edith asked Rachel to accompany them to a party. She had never danced with a boy, nor had she gone to a party in a beautiful home with happy young people. When she arrived, she was extremely flustered. What if a boy asked her to dance?

Rachel had barely arrived when a young fellow approached her.

"I'm Jack Wasserman. Would you like to dance?"

They started to dance and she felt herself trembling and her hands began to perspire. How embarrassing! He must have thought she was a nervous wreck. They finished the dance and she ran to a corner of the room without even looking back. Her very first dance and she had botched it. She hated herself. The only good thing that came of it was that she was amazed to feel for once, that she was not an ugly duckling. Jack was a handsome, tall young man and his arm around her waist and his hand holding hers was breathtaking. If he had singled her out, she might be more desirable than she thought. The next time she would be prepared.

CHAPTER 8

The World's Fair, otherwise known as the "Century of Progress Exposition," was closing. Despite the fact that it opened when the United States was in the midst of a severe depression, it was an outstanding financial success. It was built on a strip of land about six miles long and six hundred feet wide along Lake Michigan. More than a fifth of the area was devoted to lagoons. There were incomparable exhibits of science and industry as well as varied recreational and entertainment offerings.

Fern and Edith were going to attend a farewell party given for the group of entertainers they had been performing with. It was held backstage and Rachel was thrilled and excited because her cousins had invited her to go with them. She was given a glass of champagne and since she had never tasted anything in the way of liquor, she cautiously took a little sip and was surprised to find it tasted like ginger ale. Everything was wondrous to her. It was as if she had been isolated away from the world and was seeing life for the first time. She would be grateful to cousins Edith and Fern forever for having included her.

Rachel excelled in her classes and was noticed for her contributions to the school newspaper. Her classmates applauded her poetry as did her teachers. Out there in the Midwest, they rolled their R's. They found her New York accent cute. Innumerable times her classmates beseeched the teacher: "Tell her to say New York," and when she complied and said, "New Yawk," they laughed and clapped their hands and stamped their feet.

Rachel made many friends and formed a sorority with five girls. They had lots of parties and there were plenty of boys. She became an excellent dancer and was always popular. The girls were inseparable. They saw each other almost daily, attending movies together, eating at each others homes and playing Bridge together. Some of the girls had brothers who joined in. They danced with Rachel and walked or drove her home.

Just as she was beginning to like the way it was, Jake and Monroe announced that the business was failing and they should go back to New York. They had spent a year and a half in Chicago. Aunt Bella, Uncle Manny, Fern, Edith and Harry as well as all five girlfriends, saw them off. It was February, 1935.

Rachel wrote in her diary: Anne Bernstein, Adeline Berger, Janet Frank, Doris Stern and Lucille Friend came over to say goodbye. Besides, Uncle Manny, Aunt Bella, cousins Fern, Edith and Harry, they took us to the station. We went in Uncle Manny's and our car. Uncle Manny and aunt Bella brought us a big heart box of candy. Monroe and Papa remained in Chicago and would leave in a few days by car. They would attend to all the packing and shipping.

The train left for New York at ten p.m. Thanks to Danny, they had a pretty good night. He had learned from a man how to make a bed out of two seats and Natalie, Debbie and Rachel slept on it. Anna and Danny sat up on the seat in back of them. At seven a.m. the next day, they were still riding. Soon, however, they reached New York and with Danny at the helm, they left the train to embark on their next who knows what.

CHAPTER 9

When they left the train, it was nighttime. Through the last final hours of the trip, Rachel had watched the transformation of day to night. She saw the twilight softly descending as streaks of crimson faded into the sky at the ending of the day. It was awesome watching this with her face pressed against the window of the moving train.

"All aboard, New York," called the conductor. Rachel felt her heart beating fast as she followed her mother, Danny, Natalie and Debbie down the train steps and onto the platform.

"We're going to Grandma Jennie's house in Jersey City," Danny announced, even though he knew they were well aware of it. There was nowhere else to go. They had no choice.

They approached the old Fluger house. The little grey house with its shabby porch was still there and as they went in, Anna's heart sank. This was the place she had escaped from and now she was going back there. Please make it a short stay, God, she prayed.

Grandma Fluger looked awful. She was wrinkled and parched, in her eighties and suffering from diabetes. It was freezing in the house. Uncles Max and Hymie were working, Max driving his cab and Hymie driving his bus. Anna and the girls slept in one bed downstairs and Danny slept with grandpa. It was February and the temperature was seven degrees. The coal stove in the kitchen gave out a little heat, but not to the other rooms. The most bitter cold place in the house was upstairs. Grandpa and

Danny slept there. Grandma Jennie had a tiny bedroom downstairs the size of a small closet.

Somewhere in the middle of the night, Uncle Hymie came home and joined Danny and grandpa in the upstairs bedroom since Anna and the girls had taken over his bed in the living room. Poor Danny, always concerned, ran up and down a good deal of the night trying to find covers for Anna and the girls. Uncle Max, who shared the same bed with Hymie, slept in the kitchen on the floor on a blanket. Towards morning, Danny couldn't take it any more and he sat on a chair near the coal stove in the kitchen until everyone had gotten up.

After a horrible night, Rachel and Natalie went to the movies. They saw a double feature, "The Barretts of Wimpole Street," with Norma Shearer and "The Lemon Drop Kid," with Lee Tracy. Rachel loved going to the movies. She drank it all in and vowed she would some day write a good movie script.

When they returned to the house, they found that Jake had sent ten dollars and Annie was making liver and potatoes for dinner. She also informed them that they were going to Aunt Etta's the next day and would ask her if they could stay there for a while.

The world of the Freeman's was a different world. It was warm, secure and comfortable. Everything was orderly. Bedtime was eight-thirty and everyone was in bed and lights were out. Etta was an unbelievable housekeeper and cook. Each of her four children had their own room. They and the rest of the Freeman cousins down the block participated in functions of the Shul and other activities and were constantly sharing enjoyable occasions. Since Etta's children were about the same age as Anna's, they fit in. It was wonderful, except that they felt like intruders. After all, they were without a home of their own. This had to be very temporary, especially since Etta and Louis weren't too thrilled with the situation.

Rachel was enthralled with the player piano which was locked with a key. She had discovered the hiding place of the key. She found it accidentally under a vase on top of the piano and asked Aunt Etta if she could play it. At first Etta gave permission, but since she didn't like anyone in the living room except on special occasions, she said no to subsequent requests.

The player piano was sheer magic to Rachel. If you put a music roll in and pushed a lever, the notes bobbed up and down, emitting clear and beautiful music, just as if someone were there playing at the keyboard.

"Some day I'm going to play the piano," Rachel told Danny. "And I'm going to have a piano of my own and maybe even write some songs."

"You can do anything if you make your mind up to it. Never give up your dreams," he encouraged her.

"Do you remember when we lived in Richmond Hill, how I walked a mile each way to take piano lessons? Mama gave me fifty cents for a lesson and I didn't have a piano to practice on, so I went to Sarah Kleinman's house and practiced every day. Then when it started getting cold and snowing I couldn't walk so far every time to practice at Sarah's house or even to walk to the piano teacher's house, so I had to stop taking lessons. It was right before I got rheumatic fever."

"I remember. Some day you'll do it."

"I'm so glad you're my brother, Danny."

"You're a good kid, Rachel. I remember things too. When we lived in Richmond Hill you used to go into Sam Newhouse's candy store and help him behind the counter and he let you fill up a small bag of candy and you always saved some for me."

"Remember the penny Hershey bars? And the tiny silver dish with a tiny spoon. It had a pink and white candy in it that looked like cake icing. And the small tootsie Rolls, small boxes of licorices and the tiny candy dots on a long thin strip of paper? Each item cost one cent."

"Boy do I remember. Do you remember the 'picks'? You bought a penny piece of chocolate covered candy and bit into it. If it was pink you won a little something. Then there was the tar baby lolly pops. You saved the wrappers and if you had the most wrappers on a certain date you won a giant tar baby lollipop. You and Armand Baum were so close and he won."

"You have some memory, Danny. So have I. I'll always remember those days."

Then she said fearfully, "What are we going to do? We can't stay at Etta's too long. I can see she wouldn't have it."

"Don't worry. We'll figure something out."

CHAPTER 10

Grandma Fluger practically lived on anything that had sugar in it. She kept eating sugar coated raisin cinnamon buns, put sugar on her bread and on almost anything. She had a terrible craving for sugar.

"Mama, you'd better stop eating so much sugar," Anna warned her mother. She stubbornly kept on doing so. In a way, she was a pitiful character. She offered everyone the buns or other sweets she had in the house. She gladly shared her meager home with everyone. In the summer she tended her flowers in the back yard and gave them out to whoever visited her.

Grandpa Fluger was truly pathetic. He hobbled down once in a while like a frightened deer. Who knows what he ate. Who know shat he thought. A dog lived better than he did.

"Get your grandchildren some shoes," Jennie screamed and he would come down and take them to the shoe store down the street and buy them shoes. Rachel felt the guilt creep up on her as she went to the shoe store with the old, sick man, never a conversation, just the constant coughing. That was what she would remember of her grandparents.

When the family arrived in New York from Chicago, they stayed in the old Fluger house for a few days. Then Danny took Rachel and Natalie to Aunt Etta's. He then returned to join his mother and little Debbie who were left there.

It was still February, brutally freezing in the house and Annie feared for Debbie and Danny's health. "We'd better go to Etta's," she said to Danny. "I hate to come to her for anything, but what can I do right now?" So they went.

The next day, at Etta's house, Anna received a call from Jake and Monroe who were at Grandma Fluger's house in New Jersey. They had just arrived there after much difficulty. Their car license had expired and Monroe had to leave Jake in Pennsylvania in a hotel and go to New York by bus for a new license and then go back there to get him. They had to pay for the hotel, the license and a fine. The money was supposed to be for rent. They were going to sleep at Grandma's and come to Etta's tomorrow.

Jake and Monroe had a bitter argument with Anna when they arrived at Etta's the next day because of the way things were and they left the house. They were away for most of the day. When they came back, Jake said he had prospects for a job which would start the following week. Rachel took this all in. She locked herself in the bathroom and cried.

It was Friday and Anna washed the floors and did all she could around the house. Etta did the cooking. Essie, Etta and Lou's married daughter, came for dinner every Friday night with her husband, Sidney. He was a slim, quiet fellow with glasses, an accountant, and they were very happy together. Etta and Lou also had two sons and another daughter, Doris. Cousin Doris was closest to Rachel's age. She was not popular with boys, perhaps because she was prim and plain and studied all the time. She was generous with understanding but very stingy with money. Rachel marveled at the way she kept everything so neat and orderly. Of course she had her own room. That helped. But the drawers and closets were unbelievably organized.

"The Shul is giving a dance," said Doris. "Rachel, you'll go with me. I know you'll have a good time." Rachel looked forward to going, but at the last minute, Etta talked her out of it. Admission was seventy-five cents and on second thought, they had changed their mind about treating her. Rachel had wanted to go very badly and felt hurt and disappointed.

She was so blue when Doris left without her. The doorbell rang. It was Marty, one of the Freeman cousins who lived down the block. He came in every day and Rachel felt that she was the reason. She was right, for he remarked how pretty she was and asked her if she would go to the movies with him soon. They played cards and talked and she felt better.

CHAPTER 11

It was impossible to stay at Etta's much longer. It was only two weeks since they had arrived there and Etta was beginning to show her annoyance. Anna could sense it and in order to keep peace, she washed the kitchen and bathroom floors on her knees to satisfy Etta, since Etta was so meticulous. They were beginning to argue because Anna felt her sister should have been more compassionate and generous.

There was nothing to do but to return to Grandma Fluger's house in Jersey City, but Monroe took the fur machine which Jake had stored and sold it. Then he made Anna and Danny go with him to look for rooms. Etta was against it.

"Why don't you go to Jersey and save the money?" she insisted.

The thought of staying in that dismal, freezing house, filled Rachel with horror. Marty came in a few times during the day as he wanted her to go to the movies with him. She said she couldn't as she didn't know whether or not they were going to New Jersey. It was a consolation knowing someone thought she was pretty and wanted to be with her.

In a couple of days, they had found an apartment and moved in immediately. It was on Barbey Street near New Lots Avenue in East New York. Before they left for Chicago, they had put their old kitchen set with its four scratched chairs down in Etta's cellar and Etta gave them an old spring and mattress which she had down there too. Monroe and Danny got the kitchen set, spring and mattress to the new apartment. The spring, covered with some old clothes and thin blankets, served as a bed for Jake, Danny and Monroe. It was placed in one bedroom. The mattress was placed on the floor in the other bedroom for Annie, Rachel, Natalie and Debbie. Mama hung half curtains on the kitchen window as she didn't want neighbors to look in.

The living room was empty except for some bags and boxes with clothes in them on the floor. Danny and Monroe had gone to Namm's Department store and given a twelve dollar deposit on some furniture, but the deposit was returned. When they got the twelve dollars back, they used two dollars for carfare and food. They went to Jake's brother, Joe and he took them to a friend of his who had a furniture store. Joe signed for them and they gave the remaining ten dollars as a deposit on two beds which would be delivered in two days. It was the only thing to do because if Namm's refused to give them credit, the other department stores would probably do the same.

Rachel decided to register at Thomas Jefferson High School. Tonta Hecht lived opposite the school. Rachel had been to the ground breaking ceremony when she was about six years old. She had often gone to the Hecht's apartment, which was near the site of Thomas Jefferson and watched them build it little by little. Then she would go up and Tonta Hecht would give her a big glass of milk and a whole box of chocolate Mallomars.

Her three grown sons were still in bed if she went up on a Sunday morning. They joked around with her and treated her as if she were a little rag doll, tossing her up and down on their knees. Uncle Hecht always sat in a big easy chair and never spoke, but she knew he liked it when she was there. He referred to her as Rachie and smiled. It was so wonderful and safe up there. One of the boys became a very successful lawyer, dignified and intelligent. The other became a judge and the third a surgeon.

Thomas Jefferson High School was a magnificent place in 1935. The principal, Elias Lieberman, was an inspiration. He spoke at the Assemblies, encouraging the students to study and aim high. He was also a poet and had a book of poetry published. Rachel's poems were published in the school bulletin and Dr. Lieberman called her to his office and complimented and encouraged her. That was the kind of man she would marry one day. She idolized him.

Many times, after school, Rachel would go up to Tonta Hecht's house and Tonta Hecht would bring out the milk and Mallomars.

"Well, how do you like school?" asked Tonta Hecht.

"Very much."

"Did you make friends yet?"

"I met some nice girls. We're starting a club."

"Do you go with boys?"

"I'm too busy studying."

She didn't tell the whole story, how the boys in her classes flirted with her. How she tried to act disinterested and how this only made them flirt more. How she vowed that no one would kiss her until she felt she loved him and he loved her. Certainly there would be no "petting" until the one and only came along and married her. He would be rich and famous and brilliant. She would be the love of his life.

There were eight girls who finally formed the "Merry Girls" Sorority. They met in each other's homes once a week. They made dates for each other, had parties and were together a great deal, either all or individually. They shared their thoughts and aspirations. They were all sixteen. They all had sweet sixteen parties, except Rachel. First of all she was ashamed to have anyone come into her house. Anna kept the place spotless, but it was so poor and empty of furniture and such. Then too, there was hardly money for food. If not for Tonta Hecht, they would have starved.

For instance, Rachel wrote in her diary: Friday, March 15, 1935:

> "Letter came from Adeline in Chicago today . . . the two beds came . . . Heard Monroe got driver's job at the furniture store . . . We were broke today except for a few cents so I had a plain roll with butter to take for lunch and I got fifteen cents for carfare and five cents for milk and darn it, I forgot the roll. So that left me with five cents lunch hour. Fannie lent me five cents so I bought lunch for the ten cents and Fannie gave me a cake (Hoomintosh) that she'd brought for me. Went to Tonta Hecht right from school. Her daughter-in-law gave me a skirt (blue) and blouse. When I got home the beds were here, thank God. P.S. Tonta Hecht gave me milk and Mallomars.

Tuesday, March 19, 1935:

> Received a long letter from Ann Bernstein in Chicago today. Today was "Purim" so Tonta Hecht and Esther, her daughter-in-law, came over with a lot of cakes and chollies (twists). That was swell of them. It was raining all day do I didn't walk home from school. In my English class, some boys (especially one) kept yelling to me all period and

flirting. Also, boy in back of me in Biology class;
I'm beginning to dislike him.

Saturday, March 23, 1935:

Mama, Natalie, Debbie and I went to Tonta
Hecht's. We made a long visit of it. We had a bite
for lunch there and also they made us stay to eat
supper and Louis Hecht and his wife, Esther, drove
us home. They're very nice.

Wednesday, March 27, 1935:

Since I'm excused from taking gym (they let us
rest on a mat instead of doing gym), Miss Williams
(from P.T.) told me if I don't go to a doctor or
clinic and get a slip signed, she will have me
expelled from school . . . there was seventy-five
cents to our name and I needed one dollar at least,
so Papa went with me to Dr. Epstein in the
neighborhood and asked him to trust us. He was
a perfect stranger and refused to give me the
examination. Boy was I sad. Danny went with me
to Kings County Hospital as we still had the
seventy-five cents. Boy are they terrible, those free
places. You suffer plenty. I was shoved around from
nine a.m. to four p.m., waiting on lines, going
through red tape, etc., all for the lousy signature.
And after all that trouble, they didn't want to sign
the note and I had to put up a fight to make them
do it.

Sunday, March 31, 1935:

> Things have really become terrible. We have not
> even one cent in our family. There was nothing to
> eat, so Mama went to Mrs. Kleidman in the
> afternoon and she gave her some potatoes, split
> peas, jar of jelly and lent her one dollar so she
> bought some meat. At night, Mama took Natalie
> and Debbie to Tonta Hecht's. She gave them some
> supper and some bread, cake, a half box of
> Wheatena and some split peas (Look what we've
> come to).

Tuesday, April 2, 1935:

> Still flat broke. Don't eat all day lately and then
> they (our three men) bring home some change,
> let's say one dollar, two dollars, three dollars or
> even fifty cents, and we get something to eat. Then
> the next day it's the same thing all over again.

There was barely enough money to buy bread, butter and milk
each day. Also, fights, fights, fights! Annie fought terribly with
Jake, Monroe and even Danny. Annie cried and cried and told
the girls to "notice everything that goes on and to remember it so
that if anything happens to me, you should tell people it's your
father's fault and also your brothers'."

It was pathetic. Annie never had any recreation and hardly
anything to eat and was left with the kids to take care of
without money. If there was anything to eat, she gave it to
the children, even if she had nothing for herself. She fine-
combed and cut their hair, washed and ironed their clothes,
got them off to school, signed their report cards with pride
and watched over them as much as possible.

"You trust everyone," she warned Rachel. "They'd steal the whites of your eyes if they could. You'll get wise some day."

Rachel's passivity made her a sitting duck for abuse. Her mother took her frustrations out on her. Once in a miserable fit, she pulled Rachel's hair so hard that she dragged her down to the floor, leaving Rachel degraded and lost, not knowing the real reason for this attack.

Natalie was Anna's favorite for she would fight back and thereby get respect. She was down to earth, didn't mince words and made sense. Besides, she always had a certain "class." She was a natural beauty, with blond hair and beautiful large, expressive green eyes. Everyone loved being with her and leaned on her for support. She was cheerful and confident. As she grew up, she had a way of dressing things up, with a scarf, a cheap trinket or perhaps a hint of perfume and a twist of her hair. No doubt about it, she had class.

Debbie was the baby, the little blue-eyed, black-haired doll, sweet and unspoiled nevertheless.

Rachel was the eldest of the girls. She was the serious one, with her books, her poetry and her music. She was not as concerned with external things as Natalie was. She did the best she could with her straight hair and over-sized, hand-me-down clothes. It was inevitable that she was easily hurt by the selfish and inconsiderate acts of thoughtless people.

Monroe took advantage of Rachel's good nature by criticizing her appearance, especially her most vulnerable spot, her straight hair. The only one who understood her was Danny. He took an interest in her and encouraged her in her endeavors. How lucky his wife would be, she thought. He was beautiful, both on the inside and outside, dependable and caring.

Another year went by, filled with the same agony: hunger, fights and frustration. Rachel was so proud of Natalie. She remembered that when Natalie was six years old, the kids were dancing in the street and a woman came over and admired how graceful she was. Rachel, the big sister, was eleven and was watching her little sister.

"I'm her sister," she remarked to the woman.

"I represent a dancing school. Your sister is talented and I'm looking for talent. We can give her dancing lessons and it won't cost your family anything. Can I talk to you mother?"

Rachel ran upstairs and excitedly told her mother, who came downstairs to talk with the woman.

"You won't be sorry. She's beautiful and talented and we will sponsor her."

"No, thanks," said Anna. "I have better things in mind for her."

Now Rachel was seventeen and Natalie twelve. Things were happening fast. For one thing, Rachel was very busy between studying and her social life. She loved her family dearly, but was distracted from them to a certain extent.

Rachel began to be aware of the fact that boys were attracted to her, even though she felt inferior about her looks. They remarked about her beautiful skin, her vivaciousness and her dancing. Sometimes at parties, every fellow in the place asked her to dance. She was lithe and slim, weighing only ninety-six pounds for her five foot three and a half frame. When she danced, she responded to the music wholeheartedly. She was a perfect partner, following almost anyone.

Once, the "Merry Girls" went to a dance at the Roseland Ballroom. A real "sheik" asked her to enter the tango contest as his partner. She was so thrilled when one by one the couples were pulled out of the contest. She and her partner won.

It was amazing how naïve she was about sex. She liked the attention the fellows gave her, but regarded them as brothers. If they tried or suggested anything personal, like kissing or petting, she shrugged it off gracefully. Strangely, they liked being with her, chatting, dancing and otherwise enjoying themselves.

Once she went to a party. It was New Years Eve. When she got there, everyone was lying all over the place, having drunk too much. A very handsome guy, who looked like the fast type, took up with her.

"Let's have some fun," he said. He looked like a movie star.

"Sure," she smiled, flattered that such a fellow would want to spend time with her.

He pulled her down to a couch and sat down next to her and ruffled her hair. "You have such soft, beautiful hair," he remarked, "and your skin is unbelievable."

"Thank you," she said.

Rachel had met fellows like that, real gigolos who probably looked for gorgeous girls, not like her. If she rebuked him, he might laugh at her and just go away and find someone more to his liking.

"Look at this place," she said. "Nobody's having a good time. They're too drunk to enjoy anything."

"Let's get something to drink," he said.

"I don't drink."

"You're different," he said, "but I like that."

"It's snowing out," Rachel remarked. "Wouldn't it be beautiful to take a walk in the snow and welcome in the New Year?"

"Let's go," he answered enthusiastically.

It was so peaceful and lovely as they walked in the newly-fallen snow, their footsteps leaving tracks behind them. It was cold but invigorating as the wind blew soft wisps of snow across their faces. She wasn't wearing gloves, so he put her hand in his large coat pocket and held her hand in an effort to keep it warm.

He told her about his life, his ambitions and then it was midnight and the New Year had arrived. People stuck their heads out of their windows and rang cowbells and blew horns and shouted Happy New Year. He kissed her on the cheek and they exchanged New Years greetings.

They headed back to the party. It wasn't a pretty sight. Almost everyone was drunk and lying all over the place. He looked at her lovingly, "This was the nicest New Years Eve I've ever spent."

"I'm glad," she said.

He took her home. "May I have your phone number?" he asked.

It would never work out, she thought. He was so handsome and experienced and could get so many girls. I'm graduating from high school and I'll be taking regents exams and preparing for graduation. Thank you for a lovely evening and for taking me home." He seemed embarrassed, but wished her luck and left.

CHAPTER 12

It was Spring again. As Rachel walked down the block towards Fannie's house, it seemed to her as if the Almighty Artist had poured a huge bucket of green paint over the earth. This drab mound called Earth was now filled with glorious color. It reminded her of the frosting on a huge cake. People ran around like ants on the frosting of the cake. As for herself, the world had changed before her eyes into a great pageant. She was the guest of honor and was not required to pay an admission fee. Thank God she was able to notice both the good and the bad things, otherwise she might have given up.

On Mother's Day, Sunday, May 12, 1935, Anna didn't feel well, but she cooked dinner and Rachel served it. The radio was going all day and songs about mothers kept playing. Natalie had been in bed all week with fever and pains in her legs and side, but she got up and went outside in front of the door for a while. Nobody had money to buy Anna a decent Mother's Day gift. Natalie, Debbie and Rachel had saved up seventy-five cents together and gave it to their mother.

Jake had come home and said, "I almost died on the train, that's how sick I felt." Coming from him, it was a terrible announcement for he had never complained of being ill, nor had he ever gone to a doctor.

Monroe brought up the Spring outfit bit again that he did from time to time. The Chicago episode where the finisher put Anna and the girls up on the Spring on the floor haunted him. Danny had gone out somewhere.

Monroe had gotten paid for the work he did the last few days and he gave Anna three dollars towards household expenses. Then came the last straw. Jake had joined up with someone and started a fur contracting operation. He was supposed to bring home one hundred dollars, but said he had to split with the partner and that he thus had fifty dollars. He said that he had given the landlord, (who lived downstairs in their two family house) thirty-eight dollars for rent and was only able to give Anna twelve dollars. Worse than that, the landlord complained it was way over due and said we would be dispossessed.

"Don't worry, Annie," Jake said, "some day you'll have plenty of money." With that she started to cry bitterly.

"Maybe I should get a separation and the few years I have to live, I should live like a person," she wailed. She said this, knowing she was trapped, knowing she could not do that.

Rachel left the house. She would stop by Fannie's, then Helen's. She had to get away. It was so nice stopping in at Fannie's. Her mother always greeted her with a smile.

"You're such a smart girl and nice too. The boy who gets you will be lucky. And what beautiful skin you have." Fannie was always giggling. She looked like Myrna Loy, the movie star. She had slanted eyes, a lovely turned up nose and she was slim and graceful.

Fannie and Rachel next stopped at Helen's house. Her mother too was friendly and hospitable. Many times Rachel had slept over at Helen's house. They always invited her to a nice supper. Her sister and two brothers were friendly too and often drove Rachel home. They were all a little older than Helen, nice looking, ambitious and intelligent. One brother worked in an appliance retail store after school, but in later years he owned the place and was a millionaire.

Fannie, Helen and Rachel took a walk down Pitkin Avenue and
passed the Loew's Pitkin Theatre. It was a big, new theatre and
unusual because when you looked up it was as if you were
outdoors looking up at a beautiful night sky filled with stars. It
was a romantic place for couples. The other attraction was
Henrietta Cameron at the organ. She played while sing-a-long
words were flashed on the screen. It was wonderful singing to
the accompaniment of the organ and the audience loved it.

Mother's Day was a thing of the past, and after a difficult and
uneventful summer, Fall arrived. Rachel was still wearing her awful
four year old winter coat and when she got home and told her
mother that she hoped Papa would bring home some money so
that she could buy a coat and also shoes, Anna cried again. That
made for another fight with Papa and Danny and Monroe.

Rachel felt miserable and guilty. Anna could hardly walk on her
turned and worn out shoes which she had gotten way back in
Chicago. Rachel wished she hadn't mentioned the need for a coat
and shoes.

"If I get some money, I'll buy you a cheap little coat or jacket and
a pair of shoes," Anna promised.

She woke up the next morning early, as she wanted to study
some more for the history exam that she was taking that day.
When she got out of bed, Anna was in the kitchen with Danny
and Monroe. Jake had already left.

"Don't you forget it. I'm sick. I'm sick in my heart. I'm sick of
looking at these bare floors and beds." Anna had just forty cents
and gave Rachel ten cents to go to school. She went and found
out that she had passed all the other tests and took the History
test. After school she went to Helen's. She loved their Spanish
living room furniture, the red couch with its tassels, in particular.

They talked about school and boys and danced to records. Helen's mother, a pleasant, quiet sort of stout woman, invited her for supper and she was grateful, knowing there was probably nothing to eat at home.

Helen was chubby and had dimples and always seemed contented. She didn't have Rachel's troubles. Her father always appeared with a book in his hand for he was very scholarly and it was refreshing when he discussed the books with Helen and Rachel while his wife quietly prepared dinner.

When Rachel got home there was not a cent in the house and Anna was not feeling well. Rachel had to go down to the candy store and get a bottle of ginger ale and some peppermint life savers, which her mother needed, on credit, of course.

Thanksgiving Day was a sad one. Usually Jake would go down to the live poultry market and bring home a live turkey. The poor creature would spend the night before Thanksgiving in the bathtub, with the bathroom door locked. In the morning Jake would bring it to the schoichet who would kill it. Then it would be brought back to the house to be roasted for the Thanksgiving dinner. Rachel could never enjoy eating the turkey. The sight of it being alive kept haunting her and seeing it on the table was like a cannibalistic ritual. Nevertheless, it was sad not celebrating the holiday at a Thanksgiving dinner with the family.

Jake went to New Jersey with Anna as Grandma Fluger was very sick. Natalie and Debbie remained with Rachel who made them something for dinner and straightened up the house with the help of Helen who came to keep her company after she had finished having Thanksgiving dinner with her family.

There was a proliferation of "cellar clubs" in Brooklyn. Sometimes they were called fraternities. Fannie had met a fellow who belonged to one of these clubs. He had given her a card with his name and the club's name and address and his phone number on it and he had promised to call to invite her to the club soon. Fannie told Helen about this and Helen told Rachel and soon all the "Merry Girls" were included in this upcoming possibility because Fannie had told the fellow that she would like him to ask his friends to call for each of the "Merry Girls" at the same time he picked her up.

That's how it went. If any of the "Merry Girls" had a date, they would see to it that the others were invited too. Thus, the girls were taken up in a round of parties and dates, with hardly a Saturday night unoccupied.

Fannie was the most beautiful and popular and Rachel was either a tie or next in line. They never lacked an interested male and danced for hours on "Empire State" heels, the tallest heels around, yet tolerated them very well.

Helen was chubby, dimpled and cheerful and was also popular, usually to studious, ambitious fellows. She was very academic and book minded and those were the kind of fellows who found her compatible.

May was a quiet, unobtrusive sort of person, sweet and reticent, who liked to go out, but didn't care too much if she didn't. She had naturally platinum blond hair, was small and rather delicate. When she spoke, it sounded as if she barely had strength to get the words out.

Mary was loud and abrasive. She was president of the "Merry Girls" and had to have her way. She was going steady with Fred and was crazy about him. He was a nice looking chap. She had a big nose and looked like a plain housewife, even though she was still in her teens. She lived with her parents, divorced sister and brother and when Fred slept over, she washed and ironed his shirts and made a fuss over him.

When Fred broke off with Mary, she came to her senses. She got a new hairstyle and some nice clothes, and went out and got a job rather than stay home and clean and cook as she had been doing. For years, she dreamed of him coming back to her. He had succeeded in business and could get plenty of girls, but finally married her.

Dotty was average looking, sincere and enthusiastic.

Strife, strife, strife. There was a note on the table. "Tell Natalie and Rachel to get ten cents and come down to New York and we will borrow some money and give it to them. If they can't come, I'll be back with some money. It was signed, "Danny."

At one o'clock they were starved, having had nothing to eat and their mother was in bed, not feeling well. Since they had no phone, Natalie and Rachel went to Tonta Hecht's to use their phone and to tell Danny to hurry up, but Jake said he had already left. Tonta Hecht gave them some coffee and bread and butter and a sour pickle.

Jake had opened a fur shop in the city in the fur garment area with another partner. Monroe was part of it too. Danny still worked in the coal yard, but since this was Saturday and he didn't work Saturdays, he had gone to the shop.

CHAPTER 13

Just as Rachel despaired that she would have to go through another winter with her old, cheap, worn cloth coat, Jake declared that he was making her a fur coat. He brought home one of the skins to see if she liked it. She was thrilled beyond words. It was brown lapin, a sort of beaver-like fur.

She had to go in for a fitting and Helen went with her. Rachel looked out of the window of her father's small office on the tenth floor of a building in the fur manufacturing district. Across the street, immediately facing front, stood a prosperous looking building of about sixteen stories. It offset the poorness of the group of ancient red tenement buildings just to its left. To the right, in between the space presented by a rift between the newer building and a tall bank building, a step ladder of architecture appeared from the block in back. There was a slanting pattern of buildings in the background facing north, east and west. As each street hung farther away, she could see a variegated segment of skyscrapers majestically topping off the whole scene.

The majesty of it all started working on Rachel's vivid imagination again. Out there somewhere she would find a place where she could succeed. She would never know the ache of hunger again, nor the disgrace of an unfurnished home. Furthermore, she would be sure to help anyone in need. She would be a famous and loved writer.

Helen was exploring the place. Jake took Rachel out of her reverie. "Come, try your coat on." He walked out of the factory and led her to a mirror. He was wearing the traditional white coat the furriers wore and as usual, a tape measure hung from his shoulders.

She loved her father and this made her feel he loved her too. "It's going to be beautiful," she said. "When will it be ready?"

"It's almost finished. You should have it in less than a week."

After they left the shop, Rachel and Helen went to the big department stores, Gimbels and Macy's. Beautiful Christmas displays were already on view, since it was the beginning of December. Then they went back to Brooklyn and went to the movies. They saw, "She Married Her Boss," with Claudette Colbert at the Warwick Theatre. After that, Helen invited Rachel to have supper at her house.

Since it was Saturday and the "Merry Girls" had spent the last few days deciding what they were going to do that night to no avail, they got together and went to a Dance at the Temple Auditorium on Eastern Parkway. They had a good time dancing, but none of them met anyone they particularly liked.

During the week, Fannie got a call from Hy, the fellow who wanted her to come to his fraternity. He said the rest of the girls could come to the club where he was sure they'd meet some nice fellows, but he couldn't get them to pick the girls up in a blind date situation. Fannie persuaded the girls to go. She said Hy was very nice and probably had nice friends.

All the girls got spiffed up and went to Fannie's house and when Hy came they all left for the fraternity.

Hy was a natural comedian. He was very funny, but clean-cut, no dirty jokes. He was average in looks, friendly and pleasant. He was the "life of the party" guy.

The fraternity was amply furnished with a number of couches
and armchairs, a few end tables and a radio and soft lights. When
the girls arrived, there was no one there, but soon some fellows
came in. Rachel was still wearing her new fur coat and she eyed
the fellows as they came in. She was disappointed as they didn't
appeal to her. The radio was playing "A Little Bit Independent,"
and her ego, boosted by her new fur coat and the brown hat she
had bought that afternoon, made her feel as if the song had been
written for her.

Just when she felt this would be a wasted evening, three more fellows
came in. One of them seemed to like her right away and she had
singled him out as he walked in too. She was partial to the fair type
and he had light brown hair, was refined looking, slim and well
dressed. There was a mutual chemical attraction between them
instantly. He smiled and walked over to her and introduced himself
as Kenny, a member of the fraternity. He said they were all going to
a party and asked if he could be her escort. She tried to hide her
excitement and said that would be fine.

Mary, May and Dotty went directly to the party with their escorts.
Fannie and Hy went with them. Helen and Rachel asked Kenny
and Stanley if they would mind stopping off at Helen's house as
she had forgotten her gloves and might as well get them since it
would not mean going much out of the way. The boys said they
wouldn't mind. Actually, Helen, being very cautious as usual,
wanted her parents to okay the fellows and felt that if they would
be willing to have her parents meet them, they must be respectable
enough.

Then they took the streetcar on New Lots Avenue and went to
the party. Kenny and Rachel found plenty to talk about. It was
the first time she had felt that way about a fellow and it was
unbelievable that he seemed to feel the same attraction for her
from the very first moment they laid eyes on each other.

Imagine her delight when Kenny called her a few days later and invited her to a Christmas party at his fraternity. Stanley had called Helen and invited her to the same party too. Rachel asked Kenny to get some extra fellows for some of the other "Merry Girls."

The days went by quickly for Rachel. There were dates, parties, studying, fellows flirting at school, school dances, walks with the girls, visiting each others homes and sleeping over sometimes, especially after going to dances and getting home late.

Kenny took Rachel to the Christmas party at his fraternity. He got three friends to call for Fannie, Helen and May, but no one hit it off. However, Hy was at the party and monopolized Fannie and escorted her home. As usual, he enlivened the party with his wonderful sense of humor and added to the general entertainment. He seemed to have been smitten by Fannie. Kenny had eyes for no one but Rachel, but he was pleasant and tolerant when she danced with practically every fellow in the place and seemed to be content that she always returned to his side.

He had gotten a special cookie with "Rachel" baked into it and she was very pleased with his thoughtfulness. She wished it had been otherwise, but he told her he had quit high school after three years and had just lost his job as salesman and shipping clerk. She liked him very much, but where did he fit into her dream of someone educated and wealthy and powerful. True, he was only eighteen, but what were his plans for the future? She must not fall into the trap that her mother had fallen into. She wondered whether she should see him again if he called.

It was Christmas Eve and even though the family was Jewish, they celebrated the occasion as an American custom, not a religious one. Natalie and Debbie had bought Rachel some lovely stationery and Monroe had bought her a nice pair of hose which she really needed. Annie had put up a line and there was a stocking on it for everyone. They all had potatoes and onions in theirs except Rachel, who found a bottle of alcohol and a bottle of Milk of Magnesia in hers. The family was all asleep and she had a good laugh all by herself.

The family awoke one by one. It was Christmas Day. What made it an exceptional day was that it was Anna and Jake's wedding anniversary and at the same time Anna's and Natalie's birthdays. There were gifts and cards and even though they were very inexpensive they were received in a spirit of love and thoughtfulness. Rachel was very sentimental about this day as it brought the family closer together.

Annie, Jake and the girls went to the "Premier" theatre and saw "Mutiny on the Bounty," with Clark Gable, Charles Laughton and Franchot Tone. The settings were wonderful. Rachel kept thinking about Kenny. She felt as if she would cry if he didn't call, but that she wouldn't feel excited if he did. She wondered why she felt this way.

On Friday night the "Merry Girls" met as usual for their weekly meeting. Fannie said that she was going out with Hy the following Saturday and would ask him to try to get boys for the other girls for New Year's Eve.

As it worked out, Hy couldn't get fellows for the rest of the girls, so Fannie went out with him New Year's Eve alone. Mary was seeing Fred and Dotty was joining them with her boyfriend, Eddie. Helen came over and kept Rachel company.

It was the first time Rachel had seen her mother and father go out for any kind of recreation and she was glad. Annie had bought a pale green beaded short flapper-like evening dress, which was the mode of the day, sleeveless and glamorous looking. It had silver beaded fringes to match the silver beads on the dress. They had gone to the Bessarabia Young Men's New Year's Eve Ball. For weeks the family had talked with anticipation of this event and finally it had come.

Rachel recalled the name "Ashes" which was her mother's original name and she envisioned her mother as Cinderella who had fled from the ashes in the fireplace for her fabulous night with the Prince at the Ball in the palace.

Natalie and Debbie were playing in the kitchen with a couple of their friends. Outside, the earth was covered with crisp, white snow. They had been playing outside and came in with pink cheeks which the brisk winter air had bestowed upon them. The radio was playing softly.

"Did you hear from that fellow, Kenny?" Helen asked.

"I was going to tell you. He sent me a New Year's card. Can you imagine, I'm over seventeen and it was my first card, in fact, my first correspondence from a boy."

"It's about time," remarked Helen. "He seems very nice. I wonder if he'll ask you out again."

The New Year came in and it was now 1936. Helen's brother came and picked her up shortly after midnight. Rachel wrote in her diary:

> "Perhaps I think too much and that is not good. Perhaps he is blessed who lives without questioning and takes events as a matter of course. I wish I could meet someone who thinks like I do who would fall in love with me . . . I wonder who Danny and Monroe will marry some day. They're

probably out with girls tonight. Natalie and Debbie are too young to ponder about . . . I close now with the prayer and hopes that this coming New Year will be a "red-letter year" in my memory book. By that I mean that there will be only happy, glad tales to tell about my family, relatives and friends."

She finally got to bed and fell asleep. When she awoke only a few hours later, she went to the window and saw that the sky was a dim gray which soon gave way to a faint glimmer of light. There was complete silence except for the clatter of milk bottles the milkman was delivering to their door. She heard his footsteps as he ran out into the street, then grabbed the reins of his horse and she listened to the gallop, gallop, peacefully riding on.

The lights on the lamp posts went out and an awesome profusion of colors filled the firmament, a variety of pinks and purples and white and the sun came up and it was day.

It was New Years Day. What would the new year bring?

CHAPTER 14

Christmas and New Year's vacation was over and school began again. The "Merry Girls" had gone out a lot and Rachel met several fellows who seemed interested in her, but she didn't take any of them seriously. Kenny called her too and invited her to attend a banquet with him, his brother Sydney and Sydney's girlfriend, Beattie. Kenny and his brother were trying to sell vacuum cleaners for the Electrolux Company. The banquet was given for the group which made the most sales in the month. Their group was the winning one.

The thought of going to a banquet in a hotel was thrilling and she looked forward to being with Kenny again. Rachel had met Sydney, Kenny's brother, at the fraternity Christmas party. His girlfriend, Beattie, had sat on Sydney's lap with her arm around him. She showed Rachel her engagement ring and told her how happy they were and that they were making arrangements for their wedding. She was a cute girl with black curly hair and a lovely smile. Rachel envisioned herself showing similar affection to a fellow, but knew she was too inhibited, bashful or whatever. Annie had told her that "when you meet the right one, you'll know it." Then she would give herself to him, love him and take care of him forever.

Kenny told her he would be wearing a tuxedo to the banquet. That meant she'd have to borrow an evening gown or at least a semi-formal dress. She called Cousin Doris who agreed to lend her a black velvet gown that she had recently worn to an affair. It was a trifle too big but it brought out the beauty of her exquisite skin by contrast, and with her size four figure, she looked elegant.

She had worn her rag curlers all day and combed her hair out into hanging curls which she held up on both sides with rhinestone clips which matched the earrings and necklace which Cousin Doris had lent her.

Kenny arrived exactly on time bearing a gorgeous corsage which he lovingly pinned on to her dress. As he bent down she could see the admiration in his eyes. Sydney and Beattie were waiting downstairs in the car. Beattie had her head on Sydney's shoulder. Oh how she must love him.

Rachel was encompassed by Kenny's sweet smile, his blue eyes looking lovingly at her and the masculinity of his clothes. He seemed happy and content just to be with her and to please her. She felt secure, loved and peaceful being with him. Was this love? Or was this the attention she had so sorely lacked during her formative years, due to her illness and her feeling of desperation, due to the poverty and suffering she had experienced at home? She basked in the attention the fellows were giving her, especially Kenny.

She had never gotten this admiration and appreciation at home, except maybe from Danny. Monroe could be mean to her and she missed her father who was always out there trying to succeed in business. Also, she never seemed to please her mother, Anna. Then there was the fear that she would wind up unhappy like her mother. She must never make a mistake and marry the wrong man. She was only eighteen, so she could string along with Kenny and still search for her one and only. She would stick to it; he would have to be educated, rich, handsome, and powerful and theirs would be the most wonderful marriage in the world. But Kenny was only nineteen and who knows how he would make out in life.

The banquet was to her, in her limited experience and isolated life, luxurious. It was held in the Towers Hotel, which was on the same block as the famous St. George Hotel in Brooklyn. She had once been in a hotel in Chicago, but had never had a boyfriend take her to an affair in one. Everything was thrilling to her, the elegant ladies' room, the bell hops, the waiters, the coat room, the beautiful formal gowns, the marvelous dinner, the speeches.

After dinner, the tables were removed, the carpets were rolled up and the dancing began. The orchestra was assembled on a raised stage and a rainbow of various colored lights flickered in and out around the musicians and created an aura of romance.

Kenny introduced Rachel to a number of people, one of whom asked him for permission to dance with her. When they were introduced, she noticed his smile and the way he looked at her. After a while, Kenny had asked Rachel, "Would you like to dance with a nice young Irish lad?" She accepted but by the third dance with him, Kenny came to claim her. They went back to their table just as a photographer was getting ready to take a picture. Kenny promised to bring her a copy of the picture.

They decided to take the subway home and not go back by car with Sydney and Beattie. They roamed around the hotel lobby exploring things and walked down to the Hotel St. George, went in and looked around as well. It was drizzling out and a cute little kitten was out there in the rain. Kenny picked it up, petted it and tried to get it into a dry place. She thought it was very kind of him. He was so gentle and sweet. He looked handsome in a tuxedo, dress shirt and bowtie. It was so good being with him. He had a good sense of humor too and she enjoyed every moment spent with him.

When they said goodnight, she suddenly felt sick. She was getting ready for bed when she had this overwhelming feeling of confusion. The events of the evening swept past her and Kenny's presence seemed to linger with her. What if he loved her? Did she love him? What was love any way? She wanted him and she didn't. No, she couldn't let him spoil her dream.

CHAPTER 15

Rachel took a break from studying for her History Regents exam which was being given the next day. She stood up and walked to the window. There was a crackling sound on the window pane for it was hailing. The wind swept forward with forceful gusts, blowing snow and pellets of ice. The window faced the backyards, which were covered with snow, except for black stumps of bushes and trees. The roofs were covered with snow too and on them there were other black "posts" sticking out, the chimneys black with tar. It was like a picture coming to life with the action of the sweeping gusts of snow and ice. It seems that in every lovely thing, there are black parts to mar the beauty, she thought. She was feeling philosophical and wanted to write a poem, but she faced reality and returned to studying.

Helen, Fannie and May came over, but since she still had studying to do, Rachel put some refreshments on the table, gave them some magazines to read and suggested that they turn on the radio. She went into the boys' room and closed the door to avoid the noise. She studied far into the night and when morning came she kept studying until the last minute when she left to take the exam. History was her worst subject, but she gave it her best shot. One more term and she would graduate. She must not fail.

After the exam she went to see the English supervisor who had invited her to join some sort of a writer's class. She would have to stay extra periods next term for that, but she didn't mind. She signed up and then went to Helen's house for lunch as had been planned. Then they went to a movie and saw "So Red the Rose," with Margaret Sullivan and Randolph Scott. They also showed an adorable "Our Gang Comedy" film in which the kids had fixed up their basement like a movie theatre and gave a show. Rachel appreciated this because she and her little friends used to do the same thing.

At night her mind turned to Kenny. Would he bring her a copy of the picture they took at the banquet? Was he avoiding her because he was out of a job and perhaps didn't have money to take her out? Or was he just not as enamored of her as she thought. Well, it was only about a week since the banquet. He'd probably call soon, after the photograph was ready. She pondered that maybe if he called she would pretend she was busy and refuse to see him. Was that a good strategy? Would that make a fellow more anxious to see a girl, or would that turn him off as a rejection?

He called the next day and asked if she would like to go to a show that Saturday night. She decided to say yes as she really felt like being with him. If he got tired of her, it would be okay. There were other fellows out there.

She wondered about Monroe. He had a girlfriend. Words about it kept slipping out and he got dressed up and went out almost every night. He had to be in love, Rachel thought for he gave her a dollar, whereas he hardly ever gave her anything. Love might be softening him up. Whoever she was, Rachel hoped the girl would be nice to her brother. As for Danny, he seemed overly nervous lately, probably due to the hard times they were having.

Saturday night came and Kenny called for Rachel promptly. He brought the photograph taken at the banquet. They went to the Loew's Palace Theatre in downtown Brooklyn and saw the Marx Brothers in "A Night at the Opera" which was considered one of the outstanding pictures of 1936. It was filled with music and laughter. Then they took a streetcar and went to a cellar club on Rockaway parkway, but since no one was there, they started for home. It was January and very cold outside. They found a small café and went in and had hot chocolate and cake.

She felt good being with him. He was so decent, too bashful to even hold her hand. Perhaps she'd better not see him any more. Perhaps they could remain friends. What if he was really in love with her? She wouldn't want to break his heart by leading him on.

"Kenny," she said, "you should always aim high and not be content with barely getting along."

He must have understood what she was getting at because he looked sad when they said goodnight. She felt a little guilty, but was not sorry she had said it.

Rachel wrote Kenny and invited him to May's graduation party. He called as soon as he got the letter and gladly accepted. She worried about a dress for the party. She wore the same two dresses over and over. Jake said she should come to his shop after school and he would go to a wholesaler with her and get her a dress. She had seen someone wearing a flowered dress with red in it and wished she could get one something like that. She would also go down to Blake Avenue.

The streets there were lined with pushcarts. There were all kinds of things, from fruit to clothes. Fannie's parents had a pushcart there. They sold stockings and other items of underwear. She would have to go there and get some stockings, seconds, which Fannie sold to the girls. The seconds had such slight imperfections that you couldn't see them and the price was very low compared to the perfect ones.

Natalie accompanied Rachel to the city to their father's place. Jake, Danny and Monroe were there and the wholesale dress deal was off because they had no money as usual. They had just acquired a new partner and things weren't good. However, they had opened a checking account and gave Rachel a check for three dollars and fifty cents. She planned to go to May's Department Store the next day to buy a dress.

The following day, Anna went to May's Department Store with Rachel. It took them hours to find a dress close to the description of what Rachel had in mind, considering that they had such a small amount of money with which to buy it. It was red on a navy blue background, with puffed sleeves which could be worn up or down, above the elbows or almost to the wrists. The neckline fell in folds and there was a dark red pin in the folds. Rachel loved it. She would probably be a hit on Saturday, she hoped.

Kenny brought three friends to the party with him. One of them entertained by singing as he had a very nice voice. He asked Rachel to dance and so did the other two fellows. They were all wonderful dancers. Helen had also invited two fellows, both of whom were good looking and refined. Joseph was the best dancer of all and once he danced with Rachel he never stopped. His father was a doctor and he thought he might follow in his footsteps. He asked if he could take her home and she was really happy about it.

Before they left she said goodnight to Kenny. She felt sorry for him as he seemed so downhearted and she had neglected him, but after all, she was not obligated to him. He told her he had sold a vacuum cleaner and that he expected to sell two more that week. He had expected to take her home and this was a blow to him.

The next day was Sunday and the "Merry Girls" met at May's house to gab about last night's party. May showed them all the nice gifts she had gotten. May's mother remarked that Rachel was a wonderful girl, so thoughtful, for she had arrived early to help with preparations for the party.

"But she did an awful thing," remarked Helen. She made Kenny feel miserable.

"I felt sorry for him," Fannie said. "He seems to be crazy about her. Then she goes home with that guy, Joseph."

"I didn't think it was that serious," Rachel said, feeling guilty.

Rachel changed the subject. "How was your partner, Stanley, Helen?" I don't think he likes me very much, does he?"

"What's the matter with you?" Helen answered. "Do you know what he said, "Rachel is so pretty. She's what I'd call a vivacious brunette." Rachel could hardly believe it. She had sensed that Stanley had kept looking at her, but he hadn't asked her to dance. After a while they all went for a walk.

When Rachel got home no one was there. Her mother, father and sisters had gone to New Jersey to see Grandma Fluger whose health was declining. Monroe came home a little while later, but Danny had gone someplace the evening before and was still not home. Rachel put the radio on and listened to Eddie Cantor.

Valentine's Day was near and Rachel wondered if she would hear from Kenny. It haunted her the way he looked at her at the party and how sad he seemed. If he never called her again, she deserved it. However, he called a few days later and asked to see her again.

Natalie

Debbie

Rachel called Helen and told her. She was surprised when Helen said that her brother, the one who always drove Rachel home had remarked, "Rachel is some wonderful girl. Boy, will she get a wonderful fellow some day." Yet, she was never sure of herself, even through she promised herself that she would never marry a loser, and even though she seemed to be popular enough.

Fannie came over and said that she was going out Saturday with a fellow she had met at May's party. He wanted her to bring three girls for his friends, especially the one in the navy and red print dress.

Rachel told Fannie that Kenny had asked her out on Saturday and was calling to confirm it.

"Tell him you'll see him the following Saturday," said Fannie. The fellows in this group are exceptionally nice and it will be fun going out together." When Kenny called, Rachel asked if they could make it the following Saturday instead. He seemed disappointed, but said he'd call her. He also said he felt bad at the party because a cold was coming on. You could tell by the way he spoke that he still had a cold. He seemed hurt by her refusal, but tried not to show it.

Saturday arrived and Fannie informed them that the boys weren't picking them up. They would meet them at the party which they had planned.

Stanley was there for Helen, Hy for Fannie and Joseph had come to be with Rachel. May, who was not that boy crazy, decided not to go. Actually, Joseph was not certain that Rachel was coming so he had escorted another girl to the party. However, he neglected her and danced with Rachel continuously, but he had to take the other girl home. Rachel and Helen went home with Fannie and Hy.

The "Merry Girls" had planned to meet the next day, Sunday, and go to a museum in Manhattan, but Rachel did not join them as she was very tired and wanted to rest. In addition, she had a nagging backache. She spent the day studying and catching up on her correspondence to the girls in Chicago. Her thoughts turned to Kenny. After last night and other times, she realized he had a sweet character compared to a lot of others she had met. She looked forward to his phone call regarding next Sunday.

At night while she was preparing to go to bed, a terrible sickness hit her. Her heart was beating out of control and she felt weak and numb all over. Maybe it was from the rheumatic fever, she thought. They said it had affected her heart. Her face and chest felt as if they were getting dead and that she was disappearing. She called for help as she was shaking with chills as well. Anna came in with a glass of water, a hot water bag and also rubbed alcohol on her hands and arms. Jake got dressed and was going out to get a doctor, but Rachel was starting to feel better so he didn't go. She silently thanked God. Oh, how she wanted to live. Life was so dear. She was starting to have a good time. Besides, how would the family feel? Their grief would be unbearable.

Natalie had a cold and was absent from school the following day, Monday. Rachel stayed home too. They spent most of the day listening to the radio and cleaning out some accumulated junk. Natalie was eleven and Rachel sixteen, but Natalie was and had always been self-sufficient. She always knew what she wanted and could be depended upon to help Rachel with various errands. She never whined or complained and it was a pleasure to watch her dance to the tune of the phonograph records, or even without music.

Rachel didn't feel too well all that week. The "Merry Girls" took turns visiting her. Sometimes they played cards and Monroe joined them. Monroe must really be in love, Rachel thought. Too bad that girl, Esther, was cheating on him and mistreating him as well. Danny also confessed that he was seeing a girl named, Tanya. So that was why he seemed so nervous.

"I'd like to bring Esther over," Monroe declared, "but I'm ashamed of the house." Danny must have had the same thought about Tanya. Anyway, Monroe brought home what Rachel thought was a beautiful lamp. But that wasn't all. Monroe and Danny ordered furniture for a studio room of their own. It arrived and everyone thought it was beautiful. There was a rust colored studio couch, a green armchair, that is, its sides were green leather and the rest was a green and brown striped material with a few yellow stripes thrown in. Also, a modernistic shiny mahogany desk with a chair. The back and seat of the chair were covered with a Turkish type material which was brown with a binding of ecru. They also had gotten a large painting of Whistler's Mother which they hung up.

Last but not least, there was a stunning lamp. Rachel thought it was prettier than the first one they had bought. The base was brown and gold, the shade tan, and there was a place for three bulbs. It was too good to be true. They had managed to buy the furniture at Sach's on the installment plan. Monroe had also bought a small vacuum cleaner the week before.

Danny was twenty-two and Monroe was twenty-one and they had girlfriends. They were fixing up the house so that they could invite them over. Rachel was seventeen and had Kenny among others. She was so glad that things were shaping up a bit so that she would not be ashamed to invite anyone over, especially boyfriends.

Thinking about boyfriends, Rachel wondered if she would hear from Kenny again. It was almost a week since he had called her and she had refused his offer of a date. Now he called her again and said he'd like to see her that coming Saturday. She accepted and looked forward to it, but in the background of her mind lay the haunting scenario of a life of mediocre years with a man of limited capabilities, such as her mother had endured and in fact, the terrible effect it had upon the entire family, including herself. She would go along with the situation for the time being but was doubtful about the foreseeable future.

Yet Kenny surprised her with his wisdom. For instance, she had not been aware of certain things, when he remarked "It's the little things that count." Another time, when he really splurged and took her to Caruso's, an elegant Italian restaurant in Manhattan, there was an incident which set her to thinking.

She had never been to such a restaurant and was trying to appear sophisticated, when he smiled and started talking to the waiter about something casual. She felt he was being undignified at first, but then felt ashamed of herself. What kind of a snob was she? She thought she knew Kenny, but did she? He was only eighteen. What did she expect of him? Who knew what the future would hold? What could be in store for a young man who was uneducated and talked about being a baker like his father?

"Bakers make good money and are usually employed," he said. She was appalled. That would be the last straw if he ever took a job as a baker.

CHAPTER 16

Danny finally brought his fiancé, Tanya, over. She didn't say much and sat with her hat on, as if she were ready to leave any minute. She was unsmiling and stern, downright unfriendly and cold for a future daughter-in-law, sister-in-law. She and her parents and two sisters and two brothers had just come over to this country from Russia. They were Communists, no less, and proud of it. (This was to come out of the woodwork later, unbeknown to Danny, until after they were married)

Anna tried to rationalize when Danny left to take Tanya home. "She'll probably be a good housekeeper and cook and maybe it will be a good marriage." Rachel could see Tanya treating Danny like a little boy and robbing him of his youth and freedom. She couldn't see him yodeling as he often did. Maybe he had been a substitute father for so long that he was looking for a mother. He had been his mother's mainstay, sort of like a husband instead of a son. Of all the pretty, happy girls, why did he choose this matronly woman? Poor Danny, would he find happiness with her?

Things progressed rapidly from then on and before she knew it, Rachel was writing in her diary: "Today was Danny's wedding day. The wedding was held in Tanya's family's apartment in the Bronx. Her mother and father seemed to be rather poor people so I guess that was the best they could do. There were refreshments, buffet style. The older people tended to gather around the dining room where the tables were and the younger people in the living room.

So many scenes pass before my eyes now, but I am quite tired so I can't go into such good descriptions and details. It was a very rainy night, so many people didn't come. There were telegrams from many, including one from Aunt Bella and Uncle Manny in Chicago. Tonta and Uncle Hecht and their whole family were there. Aunt Etta and Uncle Lou didn't come, as Lou had been having heart trouble lately, but cousins Essie and Sydney as well as Doris and Jack were there. So was Grandma Blickstein, Papa's mother, who recently came over from Rumania. She was remarkable, over eighty and mentally and physically alert and well. She was a tiny, white-haired lady. Grandpa Blickstein, her husband, had recently died. He was almost ninety and had fallen off a horse he was riding. Tanya's whole family were there too.

A canopy was held up over the bride and groom, their parents, the rabbi and a couple of others. It was held up by four people, each holding a pole. Etta's son, Jack, was holding one pole at the end which was near me. He laughed all the time. He seemed to be making fun of it. True, it was such a poor and primitive ceremony and wedding but he should have realized it was serious. I felt bad that they couldn't have had a real big wedding, but I don't know if he had any such feelings.

There was no orchestra or musician to play the Wedding March. A couple of us started to sing it as Tanya and her mother walked down the room to the canopy. It was different when the Rabbi began the ceremony. People became a little more serious. The Rabbi said certain words that Danny had to repeat. Then I noticed that Danny had to give Tanya a glass of wine and she had to throw back the head veil and taste it.

She had rented a white satin headpiece with a veil over it, just covering her face. In a house wedding of this kind, the bride usually doesn't have a full bridal outfit . . . After that, Danny was supposed to break the wine glass with his foot. This is symbolic of the destruction of the Temple. It was on the floor wrapped in a cloth napkin. He tried twice but didn't break it. The Rabbi had just said never mind, when he gave it a hard bang with his foot, the third time, and it smashed before the canopy was taken away. I'm so glad. It's good luck to break the glass.

Then the canopy was taken down and Tanya's veil was removed and everyone started kissing everyone else and giving blessings and wishes. Then everyone started taking sandwiches, etc. People chatted and tried to be joyful for the next couple of hours and that was that.

Papa's brother and his wife took us home in their car. Rain was pounding and swishing on the car roof. What a night! What a storm! Were the heavens crying? It was a funny feeling I had coming home in that car. Danny was married. So quick and everything was over; married, a new life ahead. No more searching for love as I have to do. Would they be happy? How I hope so, dear Danny.

A couple of weeks later, Anna told Rachel that Tanya had invited them to visit their apartment. She told Rachel this on a Saturday morning.

"Is she preparing dinner?" Rachel asked.

"No, just cold cuts."

"In that case, I guess it will be all right if you tell Tanya I have an important date with Kenny and that I'll visit them soon. I'd love to go, you know that. If I had known before, I would have made other arrangements with Kenny."

At night, Anna said "You ought to see how angry she was. She said you're not a lady of your word because you didn't come and she'd never have anything to do with you as long as she lived."

Rachel was shocked. After all, she hadn't known about going there until that morning and besides, Tanya hadn't cooked; in fact, Anna said she had served frankfurters and beans. How could she react that way?

Rachel called her and she hung up, saying "I don't like to talk to liars." It was unbelievable.

The years would pass and Tanya kept to her vow. Nothing in the world would change her, not even World War II which erupted. Danny, Danny, Rachel's heart cried out, but she wouldn't bring the matter up to him. She loved him too much to risk stirring up trouble in his marriage.

CHAPTER 17

Monroe came home with a swollen black eye. He explained that the Furrier's Union caught him working "after hours." There was a big strike going on. They considered him a "scab." Anna was very worried because Danny was not home yet and she feared that someone might have run after him and even murdered him. Monroe called the police who said they would search for him. However, before long, Danny walked in and sure enough; he had a black eye too. They had also broken his glasses.

There wasn't a cent in the house and if the strike continued they would be starving in a few days. They had just worked a few hours that day and this had to happen. They were bruised and frightened. Rachel had been selling copies of the school newspaper and had collected eighty cents. It had to be used to buy food. Also, the "Merry Girls" had been selling raffles to raise money for the club. Rachel was Treasurer and was holding one dollar and fifty cents which also had to be used to buy food. She was very nervous about how she would get the money to replace that which was used.

To make matters worse, the furniture, except the boys' studio room furniture, was taken back by the store because of non-payment. Still worse, the landlord was threatening to dispossess them as they were two months behind in the rent.

After much reluctance and bickering, Monroe moved his furniture into the empty living room. Danny was married and Monroe was now alone in the room. Rachel was very distressed and wrote several poems to unburden her. She hoped that they would be published some day. Then there was the matter of Kenny. He was getting to be a part of her, yet her common sense nagged at her to find someone who would take her out of this abominable poverty. His future was questionable.

Graduation was getting closer and closer and the "Merry Girls" were talking about Class Night and the Prom. Although they were popular with the fellows and had dates, parties, school dances and attention galore from the opposite sex, it was another story as far as Class Night and the Prom were concerned. Most of the boys could not afford to escort a girl to either of these events, especially the Prom. Class Night was a celebration given for the graduates. It was held in the school auditorium. Members of the graduating class planned and presented the program. After it was over, it was a custom for the students to go out and finish it off by going to a restaurant, night club, movie or whatever.

The Prom was the big thing. It was being held in the Persian Room of the Hotel Astor in Manhattan. The girls had to wear evening gowns and the boys, tuxedos. An escort had to bring the girl a corsage and if he had no car or anyone to drive them, he had to pay for a taxi. After the Prom, they were going to meet at the Club paradise, a famous night club. It would be expensive.

None of the girls could get anyone to take them. Sammy was seeing a lot of Fannie and he was taking her to Class Night, but could not afford the Prom. She had asked Hy to escort her to the Prom, but he had to decline, evidently for financial reasons too. Kenny was the only one of the boys who readily accepted. He was thrilled when Rachel asked him and said he would be happy to take her to both Class Night and the Prom. Somehow he was the most generous of the fellows and always managed to have money to take Rachel out.

"Be careful not to let him spend too much," Danny said. "He doesn't look as if he has a heck of a lot of money to spend."

"I never take advantage of him," Rachel replied, and she meant it. She couldn't ever do that to him. He was so kind and loving and was just happy to be with her. He would do anything to please her.

"There's a song, 'If I had My Way,'" he once said, "which is just how I feel about you." The song implied that he would do anything for her if he had his way. She had felt like crying when he said it. Too bad he didn't match the dream she held in her heart. She mustn't wind up a loser.

On Class Night Fannie and Sammy came to Rachel's house. Rachel and Kenny were waiting for them and they all left together for the event. The talented graduates who prepared and presented the program were great. Everyone had a wonderful time. Afterwards, Fannie and Sammy and Rachel and Kenny separated from several other couples who were going to a movie and went their own way. They decided to go to Chinatown. The girls were very excited for they had never been to Chinatown.

"I feel like I'm in China," Fannie giggled. She was adorable. She had slanting squinty blue eyes and a little turned up nose. Sammy nicknamed her Foo. "You fit right in here, "Foo," Rachel mimicked. She was truly thrilled: Class Night, Kenny, and Chinatown and with Fannie and Sammy, whom she liked so much. Sammy's poems were always published in the school bulletin as were hers. He was so intelligent and interesting.

Rachel drank in every bit. The Chinese stores and people were so quaint. They walked along taking everything in. They went into a store which was like a delicatessen-grocery and bought Chinese nuts. It was a basement store. There were three Chinese clerks talking to some men. They spoke partly in English. There was a room in the back which had no door and in it there were many men sitting around a table, evidently gambling according to Sammy and Kenny.

Fannie and Rachel tried to appear casual when the men stared at them, even though they felt uncomfortable. Once outside they saw a Chinese man selling newspapers at a stand. Rachel went over to look at the papers and saw they were printed in Chinese. Kenny bought one for her. The headline read: "Prince of Wales abdicates throne for love." He had done this because of Wallis Simpson.

A greeting card shop had a big display of cards in the window, all printed in Chinese. In the store where they had bought the Chinese nuts, all the labels on packages and cans were in Chinese and there were odd looking meats, some hanging down on strings from the ceiling.

"It's funny but there are no Chinese girls around, "exclaimed Rachel. The only female they saw was a very fat Chinese lady who showed herself outside the door of her shop for a second because she thought they wanted to buy a paper or magazine displayed on a stand. When she opened the door, they walked away.

They left Chinatown and took a bus and rode around to nowhere just for the ride. Then somehow the idea was hit upon to go in to a burlesque which they were passing. Fannie and Rachel were the ones who really wanted to go in, but the fellows were against it. The girls had never been to a burlesque and were curious as to what happened there. Sammy and Kenny said it was so terrible that they'd walk out in the middle. They said if we went in, it would be at our own risk and we'd have to stick the whole thing out. They'd hold us down to the seats. In the end, we didn't go to the burlesque.

They still wanted to go someplace, so they took the train to forty-second street. All the movie theatres had already started their last performances as it was after one a.m. They passed Chin's Chinese Restaurant at Forty-Fourth Street and Broadway and went in. It was a gorgeous place. They sat at a lovely table in a romantic looking nook. There was a little lamp on the table with a Chinese shade. It was beautiful. There was an orchestra and they danced. They had missed the last floor show, however. The food was delicious and they each had a cocktail. Rachel and Fannie merely tasted theirs as they had never had a drink before.

It was three a.m. when they left Chin's. They decided to go for a ride atop the Fifth Avenue bus, but since no buses were running at this hour, they took a walk up Fifth Avenue. Fannie and Sammy walked ahead by themselves to talk and Rachel and Kenny walked some distance behind them.

The past summer, Rachel had started to write something to Kenny in the sand on the beach with her finger, but didn't have the heart to tell him what she had written. He sensed that it was something important that she wanted to tell him, and since she had quickly smoothed out the message in the sand with her hand, he had asked her many times what it was. She avoided telling him as she was afraid of hurting him. Actually, she had written in shorthand, which he knew nothing about, "This is the last time," really meaning it at the time.

As they walked along, she was holding onto his arm when he suddenly asked, "What was the secret in the sand on the beach?"

She felt her heart racing, but he insisted and she thought that maybe she should be honest with him. She blurted it our frantically:

"I thought we were seeing too much of each other and might be getting too serious, so I wrote that in the sand."

Her voice began to choke and she could not tell him the real reason for her having written that. After the wonderful time they were having that night and how good he was to her and generous too, she couldn't bring herself to tell him what was really in her heart.

"I really can't explain why I had decided not to see you at that time," she lied.

After she told him, she wondered how he took it, but he didn't say a word for about two blocks.

"Why don't you say something? Give your opinion."

He said seriously, "There are two reasons a boy goes out with a girl, either because he enjoys her company or for sexual means." Of course she knew he meant that he enjoyed being with her because sex was far removed from their relationship.

Maybe if he talked things out more, like Sammy for instance, she could sort things out better. She told him so. He merely stated, "It's true that I'm selfish in the fact that I keep things to myself, while you're the opposite." She felt sorry for him. It wasn't his fault that he couldn't meet the requirements of the man of her dreams. Yet why did she prefer his company over so many other fellows she met or went with?

The Prom was coming up soon and he was going to be her escort. It would be an expensive occasion for him, yet he looked forward to it. So did she. The situation between them couldn't go on forever.

He called a few days later and invited her to a Christmas party his fraternity was giving. She accepted and asked if she could bring some of the girls along too.

"I know you're not crazy about the frat," he said. "If you don't like the party we can walk out."

He was so thoughtful, so sweet and respected her so much, she told herself. He always looked nice too, clean-cut and properly dressed. Why did she feel so above him? Her life haunted her, the poverty, the desperation, her parents, her sisters and brothers.

"I'm sorry about my brother Danny's wedding. It was held in his girlfriend's parents' apartment. The reason I didn't invite you is because I felt you wouldn't have a good time. All our relatives were there and besides, I knew I'd be busy helping out. You'd have to sit around and do nothing."

"You're so considerate," he replied, trying not to be sarcastic. She felt guilty. Of course it was because she didn't want everyone to think she was serious about him.

1937
Dr. Elias Lieberman, Principal of Thomas Jefferson High
School, Brooklyn, N.Y.

The next few weeks were hectic ones. There were so many exams and Rachel studied incessantly. Helen came over and studied with her. In between, when she was not with Kenny, there were dances, parties and dates. Also "Merry Girls" meetings on Friday nights, each week in someone else's house.

Rachel and Helen passed all the exams with flying colors. Now they could relax and think about New Year's Eve which was right around the corner. Kenny asked Rachel to spend New Year's Eve with him and she accepted.

They went to Manhattan. What a gala celebration! There were mobs of people in the street, blowing horns, shouting, etc. Mounted police were on the watch, movie and newspapermen were all about taking pictures. Radio technicians broadcasted the scenes. It was thrilling. All this excitement took place around Times Square, Forty-Second Street, and continued for blocks around there.

They passed Minsky's Gaiety Theatre, the Burlesque, and when Rachel expressed her curiosity about burlesque again, Kenny relented and they went in.

"You seem to want to see what it's all about," he said, "and since I want to please you, let's go." When they were going in, he passed a candy stand and bought a large bar of chocolate with almonds. "Keep eating this," he said. "You might need it when you see what you will see." He was right. She couldn't help thinking how awful it was for women to get up there on the stage in the nude, no matter how much they might need the money. Eating the candy bar helped her hide her embarrassment.

Then Kenny took her to a New Year's Eve party at one of his friend's homes. As usual, one of the fellows approached her and asked her to dance.

"No. She's going to have the first dance of the New Year with me," Kenny protested. After that, almost every fellow in the place danced with her.

"There's a party at the frat, too," said Kenny. "Would you like to go?" They did. He had bought her a beautiful mother-of-pearl compact and gave it to her just before they left. She thanked him genuinely. Then they talked about New Year's resolutions. I made one that I'm really going to keep," he said. "I'll tell you about it some other time."

When they arrived home in front of her house, he said, "I made a resolution that I was going to kiss you good night tonight." He put his arms around her and pressed his lips to hers.

After he kissed her, she turned very quickly and just raced up the steps into the house without turning to look at him. When she got inside the door she sat down stunned for a few minutes. She had vowed never to let anyone kiss her until she was sure she was going to marry him, yet she permitted him to kiss her. After all, he meant more than any other male to her and he had been seeing her for almost a year now. Her rule was too strict, she had reasoned. His kiss was so sweet, so beautiful. Until now they had been loving friends. Now it was more than that. She had wondered when this would be coming and was really glad about it. True, he respected her so very much but he was still a man and this seemed more normal. His kiss had not filled her with passion, however, just a wonderful feeling of closeness.

She was afraid, would she wind up like her mother after all, or would she suddenly meet the man of her dreams and as her mother

always said, "When the right one comes along, you'll know."
What was love anyway, she pondered? Was this love? If so, why
couldn't she make up her mind about Kenny?

She tossed and turned all night, trying to reason things out.
Besides, she was worried because she still had no gown for the
Prom. Helen said her friend, Rose, had just bought a pink moiré
gown and since Rose was the same size as Rachel, maybe she
could ask her to lend it to her for the Prom. Helen went to
Rose's house with Rachel to ask about borrowing the gown.

"I only wore it once. I got it for six dollars, wholesale. I'll sell it
to you for five dollars." She didn't want to lend it to Rachel.

"Rose, I don't want to borrow your gown now. Can you bring
it over so my mother will see it and perhaps buy it?" Helen
knew the Prom was only a week away and that there would
probably be no money to buy the gown. "Why don't you
lend it to her," Helen insisted angrily. By this time she and
Rose were practically yelling. Rachel felt very uncomfortable
seeing how nervous Rose was becoming. It was understandable.
You couldn't exactly blame her. Who would be happy to lend
a new gown to anyone?

"I'll see you in school tomorrow and talk it over with you, Rachel,"
Rose promised.

"If Kenny calls to ask what color my gown is, what will I tell
him? He might want to know the color in order to get a corsage
to go with it."

The next day, Rose met Rachel at school and said she had decided
to lend her the gown. What a close one. She had dreaded telling
Kenny that she wasn't going to the Prom for she figured he must
have told his friends and it would be a shame to change plans.

Sure enough, Kenny phoned that night and she was able to tell him her gown was pink. He would never know she borrowed it.

Kenny sounded exuberant. "I have good news. My friend, Kermit, is lending my brother, Sydney, his car so Sydney is going to drive us to the Prom. I'll call for you at eight-thirty." He didn't mention anything about their first kiss, but his voice seemed to indicate his feelings. He had never sounded happier.

"Don't worry. I'll be wearing a tuxedo," he added.

Will he bring me a corsage? Will we go to a nightclub? Her excitement was building up. She was more fortunate than most girls. They couldn't get anyone to take them to the Prom. They would miss this memorable occasion. She was grateful to Kenny.

When the bell rang on the night of the Prom, she jumped to answer the door. There was Kenny in his tuxedo, looking happy and handsome. His brother, Sydney, and his fiancé, Beattie, were waiting in the car. She had her head on his shoulder. When they got in the car, there was a long florist's box on the seat beside Rachel. She picked the box up as it was in the way.

"It's for you," Kenny smiled.

"Oh, thank you so much," she beamed. She opened the box and in it was the most beautiful corsage she had ever seen. It was made up of all colors, pink, red, white, orchids, carnations and sweet peas. Pretty silver ribbons and green ferns were beautifully and artistically arranged. There was also one white carnation in the box, for Kenny's lapel.

"It's gorgeous."

His face lit up. "Nothing is too good for you."

The car stopped in front of the Hotel Astor on Forty-Fifth Street and Broadway where the Prom was being held. It was thrilling to walk through the luxurious lobbies and go up in the ritzy atmosphere in the elevator. The elevator stopped at their floor and they entered the huge ballroom.

Rachel was stunned at the glamorous panorama which greeted her eyes. These were mostly students from her school with their escorts, yet it was as if everyone had been transformed into high society millionaires this was the atmosphere she loved, rich and elegant. The gowns took in every color of the rainbow. Corsages with delicate tinsel ribbons, tuxedos, silver and golden slippers, dainty golden and silver evening bags, elaborate hairdos. The walls leading to the dressing room were covered with mirrors. She glanced into them as she walked by and couldn't believe this was her.

When she walked out of the dressing room, Kenny was waiting for her.

"Do you know, after looking around, I see you're the most beautiful one here." It made her feel so good to hear him say that, but she was also a little embarrassed. She had spent the day giving herself a facial, with a formula she had concocted herself out of oatmeal and things. She had manicured her long fingernails and set her hair with her rag curlers which resulted in her fixing a head full of hanging curls. She had also put on her favorite perfume. Her sandals had "Empire State Heels," very high and thin and graceful. She was used to dancing on those heels. After all, she weighted only ninety-six pounds. The heels could carry her.

The Prom ended at twelve-thirty, after midnight, and almost everyone met at the Club Paradise. It was a thrilling experience for Rachel since it was the first time she had ever gone to a nightclub. There was a stage revue, featuring Bert Frohman as Master of Ceremonies, a marvelous orchestra and a delightful supper. They had soup, roast chicken, salad, green olives, French fried potatoes, an ice cream dessert and demitasse.

The dance floor was filled with all the couples from the Prom, who danced between courses and went around collecting autographs from their fellow graduates.

After the nightclub, Rachel and Kenny walked around up to Times Square. Kenny claimed he was still hungry, which was not so astonishing, because the menu at the Paradise was served in rather small portions. Rachel wasn't that hungry, so they went into a small coffee shop and he had coffee and a doughnut and she had nothing. Soon they were on a home-going train. The train was filled with many couples who were also going home from the Prom.

When they reached her door, they spoke for a few minutes and he kissed her again. She did not run up the stairs as she had the first time he kissed her. His kiss was warm and sweet and after he had kissed her, he hugged her and pressed his cheek to hers.

When she got inside the door, she had a troubled feeling. Will this really prove to be love or will we eventually drift apart? Time will tell, she thought. It was very confusing to her. She knew that her childhood and youth would always haunt her and play a part in her decisions.

CHAPTER 18

Anna was crying. Jake had just come home from court where he had gone to answer the dispossess that Rosie, the landlady, had hit them with. The furrier's strike was still on in New York and Jake sadly informed the family that he was leaving for Cleveland again to try to get work there.

The court had given them five days to evacuate the apartment or face eviction.

"Mom, I'm going downstairs to see if I can get Rosie to wait a little longer for the rent," Rachel said. They were two months behind. She rushed out the door without waiting for Anna's answer. Rosie was a middle aged woman, an overfed, fat, beer drinking, self-satisfied slob with no compassion. She and her equally dispassionate husband owned the two family house where they occupied the lower apartment and the Blick's the upper one.

Rachel knocked on the door. "Who's dat?" Rose asked.

"It's Rachel from upstairs." The door was open, so she walked in. Rosie was just finishing a bottle of beer.

"Please don't put us out in the street. My father went to find a job. You'll get paid. We're honest people."

Rosie went on in her boisterous way, "It's not me. It's my lawyer. I have nothing to do for it no more. I no ken help it. Listen dolling, the court gave the notice. You be out on the street Wednesday if you no pay."

Rachel saw it was no use. She went out and slammed the door. Now that graduation was over, she had to find work to earn some money. Danny had gone to the Department of Welfare and they were scheduled to go back there tomorrow. They had given him a list of apartments. The maximum rent had to be thirty dollars. Monroe was driving a taxi and gave Anna a few dollars.

The next day Rachel ran around looking for a job, and then she went to the Department of Welfare to meet Anna, Danny and Monroe. It was raining and her hair was coming down. When she got there, she felt terrible. She felt that everyone was looking at her. She was ashamed and miserable.

Her mother and brothers were not there yet. She walked in and out, eyes lowered. What if anyone should recognize her? Finally the three of them came down the street. Monroe yelled at Rachel, "If you don't fix your hair, I'll fix you. How she wears her hair!" Danny came to her defense,

"What do you want from her? It's raining." They were all still outside.

"Keep your coat closed," Anna admonished her.

What a coat, torn, had to sew it every day and the cloth covered buttons were coming apart.

They were called into an office to be interviewed. A young woman, Miss Friedland, dug into them with questions. It was humiliating.

"Since you haven't found an apartment yet from the first list, get another list of apartments from the front office. Also, send in information as to the places your husband worked at for the last seven years," she said to Anna.

Monroe, Danny and Anna went apartment hunting. Rachel went over to Fannie's house. Her sister had gotten temporary work in a factory and said she could get Rachel in. She went to the factory the next morning and they put her on.

The boss was a quiet man who walked around just checking up. The Foreman was a gruff, balding man who put her to work pasting and trimming parts of the wallet they were manufacturing. It was tedious and tiring and she detested it. She did the same thing all day long until she felt she couldn't stand it any longer. The only thing that sustained her was the fact that she had a date with Kenny that weekend.

Anna, Danny and Monroe searched for rooms and finally found an apartment for thirty-three dollars a month. The next day was Saturday and they all went back to the Department of Welfare to inform them. Then Anna sent Rachel and Natalie to the apartment with a five dollar deposit which was all that could be scraped up. There was also one more dollar with which Rachel was told to buy sugar, bread and salt to bring to the new apartment for good luck, which was a Jewish custom. They usually bought a new broom too, but they couldn't afford it.

The new landlady was a very nice woman. She said she usually got a ten dollar deposit.

"My mother went to see her mother in New Jersey as she's sick. Don't worry," said Rachel. "When we move in Wednesday, we'll pay the whole rent."

"All right, I'll see you Wednesday morning. Good luck."

Anna was home packing when they got back. She wasn't feeling well. She wanted them to get Tonta Hecht's daughter-in-law, Esther, over. Rachel went to the candy store and called her. She also got some cartons so that they could continue packing. Esther was truly a good friend. She came right over and started to help.

They had to go back to the Department of Welfare on Monday morning, despite the fact that Monroe was afraid of losing his taxi job and Rachel her new factory job if they took off from work. Miss Friedland was annoyed because they did not have a record of Jake's employment as she had wanted.

"He is in Cleveland trying to find work since the furriers are on strike in New York, Monroe said. He looked terrible, as if he were breaking down. He had been waiting in the outer office looking as if he'd go insane, in a corner, ashamed, with his head bowed. Danny was putting up a front, trying to act calm. Rachel was a little hardened by this time, having been there several times before and strengthening herself to the situation. Anna had gone out and was waiting in a candy store a block away as she couldn't take it.

They didn't have Jake's address. He had written and said that there was nothing in Cleveland and that he was going to Chicago with a salesman. If he found nothing there, he'd come home. Monroe related this fact to Miss Friedland.

"He will have to be reported to the police. Since we don't have his address, he is in essence, a missing person. He will also have to see a mental hygienist to cope with his inability to face realities."

"All this for one month's rent," Rachel lamented. Her misery was interrupted by something that was going on outside. Some women had started a demonstration. It began getting louder and more heated as more people joined in. "Increase relief forty percent." Then a stout loud shouting woman walked in. She held her coat open and her hands were on her hips.

This was done to display a bright crimson cotton dress, the symbol of Communism. She walked about boldly, kibitzing with the officials and daring everyone to join them outside. She seemed very sure of herself and showed her defiance in no uncertain terms.

"You can prepare to move," declared Miss Friedland. You will get a check in Wednesday morning's mail, thirty-five dollars for rent, thirteen dollars for the moving van and sixteen dollars for food for two weeks.

Wednesday morning, Danny walked in at seven a.m. sharp. The moving van came at nine fifteen. Selfish Rosie and her stupid husband seemed to be enjoying the festivities, as they stood outside the house. The van got there before the eviction people had a chance to evict them. However, the mail had not come yet. Faithful Danny, he needed Rachel and she needed him. Monroe had gone to work to drive the taxi.

"What if the money doesn't arrive in the morning mail?" Rachel asked, fearfully.

"Listen, Butch, no court would condemn us for what I plan to do. I've thought it over. If the money doesn't arrive in the morning mail, it would probably come in the afternoon mail. I'm going to make out two checks, one for the rent and the other for the express, with the hopes that the new landlady and the express will still have the checks in the afternoon.

Then when the Department of Welfare's check arrives, we'll cash it, give them the cash and get back our checks. We'll make sure mama stays at Hecht's until everything blows over. Then we'll tell those people she had gone to the bank for cash and if they preferred, we'd give them cash later and take back the checks. They probably would prefer cash, so it won't look flooky." Dear Danny, always coming to the rescue.

CHAPTER 19

The new apartment was still in East New York, but closer to Brownsville. It was a six-story walk-up tenement building. An elevated train took a curve right outside their fifth floor windows. They had to keep some of the shades down so that the passengers could not look in. The screeching, when the train turned the curve, was intolerable. Rachel could not sleep for weeks until she got slightly used to the din.

She had persevered and worked in the factory for three weeks. One day she actually cried because she felt she was going insane from the monotonous, routine job of pasting two places of a wallet together, and then trimming the edges. She was part of the assembly line. This factory work was not for her.

She started walking the streets of Manhattan trying to find a "real job." There was hardly a building that was unfamiliar to her. She was fascinated by the Times Building with its giant electrical sign which displayed news flashes. Adjoining it was Walgreen's where she so often looked in longingly, not having five cents to spare for a soda.

How well she knew Sixth Avenue with its starving men in tattered clothes, gaping at Help Wanted signs in front of the employment agencies. There were also women and girls, even couples, looking for work. The wages were low and throngs of applicants were unemployed and competing for the limited positions.

She filled out applications and lied about her experience, but during interviews her remarks indicated that she didn't have much experience. She was told to "dress older" by one personnel director. She was eighteen now, but looked younger. Girls were fighting for jobs as secretaries in law offices which paid eight dollars a week, six days a week. She hated legal work.

She applied for a secretarial job in advertising, newspapers, magazines, and radio stations without success. They always liked her, but said she needed experience.

Kenny took her out constantly. It was almost summer again. They spent one glorious afternoon in Prospect Park. He had come to pick her up at three o'clock when she told him that Mary and Fred, who were seeing each other again, wanted to join them.

"I couldn't say no when she called me last night, yet I thought I should ask you how you felt about it."

He seemed disappointed. "If you want to, it's okay with me."

They walked to Mary's house and found that her plans were changed and she couldn't go out with them. Kenny seemed relieved. They took the bus to Prospect Park.

"You know, I like being with you alone," he said simply.

She felt the same way, only she didn't say it.

They changed buses, from the Sutter Avenue bus to the Prospect Park bus. When they got off the first bus, he said, "Let's go into the pet shop and buy some food for the pigeons so that we can feed them."

"Why not feed them peanuts?" she asked.

"I used to raise pigeons. They don't like peanuts that much."

Then he proceeded to name the different kinds of pigeons.

There were always little surprises like that. He was interested in so many things, including people, but he never bragged. Many times his intelligence and creativity startled her. He began talking about his parents, sister and brothers. He came from a wonderful family, but only just lately brought it up.

It was so nice spending the day in Prospect Park. Couples walked hand in hand as they did. They fed the pigeons, went through the zoo and then sat on the grass eating ice cream pops. Later they played catch ball. Then they sat down on the grass again to rest.

"Dotty's mother is making her a graduation party. She's planning a moonlight cruise. Would you like to come?" she asked him.

"That would be great."

"May and Fannie are having graduation parties too and asked me to invite you. And Mary's sister is giving her a surprise birthday party," she added.

She could see he was very pleased at the prospect of being with her at all of these occasions.

"By the way, our Frat is having its closing party," he announced. "I hope you can make it."

"Thank you. I'd like to come."

If only she was sure that she loved him. If only the future looked more certain and promising. He had just quit his job as a shipping

clerk for a dress manufacturing firm. He spoke about the
possibility of getting a job

1936
Prosepect Park, Brooklyn, N.Y., The Boathouse

as a baker. That would be the end of it. If he settled for being a
baker, forget it. Many bakers worked all night and slept in the
daytime. For one thing, she was afraid to be alone at night. Also,
she pictured him coming home with flour on his shoes. She
would be burying herself alive if she married him, she thought.

No, they were getting too used to each other and she was confused
about what love really was. She'd have to tell him that they'd
have to stop seeing each other for a month and then see how they
felt. She would tell him after Dotty's cruise and all the other
parties.

They got up, brushed off their clothes with their hands and went
rowing. The boathouse was closing a little earlier because it looked
like rain. They turned the rowboat in and started walking towards

the edge of the lake. There was a little refreshment stand there where a radio was playing and several couples were dancing.

It was beautiful there by the lake, under the trees, with the soft music playing. While rowing, they had passed a bush which overlapped the water and he had plucked a huge purple flower which he gave to her and she had pinned it on her dress (rhododendron, she found out years later).

When they left the park and reached her house, he said, "I had such a wonderful day." He didn't kiss her good night. She felt he was reading her mind.

He called her the next day. "Would you like to take a walk? The weather is beautiful." His call was unexpected, but it was timely for she really needed someone today.

"My mother isn't feeling well, but if you'd like to come over, we could go out for a while because Danny and Tanya are coming and my mother wouldn't have to be left alone."

Anna was sick a great deal lately. Rachel tried so hard to please her, but she seemed to take her frustrations out on her. She continuously scolded Rachel in no sweet tones. Jake was in Chicago again trying to earn some money as a fur salesman because the fur market was terrible in New York. Rachel tried to make excuses for her mother. Papa is away a lot, there is never any money, she has no fun, and she works so hard in the house. Her life is no "bed of roses."

Her mind would turn cartwheels. She loved her father. He was so good natured and soft spoken. He never berated her. Yet, he was away a lot and never had interest in the house. Take Uncle Lou Freeman, for instance. He knew everything that was going on in his household and was there when Aunt Etta needed him. He supported his wife in the discipline of his children. He demanded respect from everyone. Jake let people make a fool of him. He was by no means stupid but just didn't assert himself. If he was to be anything, he had to make money. So far he was on the bottom rung of the ladder.

It was a good thing that Kenny had come over. Rachel was very depressed, and for the first time really showed it. She was miserable over the situation at home, her mother, father and the poverty. She was out of a job, and hardly had anything to wear. Also, she owed the "Merry Girls" club fifty cents in dues and Fannie thirty-five cents for stockings she had bought at Fannie's parents' pushcart on Blake Avenue. She also owed a girl she had met at an employment agency fifteen cents. It was terrible staying in the house trying to help and please and getting abuse for it.

When Danny and Tanya arrived, Kenny was already there and they went out for some air. Her mind was churning again. She loved being with him, but what about the future? She didn't want her life to be like a bubble blown out of a pipe becoming bigger and bigger until it burst into nothingness.

They went back upstairs and Rachel prepared supper and everyone ate except Monroe who suddenly complained of pain in his stomach and right side. Danny and Tanya left and Kenny and Rachel went into the studio room and played a game of checkers. It was about ten p.m. when Natalie had to go to sleep in the studio room, so they went into the living room.

They went in to see Anna in the bedroom off the kitchen and Monroe in the bedroom off the living room. They both felt worse. Rachel was close to tears, running back and forth to help them. She was afraid Monroe might have appendicitis. Jake was out of town.

Kenny asked, "Rachel, would you like me to stay over night incase you might need some help?" Did she! She didn't know what to answer because there was no commitment between them and it wasn't usual to have a fellow sleep over in that case, even in an emergency. She went into her mother's room and asked her and she said yes because she really was afraid.

Kenny slept on the couch in all his clothes except his vest and jacket. He was really a friend in need. He called his mother to let her know he wouldn't be home.

In the morning, Rachel asked Natalie to wake Kenny up. It was good to have him there, but she was too timid to wake him, so she prepared some breakfast for everyone. The girls left for school and Kenny for work. Later he called to find out how things were. Both her mother and Monroe were feeling better.

"Great," he said. "How about seeing me Saturday?"

She wanted to see him, but was afraid that he might grow to care too deeply for her so she said, "Would you rather see me Saturday or Sunday?"

"Both. Would you like to see a Broadway show Saturday?"

She wanted to badly. "It's so expensive."

"Don't worry. What would you like to see? I'll try to get tickets."

"'Tonight at Eight-Thirty'" with Noel Coward and Gertrude Lawrence."

He got the tickets and picked her up Saturday. Dottie and Eddie and some friends were seeing another show right across the street from their theater, so it was arranged that Kenny and Rachel would meet them after their show was over.

They crossed the street and saw people streaming out of the theater, but there was no sight of Dottie and Eddie. They had probably gone already.

Watching the people come out of the theatre filled her with uneasiness and apprehension. Women and men wearing expensive evening gowns, ermine wraps, jewelry, tuxedos and top hats, swarming out of the theatre. Her dream of possessing wealth and prestige was being challenged. Kenny, although far from lazy, was not one of these "successful" men. The terrible taste of poverty hit her again as she compared the style of these people to her possible future life with him.

A tall young man in evening clothes, top hat and all, spoke gently to an elderly woman who wore a beautiful long gown, her shoulders ensconced in a chinchilla cape. She probably was his mother. He held her under the arm as he escorted her across the street. So wealthy, so kind and alone, she thought.

Maybe it would be better if she stopped seeing Kenny and searched for her ideal. Would she be sorry for it some day if she did? Kenny would probably wind up making a fair living and feel comfortable that way, while she would feel stunted and regretful being married to him. She would probably be cutting herself short if she didn't seek a more ambitious man with a greater zest for living. Yet, Kenny was so good, so sweet. She couldn't bear losing or hurting him. She would have to make a decision. Time would tell.

CHAPTER 20

At last came the long awaited Moonlight Cruise in honor of Dotty's high school graduation. All of the "Merry Girls" were there, Fannie and Sammy, Dotty and Eddie, Rachel with Kenny, Helen with Stanley and Mary with Fred. Also, May had asked Monroe to escort her, so he was there too although he felt a little uncomfortable since the crowd seemed a bit younger than he was.

As they were waiting to board the boat, the sky became dark. There was lightning and thunder and a few drops of rain fell. A storm was threatening. They certainly needed one because it had been an unbearably hot day, in fact, the hottest day of the year.

As they waited at the dock by the water, huge zigzag and curved streaks of lightning appeared in the sky. In spite of the weather they all took a chance and boarded the boat. They were lucky for as suddenly as it had started, the storm passed over and all was clear again.

They were on Bobby Sanford's Showboat. It was a beautiful three-deck streamer. They watched the wonderful Broadway Revue and when it was finished, they met the performers and got their autographs, which they signed on the program sheets. Then there was dinner and dancing.

Kenny guided Rachel to the upper deck and they sat quietly in the darkness, looking out at the black water, when he suddenly put his arm around her and pulled her towards him, slowly and gently kissing her several times on the lips.

"I wanted to kiss you in Central Park by the lake, but I thought it best not to," he remarked. She did not answer because she knew he was right and that she was sending him a pretty clear message by her actions and behavior. He knew she liked being with him, but wasn't sure of her feelings. As she was only eighteen, he would pursue cautiously until she made her mind up.

"Would you like to go to Coney Island Sunday," he asked.

On Sunday they met all the "Merry Girls" on the beach, together with their boyfriends. Rachel felt it was the most enjoyable day of her life. Mary had a locker there and invited her to share it. She was glad that it spared Kenny the expense of renting a locker for her.

Another surprising thing about Kenny was that he was a terrific swimmer and with tolerance and patience, he taught Rachel how to swim a little. They all joked and sang and had a grand time on the beach. The sun, sand and water and murmur of people were soothing to Rachel. Kenny held her hand almost all day. He did it bashfully at first, but then it seemed as if he wouldn't let go. They were lying on their backs trying to get sunburned and he fell asleep still holding her hand.

In the evening, the couples dispersed and Kenny took Rachel to the Cosmos Cafeteria where they ate. Later they danced on the rooftop at the place where he had taken a locker for the season.

"Would you like to see the famous side-shows of Coney Island?" he suggested.

"That would be fun," she replied. They walked along the crowded avenue. Lots of people stood in front of each of the various side shows. There were colorful life sized posters in front of and describing each exhibit and a "Barker" who tried to entice people to come in.

Among these side shows, was the "half-man, half-woman" exhibit. The "freak" was flat-chested on one side of the chest and wore part of a brassiere on the other side. There was "The Incubator Babies," the "Seal Man," a woman without hands who could sew and play a xylophone with her mouth, a giant-sized boy, an African dancer and others.

They walked around for a long time enjoying "The Bowery" as this avenue was called. There were countless stands offering pineapple drinks, frozen custards and malteds and all kinds of games where you could try your skill at winning cupie dolls and other prizes.

They went on the miniature "Drive Them Yourself Cars" twice. It was fun being bumped by other cars and trying to steer clear of bumping. The little cars were protected by rubber bumpers. Kenny was generous and thoughtful and Rachel enjoyed every minute of it. There was so much to explore. Luna Park was thrilling. They danced on the huge dance floor. There were brilliant lights everywhere. Luna Park was a dazzling spectacle. It was so exciting.

1936
Luna Park Coney Island N.Y.

They sat on a rail not far from the carousel. As they watched the up and down horses, Kenny seemed anxious for an answer.

"Do you like being alone with me?"

He was holding her hand. She couldn't avoid answering him this time.

She felt like telling him the truth, that being with him was the most beautiful times of her life. Yet, she didn't want to lead him on too much, for the future was so doubtful, with her high expectations.

"Yes," she said, trying not to sound serious.

He didn't want to lose her by being persistent. After all, she was only eighteen and he was nineteen. For the time being, he was satisfied. They needed more time. He would have to pave a way in the world for them first, if they were ever to get married.

As they were going back to the dance floor, who should come over to them but two girls dressed beautifully, both in white silk suits. They both had black hair and beautiful faces and figures. They ran over to Kenny and greeted him enthusiastically. Who should they be but Kenny's sister, Florence, whom he frequently mentioned, and his cousin, Dolly, whom he also sometimes talked about.

It seemed to Rachel that he had it all arranged that they should meet "accidentally on purpose." He probably figured that if it looked like a chance meeting, Rachel wouldn't think he was getting too serious. Rachel's impression of them was that they were refined and sweet. She remembered how excited she had been to meet Tanya, the one Danny was to marry. They must be excited meeting their brother's "girl."

The two girls were sixteen, as Kenny had mentioned. They said they didn't go swimming on Saturday since they and most members of their families observed the Sabbath. They were here to enjoy the evening. Rachel's insecurities came up. With a sister and a cousin such as they why did he think she was so great? His parents owned their own house. Maybe they were not as poor as she thought, she with her grandiose dreams.

Kenny was working as a shipping clerk in another dress place for a measly fifteen dollars a week. She was puzzled about the whole thing. She felt as if she might be in love with him, but wasn't sure what love was. And what about her dream? She was not going to rush into anything. Time would tell.

His sister, Florence, and cousin, Dolly joined them for about an hour. They all went on some of the rides, then they left. Kenny and Rachel took a walk on the boardwalk, then sat down on one of the benches. The thrashing of the waves in the night made an awesome sound and the salty air and breezes were invigorating. It was getting late and they headed towards the subway and home, still hand in hand.

Dotty came over the next day as she and Rachel were planning to go away on a week's vacation together. Tanya had gone away on a two week vacation with her two sisters and Danny was going there for the weekend. Danny's friend would be driving them. It was a place in Highland Mills, near the Hudson River and adjacent to the West Point Military Academy.

At about ten o'clock at night, Kenny came over unexpectedly on a bike that he had rented. He talked her into riding on the handlebars. She was afraid, but she went and found it to be more fun than she had expected. It made her feel so young.

Natalie was there when he had come in. "Does Rachel know how to swim?" she queried.

"About ten strokes," he laughed.

"I heard you're such a good swimmer. You should be able to teach her."

"Don't worry, I will," he answered.

"We probably won't go swimming anymore, because when I get back the summer will be over," Rachel remarked.

"But there will be plenty of other summers, won't there?" he said.

Was he looking forward to many other summers with her, perhaps even as her husband? She felt a twang of realization. She had not thought of next summer with him, just figured that the summer was about over and that she wouldn't be going to the beach with him anymore.

Rachel and Dotty left on their vacation. When they arrived in Highland Mills, they discovered they were at a camp, not a hotel. Dotty wanted to leave and go to Mountaindale in the Catskills where her family had rented a bungalow for the summer. But since a storm was coming up, they stayed.

There were no young American people there, just mostly middle aged and older Europeans and what was worse, most of them were Communists as they found out the next day. Poor Danny, Rachel thought, when she learned Tanya and her sisters were also Communists. Look what he had fallen into. He was only nineteen years old; she looked older than him.

They decided to stay out the week. The good points were that the meals were marvelous and they had been given an adorable little "bunk" which they loved. Well, they would have a good rest at least. The magnificent country grounds and fresh air were something too.

The "bunk" was a little green and white bungalow. It contained a double and a single bed, two closets, a dresser, chair and there were flowered curtains on six windows. There was a little porch on which there were two benches, one on either side of it. The whole place was cute and tiny. It had no sink or toilet, as did the other accommodations there, but it was in the most beautiful area in the camp, so they didn't mind walking almost a block to the dining room or bathroom and about four blocks to the casino, office or pool. They got accustomed to it.

Looking out from their "bunk" they could see the tennis court, and further back bushes, trees, hills, mountains, and at night, the moon and the sky covered with millions of big and little sparkling stars. The stars were unbelievable. It was the first time they had seen such a sight. It was visible to the naked eye because they were situated high up in the mountains.

West Point, where the cadets were, was about nineteen miles from Highland Mills. These cadets were being trained to serve as officers in the Army and were probably the choicest young men in the United States. They had to be college graduates and pass rigid mental and physical examinations. Congressmen from each state selected only two from their state to attend West Point, so they were the "cream of the crop," healthy in most cases handsome and exceptional all around.

One day, Dotty and Rachel, wearing their identical blue bathing suits, which the "Merry Girls" had bought with their dues money, were wading in the lake, when two very handsome fellows seemed to come out of nowhere in the water and swam towards them. One was blond and the other dark. They explained that they had swum over from the other side of the lake, where they and several hundred of their fellow West Point Cadets were camping. The blond one seemed to favor Rachel and she was thrilled because she was partial to fair men. The other one seemed to be giving Dotty the eye. They conversed for a while.

"May we meet you tonight?" the blond one asked.

"Yes it would be wonderful," the dark-haired fellow reiterated.

"We could get away from our camp in time to meet you at night, but we'll have to be back in camp by ten," the blond one said, looking directly at Rachel.

"We'll meet you outside of the dining room about eight," Rachel said.

The girls got through with dinner at eight-thirty and when they came out of the dining room, they found not only the two cadets waiting for them, but they had brought ten more cadets with them. They all marched into the casino, Rachel on the arm of the blond one and Dotty on the arm of the dark one. All eyes were upon them. Rachel and Dotty were thrilled beyond description.

The blond cadet's name was Bill and he was from Missouri. Rachel was enchanted with his voice and accent. When they danced, she could feel the powerful muscles in his shoulders and arms. She had never seen anyone so physically fit. He was as straight as a beam. His strong white teeth gleamed when he smiled. He was the personification of manliness. She couldn't believe he would be interested in her, but she tried to conceal her emotions.

Just as she was enjoying all this Abe, the dark-haired cadet, cut in.

"May I have this dance?"

He danced three dances with her. His name was Abe Goldstein, probably the only Jewish cadet at West Point, she thought. He was gorgeous too. He was from California. Although Rachel favored blond men, she was immediately fascinated with Abe.

"You seem like a wonderful girl," Abe remarked. "It would be difficult to forget you."

He was the most romantic person she had ever met. It would be easy to fall in love with him, Rachel thought.

Just then, Bill pulled her away from Abe. "You're not beating me to it, Abe," he remarked.

Here were Abe and Bill, probably the two most handsome cadets at West Point, competing for her. She wondered if she would ever see them again.

After a few more dances, they went outside to where the cadets had parked their cars. Rachel and Dotty sat on the running board of Abe's car. He put the radio on and tuned in to some soft music. Rachel was talking to Bill, resplendent in his uniform, as he sat on the grass beside her. She felt something on her arm and it was his lips.

"What brand of perfume do you use?" he asked.

She had put on some new face powder and perfume that evening. It really had a beautiful scent.

"I think you can smell the aroma better from a distance," she quipped. She laughed and the others joined in the laughter.

She told Bill how she hated war and she couldn't imagine someone as nice as he was to be training for war.

"I hate war too. Most of the cadets hate war. But we're training just to have a good defense so that other nations would be afraid to start a war with us."

How naïve I am, Rachel thought. I don't know anything about politics or war. Why did I have to say anything?

They finally had to leave and invited Rachel and Dotty to come to West Point during the weekend. It rained furiously all weekend so they didn't go.

Rachel received a loving letter from Kenny saying he missed her, but hoped she and Dotty were having a good time. She had promised to send him a picture of herself and Dotty in front of their bunk, so she did, together with a letter describing everything.

He wrote back, "I showed everyone your picture. Thanks so much." And he ended, "So long now to a beautiful senorita. Let me know when you are coming home."

The camp was having an Amateur Hour and Rachel participated. She sang "The Glory of Love" and got a lot of applause. She almost won, but didn't because she had never sung in public before and had stage fright. Then some new people arrived and several fellows vied for her attention. She forgot to write to Kenny to say exactly when she was coming home.

When she got back home, he called and she agreed to see him again. He didn't seem to want to say good bye and as they talked on the phone, she was aware that she was truly glad that she would be with him again.

After she had returned from the camp with Dotty, Kenny took her to Coney Island where the annual Mardi Gras was taking place. This was the official closing of Coney Island for the season. You walked around on Surf Avenue. There in the midst of the happy throngs of people, you could enjoy the amusements of Coney Island for the last time that year. People threw confetti on each other and there was a big parade. Kenny bought red felt Mexican hats, tied the laces under their chins and they wore them as they walked hand in hand, laughing and enjoying everything.

Then they went dancing in Luna Park. On the way they passed a small crowd surrounding a man with a huge scale.

"If I don't guess your weight within three pounds, you win a prize, he hawked.

Kenny asked, "How much does she weigh?" pointing to Rachel.

"126," he guessed.

"Wrong," laughed Kenny. "She weighs 96."

She won a fancy colored cane not worth much, probably fifteen or twenty-five cents at the most, and the chance cost twenty-five cents.

Kenny took her to the Cosmos Cafeteria. Then he suggested the "Funny House." They walked in and passed a mirror that makes you look funny. Then they proceeded through vestibules that were quite dark, no turning back possible.

Rachel was beginning to get scared for it had gotten so dark that it was pitch black. She tried to endure it and luckily it was only for a minute or so, when they turned a bend and got to a lighted place where there was an old carriage. It was the "Old Barn."

Everyone walked in a line, one following the other, through narrow passageways, not knowing what came next.

She clung to Kenny with all her might. All of a sudden, they turned another bend. It seemed there were rags on the floor or something like that and they jumped over them, because they feared it might be a trap. You might get caught and fall in.

The place started to get darker and darker until it was absolutely pitch black, even more than the previous darkness. Rachel became hysterical and cried out, "Light a match, Kenny." He said it wouldn't be safe and took her around. She thought she was dreaming and felt as if she would faint dead away, when they saw a light. Something came back to her. What happened there had subconsciously triggered off some old feelings. One was when she had her tonsils removed at the age of ten, when they had put a mask over her face and had given her ether. She felt as if she had entered a dark tunnel as the anesthesia quickly took effect. The other time was when they took her to the hospital in an ambulance with rheumatic fever and covered her face; it was raining.

She pretended that she had screamed in fun as she didn't want to tell him the miserable past. Anna had taken her home from the hospital despite the Administrator's warning that she would be an invalid for life, no marriage, no childbirth, no career. Anna did not heed him and neither would Rachel. She would live a normal life, no matter what.

Now that summer was over, Natalie and Debbie were preparing to go back to school and Rachel would have to put all her efforts into finding a job.

Anna went shopping with Rachel and bought her a black dress, princess style, with long net sleeves (which would hide her skinny arms), and a red pin and earrings to brighten it up. She also bought her a pair of high heeled shoes, suede and patent leather, and a bag. The Jewish High Holidays were coming and this was supposed to be for the holidays.

Kenny had asked if he could see her that coming Saturday and also during the holidays. She knew she couldn't get two outfits and since she had to wear the dress on their date Saturday, she had to decline seeing him during the holidays. She'd be embarrassed wearing the same outfit twice in a row and she couldn't tell him the reason. That was the bad part of it.

Kenny wanted to see her as much as possible. She had told him they ought to separate for a month to test their feelings for one another.

"How do you know I have to test my feelings?" he replied, but he went along with it.

Rachel went to parties, dances and met many more fellows during that month. The same thing happened as in the past. She would enjoy the freedom of being sought after and meeting new fellows, only to be glad when she was back with Kenny again, but she was still uncertain about things.

Fannie came over and told her that Kenny's friend, Hy, had invited her to a party at the fraternity. Before they had agreed to separate for a month, Kenny had also asked her to go to the party. Fannie told her that Kenny had escorted a pretty blond girl to the party. Rachel couldn't blame him, but she felt a pang of jealousy and uneasiness about it. Fannie sensed her distress and said, "Don't worry, she was very sweet, but you're prettier than she is."

When the month of separation was just about up, the bell rang and a boy called her to answer a phone call in the candy store. Her heart leaped. She was sure it would be Kenny, but when she got to the phone it was another fellow who had been dating and pursuing her. He was tall and handsome, with deep dimples when he smiled. Yet, she knew he wasn't for her. He called to invite her to a Halloween party his friends were giving. She accepted, but asked him to bring some fellows for some of the "Merry Girls." He said he would call her to let her know.

When she went back upstairs to her house, Anna was baking. Danny was supposed to come over with Tanya because it was her birthday. Anna prepared a nice dinner as well, but they didn't come. Tanya was a very rigid type of person whose main interests were herself and her equally cold family. Rachel couldn't see how Danny could stand her, no less love her. She was selfish and possessive, whereas he was so kind and caring.

Again the bell rang, summoning her to the candy store again for a phone call. She ran down the three flights of stairs and over to the candy store. This time it was Kenny. She would be seeing him again that weekend. Anticipating this made her happy.

The month of separation was over and she was excited when Kenny arrived. He looked a little thinner, but was still as nice as ever. They went downtown to the Metropolitan Theatre and saw a wonderful picture, "The Great Ziegfeld." It was cold out and she put her hand in his big coat pocket to warm it up.

"Is there room enough for mine too?" he asked. He entwined her hand in his in the pocket. He said he had taken a federal government exam for a Post Office job, had given up the baker's job and was again working as a shipping clerk in a dress house. He had worked there before and they took him back. She decided to turn down the previous invitation to a Halloween party and accepted Kenny's invitation to a Halloween party instead.

CHAPTER 21

Some girls on the block mentioned that they were working for the Lucky Strike Hit Parade. Coincidentally, Helen came over and said her friend, Rose, was working there too. One of the girls told Rachel to come down and try to get hired.

When Rachel got there, she discovered that no one could get into the building unless they had a certain pink identification card. These cards were given only to the employees. Rachel couldn't believe the mobs of girls and boys too, who were trying to go in. They were all told to wait outside and "perhaps there would be some openings."

But after hours of waiting, there proved to be none, so she went home disgustedly. At night, Rose came over and believe it or not, she had a card for her.

The next day, Rachel went again and got in and was employed. It was awful. She was put into the hand addressing department. There was also a typing department where the cards they were sending out were addressed by typewriter. Rachel didn't know what was worse. That day she addressed six hundred cards by hand and earned one dollar and twenty cents.

She endured this job for two weeks and quit. The Lucky Strike Hit Parade job was an interesting experience, however. She would always remember it. It was really a contest. She saved some of the cards that people sent in and tucked them between the pages of her diary.

The most popular songs of the day were "When I'm With You,"
"A Star Fell Out of Heaven," "Until the Real Thing Comes
Along," "A Rendezvous With a Dream," "When I'm With You,"
"Did I Remember," "These Foolish Things" (Remind me of you),
and "It's a Sin To Tell a Lie." People had to choose what they
thought were the best selections after the Lucky Strike Orchestra
played fifteen numbers. They sent postcards in, listing them in
the order of which were most popular that week.

Rachel walked her feet off, going to every possible employment
agency. There were always dozens of girls going after one job.
She advertised in the New York Times and got incredible phone
calls, all kinds of offers, some legitimate and some suspicious.
She sat in her father's office waiting for the calls, since they didn't
have a home phone.

She was very naïve and inexperienced, but careful enough with
the people who called. In between interviews she spent time in
her favorite place, the New York Public Library on Fifth Avenue
and Forty-Second Street. She read anything she could get her
hands on regarding the writing profession.

She applied to magazines, newspapers, etc. She almost accepted a
part time position at the apartment of an author, but at the last
minute copped out. He seemed brilliant. It was like a dream there in
his private library, walls covered with books from floor to ceiling,
but she didn't trust being alone with him in the apartment. True, she
did find some of his articles in the library, but they were political in
nature and now he was going to write a book on sex.

It's a good thing Danny was in her father's place when a man
called in to answer one of the advertisements she had placed in
the New York Times. He said his name was Mr. Phillips and he
was calling from Cuntiform Corporation, three twenty-eight West
thirty-eighth street.

"Are you the girl who advertised?"

"Yes."

"Did you graduate from high school?"

"Yes."

"How old are you?"

"Nineteen. I stated that in the ad."

"Could you be a receptionist?"

"Yes, I think so."

"How tall are you?"

"Five feet, four inches."

"What color hair?"

"Light brown."

"What size?"

"Three."

"What size bust?"

"Thirty-two."

"Do you wear a brassiere?"

"What difference does that make?"

"Well, I want it to appear as if my girl didn't."

She got angry. "What do you mean? "What has that to do with the job?" What kind of place do you have?"

"It's a lingerie place."

"Do you want a model?"

She would go along with this and see if she could get him to break down and let the true goods come out.

"No, I don't want a model," he answered. She felt safe because Danny was there.

"Do you wear a brassiere?" he persisted.

"Well, if yours is the lingerie business, you'd want everyone to wear one so that you could make more sales." Then she changed the topic and asked him his name and address and when she should come.

"Do you really want to come?"

"If I could possibly arrange it, I'll be down this afternoon." He asked her to repeat the name and address to see if she got it straight. She was smart enough to know that Cuntiform was a dirty, made-up name and that he wanted her to repeat it to make fun of her. At this point, she purposely said aloud, "Danny, come here. I think this guy is kidding."

And when Danny reached for the phone, the skunk hung up. Then she called information to check on him. There was no phone at that address for such an organization. Thank God for men like Danny and Kenny. They were so sweet, so clean.

What a winter. She got part-time jobs, temporary jobs, had plenty of dates, and met plenty of eligible fellows who she could have had, yet somehow it always reverted to Kenny.

It was March before they knew it and Kenny came over at two-thirty on a Sunday afternoon. It was damp and slushy, that is, a wet snow was falling lightly. They went to the Loew's Pitkin and saw Fred MacMurray and Gladys Swarthout in "Champagne Waltz." They also showed "Bulldog Drummond Escapes" and a Mickey Mouse cartoon. Besides that, Henrietta Cameron played the organ while lyrics were flashed on the screen and the audience sang.

When they got out of the movie, they went to the delicatessen on Sutter Avenue to eat. He took her home and stayed about four more hours until one a.m. they got into a serious discussion. Rachel told him her innermost feelings, how she wanted to marry someone wealthy and perhaps even famous. She tried to find out if he really ever harbored the desire to attain either of these two goals.

"Of course I'm ambitious," he said. "However, sometimes people of small means are happier than the kind you mentioned. You haven't seen much of the world yet, Rachel. If you'd been around more, your beliefs might not be the same." He went on, "You know, I'd like to be a buyer. A cousin of mine is married to a buyer who makes one hundred dollars a week."

"One hundred dollars a week isn't too bad," she said. Yet in her heart she thought, is that all he's looking forward to? Well, I'm young yet so there's still time to find out.

"Is there anything you like about me?" he asked suddenly? "You know, I have one very good point, that is, the way I feel about you." With that, he leaned forward and kissed her.

He continued, "You must have thought it strange that I haven't asked you to my house. Knowing how you feel, I've hesitated to ask you. My family would like to meet you, especially my mother. It's about time I did, but it's true, you bring a girl over to meet the family when there's a commitment between them."

"I think it's foolish that boys think they have to be really and definitely serious before inviting a girl over to meet the family. As far as I'm concerned, I would go and just visit as I would any friend's home."

"You know it's not that way," he said.

"We have a big Seder at our house," he continued. "Everyone comes. They'd think we have made up our minds to get married. It would be hard to explain."

He seemed upset. After thinking it over, he said, "Rachel, as long as we've had that understanding, how about coming to our Seder?"

She was really excited at the prospect of meeting his whole family, but was worried about the lack of an outfit to wear. She was still wearing her winter clothes. She certainly couldn't come in her fur coat, for instance.

"I'd really like to come," she said. It would be wonderful meeting your family."

Rachel got up early the next day, Sunday, and got her father on the side and asked him what he thought of it.

"I wanted to ask you first, because Mama might think it's wrong to go unless I was engaged to him."

She also thought that by making her father part of the situation he might be more serious about getting money for her to buy a dress and some accessories, including a Spring coat.

She continued, "After all, it sure will be an experience meeting his father and mother, brothers, sisters and other relatives and to see his home. It might help me make my mind up about him after I see the place he was brought up in and the people who are a part of it. That really counts a lot, you know"

Jake liked Kenny. "I think you should go. I'll get you the money for the clothes." She felt good about going, good about the fact that her father liked Kenny. Everyone liked Kenny.

All week she continued desperately to try to find a job. Each day was filled with anxiety waiting for Jake to bring home the money for her outfit. Now it was Friday, a day before the Seder and he still had not come up with the money. He made daily promises, but the money did not come in. "Please God," she prayed. "I have to buy the clothes and be dressed by six p.m. tomorrow. I can't go with a winter outfit."

Friday evening arrived and her father came home, but without any money. What hurt most was the fact that even at this late time, she still wasn't sure, by the way Pa, Danny and Monroe talked, whether or not she was going to get it and buy something to wear the last minute. Somehow or other, though, she had to confront them and as a result, a quarrel ensued. She didn't sit down to eat supper with them, put on her coat and went out although she was hungry and it was windy and rather cold outside.

She spent a miserable hour walking up and down the street and standing in the hall. When she went up, they had finished eating but were still sitting around the table.

"I have to know for sure, otherwise I'll have to call Kenny and tell him I can't be there."

When they said they couldn't possibly raise the money the next day, every hope died. She would call him and say she couldn't come because she was working at the department store, her present temporary job. She would say that they were running a sale and had called her to ask her to come in. Oh, how it would hurt him, she thought.

What would his family think of this girl whom he cherished so much? She pictured his mother bustling and sweating to prepare everything and then seeing her son in despair and disappointment. He would be humiliated before his family as to what a bad choice he had made. She doubted that he would even believe her alibi, yet she couldn't bring herself to let him know that she couldn't even get an outfit to wear for the occasion.

Rachel waited until noon the next day before calling him as she wanted him to think it was lunch hour and she was working. She trembled and her voice was shaky. He had nothing to say when she told him, just six hours before he was to pick her up. Oh, he must have hated her. He must have been deeply hurt. What if he thought this was a sneaky plan on her part, just to avoid coming.

She was miserable. Just for a few dollars for clothes, to lose him. His family would probably tell him it was better for him to have found out her character now than later. Yet, if he loved and trusted her, he might come back, but she wouldn't blame him if he couldn't forgive her, that she had been stringing him along all this time.

She had to get away from things, so she went to Helen's house. They were very nice to her. Rose was there too so Helen's brother took the three of them to Floyd Bennett's Field, the airport. In the evening, they went to the "Biltmore" and saw "On the Avenue" with Dick Powell, Madeline Carroll and Alice Faye.

After the movie, Rose went home and Helen's mother asked Rachel to have supper there and sleep over. It was a good thing she was there so that she was able to keep her mind off of things a little. It was almost too much to bear.

It was two weeks after Rachel had phoned Kenny saying she couldn't come to the Seder. Each day she waited, hoping to hear from him. She could not bring herself to tell him she couldn't come because she had nothing to wear. It might get back to his family too, and she would be humiliated. Perhaps they wouldn't like the fact that their son was thinking of marrying a girl from such an impoverished family. She would merely have to tell him that she didn't break the appointment on purpose and that he'd have to have faith in her.

Kenny's friend, Hy, was still dating Fannie on and off. Rachel decided to call him to find out how Kenny was. Hy came over as she told him she had to see him. He said that for the past two weeks, Kenny stays in his room when he's home and cries

Rachel was torn with remorse. In addition to what had happened between her and Kenny, she was still out of a job and searching frantically for one. The temporary sales job was over. She remembered a movie in which a girl "ran wild" to forget. She accepted some dates from fellows she had refused to date before and tried to join her friends as much as possible, but she could not get Kenny out of her mind.

After Hy had told her how badly Kenny felt, she wrote him a letter:

Dear Kenny,

There is something I must ask you. Did you believe
I was being honest when I didn't come to the Seder,
or did you think it was on purpose?

Please don't be afraid to tell me the truth, even if
you don't think it sounds nice, and please answer
my mail.

Then she called Fannie and they went to the "Cinema" and saw
Greta Garbo and Robert Taylor in "Camille." It was a beautiful
love story and she cried all through it.

The following day she went on a job interview in Long Island.
She had never been out there. It took her two hours each way by
bus. It was gorgeous out there, not like East New York. She
drank in the lakes, the flowers, the greenery and the quietude.
Wouldn't it be wonderful to be married to a successful man and
live in one of these beautiful homes? Her family would come
out and visit her and perhaps her children.

As usual, the man who interviewed her said he'd let her know.
When she got home, there was a message, another job interview
for tomorrow. She went. So did about twenty other girls. That's
how it was.

When she got home from the interview, there was a letter from
Kenny. He had answered right away. He said he believed she had
broken the appointment because either something more to her
liking had come up or because she had regretted making it.
Furthermore, he didn't believe she was working late because he
found out the store where she was supposed to be working was
closed.

He said that she had also added when she called him that morning that she was going to her aunt's house and couldn't see him that weekend. "You said you were going to your aunt's house even before I had asked to see you and you seemed anxious not to see me." How sad it was. The truth was that she was trying to avoid seeing him until she got something decent to wear, having nothing but winter clothes. If he only knew.

Rachel wrote him immediately and said she was disappointed in him for having doubted her intentions, but deep in her heart, she knew he was right. Nevertheless, he called and asked if he could take her to a wedding which he was attending Saturday night and apologized "for acting so foolish." She knew she'd have to borrow something to wear somehow, but she couldn't say no.

The wedding was wonderful. The bride's and her attendants' gowns were gorgeous. Everyone greeted Kenny as if he were really someone special. His ex-boss and co-workers from the dress manufacturing firm seemed very fond of him. He brought Rachel a gorgeous corsage made up of little orange roses, sweet peas and orchids. She felt as if he must really love her if he could forgive the incident regarding her not coming to the Seder.

The next day was Sunday and they spent it in Prospect Park. They listened to a concert at the Brooklyn Museum and then explored the whole third floor of the museum. By the time they got to the zoo it was closing, so they only saw the seals. They went through the Botanical Gardens then decided to go rowing on the lake. It began turning dark and the water started to get rough and it started to rain. It was lightning and thundering.

Kenny was afraid to let Rachel stay in the boat so he put her out near a shelter, said he wanted to take the boat back to the boathouse by himself and then come back for her. Rachel didn't want to leave him alone on the lake in a storm. She was wearing his overcoat and he was only in his suit for she had been a little cold and he put his coat over her jacket. He insisted that she get out of the boat but she was afraid to let him go alone, so she trailed him alongside the lake. It was completely dark by now. She ran down the road until she got to the boathouse. It was raining hard and she was drenched.

She waited there for about twenty minutes, but Kenny didn't show up. She was beginning to get frightened when she finally saw him approaching. He had gotten to the boathouse before her and had rushed back where he had left her, but since she wasn't there, he figured she might have followed him to the boathouse so he had raced back there again.

His suit was soaking wet and his hair and face as well and he was out of breath. He didn't say anything, but took her hand and led her to the boathouse where they had a sandwich and a hot drink.

As they walked out of the park, he held on to her hand. She noticed that he was very deep in thought and troubled.

"Kenny, I'm really sorry about the Seder. I'll tell you the real reason I couldn't come, but not now." She felt her face turning hot. He didn't reply.

At that moment, she felt this must be love. She was always wondering what love really was. Perhaps it meant that you didn't want to see the one you love unhappy. She couldn't hurt him any more.

"Kenny, I want to make you happy, but I need some time to sort out my feelings. I love the present, but I'm afraid of the future. Let's separate for a month. By that time, maybe we'll both have jobs and feel better in general."

"Every day counts. A month is a long time, but if that's what you want." When they reached her house, he didn't want to come up but relented. She made him something to eat. He seemed very dejected and when he left, he said, "I'll call you in about twenty-five days."

CHAPTER 22

During the month of her separation from Kenny, Rachel searched desperately for a job. She also went out as much as possible to dances, parties, on dates and with her girlfriends. Now the month was over and Kenny called as planned.

During the course of the conversation, he told her he had been working as a baker and would join the Baker's Union. Her heart sank when she heard this.

"Oh, I suppose it's just for a while," she said, hopefully.

"I don't know. It's the only thing I can do. My father's a baker, you know. I can't run around making a small salary all the time."

"But bakers don't make that much."

"That's wrong. They do. You always care what people think."

He said he'd be over the next evening, Saturday that is if he didn't have to go in to work, since he sometimes had to work the night shift.

That did it. Her worse nightmare was coming true. He was right. She did care what people thought. Take Helen, for instance, she always bragged about the dates she had with college fellows and intellectuals. She would probably marry one of them.

Even Fannie who was not the studious type, was going with Sammy, definitely a brilliant guy who was active in school events and wrote poetry for the school publications. She, Rachel, an honor student, was going to put herself in a trap like her mother. Be careful, she warned herself.

Maybe if she could succeed with her talent for writing, things might open up for her. She would try to break into that field, perhaps first in the office of an advertising firm or a publishing office or something like that.

She cherished the letters from Danny that he had written to her when she was in Chicago and he had remained in New York for a while. He wrote that he loved her letters. He encouraged her to write and said he knew she would someday make it, that she was a born writer.

Kenny kept the date for Saturday night since he found out he was not working that night. When he left, they both knew in their hearts that this might be the end, that they might never see each other again.

The department store where Rachel had worked periodically called her in again for they were having a three-day sale. This time they put her to work in the Infants' Department. She loved the experience; all babies' things; so adorable. She was amazed at the unbelievably small garments. She found it hard to believe a living person could be so tiny. Clothes about four inches square, tiny bonnets, shoes, dresses, shirts, slips and bloomers. There were also diapers, bottles, tiny combs and kimonos, all so adorable.

She told Fannie, "You ought to see the proud young parents. They come in carrying their little darlings. I put a tiny, newly-bought bonnet on a wee sweet baby and tied the ribbon around its delicate little neck while the young mother held her baby. I immediately loved this innocent little one. Having your own baby is probably the most thrilling thing in the world."

Fannie merely giggled in her own lovable way. "That's sweet," she replied.

The sale was over and Rachel was back in the same situation as before, job hunting. It was June now and she was nineteen years old. She couldn't stand it at home. She pitied the whole family and wished she could do something about things, but she was helpless.

Fannie's sister had just left to start working as a bookkeeper in a Catskill Mountain hotel.

"You ought to go to the same employment agency which got her the job," Fannie said.

Rachel went to the agency and sure enough she also secured a position as a bookkeeper in a hotel in Ferndale, New York in the Catskills. It was rather a small hotel, having sixty-five rooms. Anna was glad she was going away as she would avoid another summer of misery at home and the heat of the apartment and the city. She would also probably get more and better food to eat and the benefits of the fresh air and sunshine of the country.

Anna washed, ironed and packed a valise. She had bought a couple of new items for Rachel to wear. Roy Ellstein, the owner of the hotel came to pick Rachel up to take her up to the hotel as he had come in to the city and was going back. Anna, Natalie, Debbie, Danny and Monroe waved goodbye as the car left.

CHAPTER 23

It was a relief to spread out from the closeness of the city into the vast freedom of the country and to feel the heat of nervous tension already being cooled by the green tranquility therein.

Rachel sat beside Roy Ellstein in the noisy little battered car as they drove to his hotel, the "Friendship House," in Ferndale, New York, a Catskill resort.

"Isn't it wonderful," she said. "Look at that little house way up there on the mountain. I wonder who lives there."

The squat, chunky man seemed not to hear her. He just hummed and kept on driving.

"I hope we can get the place in order," he remarked after a while. There's so much to do. I have to stop in at the butcher in Monticello first."

When they reached Monticello, he asked her to come into the butcher shop with him. "Marty, this is my bookkeeper. Better watch the bills. She'll be checking them," he laughed robustly. She felt so important.

When they reached the "Friendship House" Hotel, Mrs. Ellstein came out to meet her. She was a stern woman and eyed Rachel up and down suspiciously.

"Meet Herta, the chambermaid," she said, as a young girl of about seventeen came towards them on the lawn, carrying a pile of sheets and pillow cases.

Herta said hello and continued on to do her work of cleaning up the sixty-five rooms which had been unoccupied since the previous summer. Then she would make the beds. The first guests were to arrive in about a week.

Mrs. Ellstein showed Rachel around the small office. "Here are the keys to the rooms. When guests arrive, show them to their rooms. You can also start mailing circulars to people and checking the bills. Make sure they're right." She went on and on. "The lawn chairs, benches and tables have to be painted, also the fireplace in the main dining room. You can do that before the guests arrive. Wait here; I'll get the paint."

She returned in a few minutes with a handyman who helped her carry the cans of green and red paint. "Before you start painting, you'll have to dry all the dishes. They're washed already. I'll show you what shelves to put them on."

Rachel worked like a beaver. Her pay was to be sixty dollars and room and board for the whole summer, yet she dreaded going home, so she had to put up with it.

"Bring all the linens from the upstairs closet to the office closet and give them out to the chambermaid. Keep a close watch on them."

"I'm still better off than Herta," she reasoned. I don't know how that poor girl can do what she does. Herta was about seventeen years old and was the chambermaid. She made all the beds up, washed floors and did all the cleaning of the sixty-five rooms in the hotel. Her parents were trying to make a living running a grocery/delicatessen in the German section of New York City. They had emigrated from Germany. Herta was very intelligent and wrote beautiful poetry which she read to Rachel before they turned the light out at night.

Rachel applied herself, taking charge of the office. She made a chart up of all the rooms and the amount of beds in each one and went around fitting all the keys to their doors and tagging them appropriately with their room numbers. She sent out five hundred circulars, checked the old guest lists, set up file folders, and took care of correspondence and bills and what not.

In addition to this, she washed and wiped the dishes of Ray and Hilda Ellstein, Herta and the two hired men and herself and helped to set the table for them and remove the dishes after they had finished eating. They were all working in preparation for the arrival of the guests.

Mrs. Ellstein called her to satisfy her slightest whim, such as shutting a door, getting her some water and even setting her hair. During the first few days, Rachel had to rake the entire lawns which had just been cut, and raked up all the dried leaves which had been there all winter, about fifteen bushels full, and carried them cut to the grounds in the back of the hotel, where they were burned. She had been hired as a bookkeeper, but was being exploited.

Rachel and Herta shared a small room on the top floor of the house. All sixty-five rooms were in this one building, a grey wooden structure, which also included the kitchen, dining room, lobby and office. There was also a barn-like huge "casino" where the entertainment and dancing was held.

Rachel and Herta would fall asleep exhausted at night. They shared a room and one bed. They would talk softly so that the Ellsteins, who slept in the next room, wouldn't hear them.

She and Rachel became good friends. They both wrote poetry and shared their poems. Herta was the picture of health, strong and agile, not delicate like Rachel. She knew how to take care of herself.

At night before going to bed, Herta put cold cream on her hands and then encased them in cotton gloves for the night. She brushed her strong white teeth vigorously. Despite working very hard, she was cheerful and never complained. It was pleasant being with her, but she did not stay out the season.

When Herta left, Mrs. Ellstein put Rachel in a shack way out in the woods with Rosie, a fat, smelly, middle aged, sometimes drunken chambermaid. The waiters laughed and joked about Rosie, something about her being a whore. It was frightening to have to sleep in the same bed with her out there in the wilderness away from the hotel proper.

At first Rachel was terrified of her, but then she started to confide in her, telling her of her feelings of despair, all about her life and amazingly, Rosie responded with understanding. But Rachel knew she wasn't going to spend the rest of the summer that way.

When she had some brief time off, she befriended some children who were vacationing at the hotel with their parents. The two little girls and their parents had adjoining rooms, the choicest in the entire hotel, completely modernized. The girls adored Rachel. Their parents wanted to go to Europe and asked her if she would sleep with them and in general keep an eye on them.

When Mrs. Ellstein heard of the situation she was livid. "This is the last time I'll employ fancy help," she said, as Rachel moved her belongings into the children's' room. Nevertheless, Rachel enjoyed her new quarters. She told the girls bedtime stories which she made up spontaneously and cuddled with them and they giggled and were very happy with her.

There was a group of entertainers who were part of the great Jewish Maurice Schwartz Troupe. Everyone was excited when they arrived, especially Rachel for she was enamored of show business and was anxious to mingle with them. The leading actress, Celia Lipson, and her husband, Milton, befriended her. Madame Lipson, as she was referred to, performed in the shows at the hotel and her husband played piano in a four-piece band there.

The actors were very professional and whenever they needed an "extra" in their performances, they called upon Rachel who learned a lot from them. She was intrigued by their hustle and bustle backstage and even by their arguments and warnings against "upstaging." They said their lines in Yiddish and since Rachel could speak Yiddish because of listening to Anna, Jake and Tonta Hecht, she came in very handy. Not only the performers, but the guests as well, commended her and encouraged her to continue to act.

One day the group had an argument with the Ellsteins. They packed and left in a huff. Rachel couldn't stand the Ellsteins anymore either. The parents of the little girls she was taking care of came back and Rachel decided to leave too.

Mae, one of the "Merry Girls," was spending the summer with her parents in Hurleyville and as she had no other place to go to, she hitch-hiked to Hurleyville.

When she got there, exhausted and troubled, Rachel found that Mae's mother had returned to the city on business and that Mae was there alone with her little brother. Her father worked in the city and came up to the bungalow on some weekends. Mae and her brother welcomed her and she spent the night there.

In the morning, she hitch-hiked to a hotel where Celia Lipson and some of the Maurice Schwartz actors were now performing. They had given her the address before departing from the Friendly House Hotel, just in case she needed them.

Lipson and the rest greeted her warmly. They got her some dinner and the next day the actress set out with her to help her find a job. They hitch-hiked to the White Sulpher Springs House where her husband was working as a pianist.

The governess there had just quit and Mr. Lipson spoke to the boss and she got the job. The hotel was larger and more exciting than the Friendly House.

At night, the dance floor was filled with fellows and girls from the neighboring bungalow colonies and the young people sat on chairs and also on the side rails of the huge porch. Rachel was free in the evening, since the parents put their children to bed. The children ate in the Children's dining room and after that the adults had their dinner.

While the parents ate, Rachel gathered the children in a circle in the main lobby and told them stories. She made these stories up as she went along and the children were wide-eyed and delighted. When the parents came to claim their children, they were so fascinated by these stories, that they sat and listened too.

Rachel had become part of the social staff. Mr. Lipson and the rest of the orchestra were like her own family and the actors welcomed her in their group too. However, the orchestra had a quarrel with the four bosses and left and she found herself alone again. She had made some friends, among them a young woman, Lillian, who invited her to sleep in her room rather than the one she had been assigned to in the worker's quarters.

The end of the summer was approaching and since most of the children were gone, there was no further need of Rachel's services. Rachel talked the boss into letting her stay an extra week, since a few kids were still there and Lillian wanted her to stay with her. She told him she would pay him a few dollars for food and stay in Lillian's room. At last she had a good rest. The thought of going home upset her, although she loved her family.

At the end of the week, just as she was preparing to go home, she received a phone call. "This is Milton, Celia's husband. I'm at a ritzy hotel in Woodridge, "The Lake House." They need someone to direct the children's shows. I know you have talent and could do it. You'll get to write your own material and direct the entire show. Come here right away. You've got the job."

She was both elated and scared. One of the actors who had been in Celia's group, had remained at the White Sulphur Springs House, where he and a couple of other actors had gone with Milton and his orchestra after quitting the Friendship House. He was an older man and always tried to get Rachel to go out with him. He was furious at her refusals and when he heard of her getting the job at the Lake House, he lashed out.

"How could you have the nerve? I once worked there. It is a very swell place. The girl who had that job was an elocution teacher. You'll be fired in no time."

She told two of the waiters about it and one of them drove her and her valise to her new adventure at the Lake House. She was taken into the dining room where the children were having lunch. It was unbelievable to her that she could at last be in a position to try to prove her abilities.

The waiters were very attractive young men, mostly college students who were trying to work their way through college.

They eyed her up and down, "So you're the new governess. Good luck!" They plowed her with lamb chops and other delectables, which she loved and kept coming over with various luscious dishes. "Come on, eat." She was so thin and they treated her like they were her big brothers, bent on fattening her up a bit. "We'll take care of you," they said. She was still about a size three.

One of the guests, Norbert, stood by her side constantly and in the evening he called for her at her cabin which she shared with the owner's daughter. He took her to the casino for dancing and entertainment. Also, the boss's nephew fell for her in such a way that he told her he loved her. She was asked to dance every dance with various fellows and without a doubt was the most popular girl there, not excluding the guests.

She planned and wrote all the material for her children's show in her secret hide-a-way. This is how she described it in her diary:

> "In front of me stretches a square, olive green lake, hemmed in by the Irish green structures of nature. I am sitting on a very worn old quilt on elevated land about twelve feet from the water's edge and am gazing down at the breathtaking beauty before me. Once in a while, I glance to the left, the right or in back of me. About six feet to the immediate left, I see a bed of goldenrod stretching its slender legs and bending its yellow head to and fro.
>
> Beyond the bed of goldenrod and forward, on the lake's shore, rises a variegated school of bushes. Still further down, strong, cool trees top off the whole scene majestically sweeping clear around the entire lake and ending here, just a few feet to the left of me by this tiny paradise which I now occupy in seclusion. The lake is covered mostly

by green stagnant moss, making it seem like some
lost, hidden remnant of a time gone by."

Nobody knew where she disappeared to, but one day she found this
notation on the lobby bulletin board: "Do you know where our
Children's Drama Director hides? Who can unlock the mystery?"

Once a week, Rachel had a few hours off. She went to this
abandoned lake, hidden amongst trees and foliage, off the main
road, about three quarters of a mile away from the hotel. This
was her haven. She sneaked away by herself, taking along, in
addition to a notebook in which to write her material, a book to
read and stationery on which to write letters home.

One day she was standing in front of the main building when a
handsome young man approached her. He had just checked in
with his parents and some friends of theirs. His brother was a
pianist in the orchestra. She was wearing a plain little dress that
Anna had bought her for three dollars. It was Alice blue and had
a white lacy collar.

"You look beautiful," he remarked. "What are you doing here?"

"I work here."

"What do you do?"

"I write and direct children's shows. We're putting on a show this
weekend."

He reminded her of one of the West Pointers. She couldn't believe
he meant what he was saying. I'll bet he tells that to all the girls,
she thought. But he really did seem sincere. In fact, she felt that
maybe he was the one she had been waiting for all her life. He hit
her like electricity.

He danced with her at the casino that night and all the fellows in the orchestra kept gaping at them and sort of giggling. At one point, he sat in with the band and played the drums and the guests applauded his dexterity. "A big hand for my brother, the pianist," he announced, "and for all the wonderful musicians."

Then he returned to her and resumed dancing. Finally he asked, "Would you like to go for a walk?" She felt as if she had known him for a long time, even though she knew nothing about him, except that he was attending college and was here with his parents and their friends and that she was incredibly attracted to him.

His car was parked in a spot about the distance of a block from the hotel. It stood in an area laden with bushes. She was so innocent about sex that she thought nothing of it when he suggested they sit in the car. It was wonderful being with him.

"I'm going to the city tomorrow. Would you like me to go to your parents' house and bring back anything you might need?"

"No, thank you. I don't need anything." How lonely she was. Did he know? Did he care?

He seemed genuine and she was thrilled that he was interested enough to want to meet her parents. He talked about his life and feelings and problems and she listened. He put his arm around her shoulder in a loving but respectful way. Hours went by until she finally said, "I could go into the kitchen and bring you something to eat and drink."

He thanked her and she went back to the hotel kitchen and brought back some cake and milk. They enjoyed the refreshments and talked until the dawn appeared. Then they went back to the hotel.

Later that day, the musicians winked at her knowingly.

"Oh, so you spent the night in the car with Marty!" She merely smiled and ignored them. She knew she had done nothing wrong, nor had Marty. He was a real gentleman and she felt like it was love at first sight, but as usual, she had given him no encouragement, just as with the other fellows. She just never believed that she could be loved and had never let anyone even kiss her, except Kenny.

And now the summer was over. It ended with a magnificent outdoor buffet, enhanced by balloons, decorations and music, which the owners gave every year during the Labor Day weekend.

She had met all kinds of young men while working in the Catskills, but never took their professions of love seriously. She always found a way to elude them, never believing them and they seemed to want her more for it. She felt they wanted something and she would save that for the one who really loved her and whom she would love in return. He would be handsome and rich and would rescue her from the awful poverty and struggle which she had endured as far back as she could remember.

After the Labor Day weekend, the hotel officially closed. It would not open until the following June. Rachel called her mother.

"Hello, Mom. My job will be finished this week. I know it's so hot in the city and Debbie could use a country vacation. There's a bungalow colony where I could rent a little bungalow for the two of us. Mae's mother is coming up and she said she would bring Debbie here. Her husband is driving. Please say yes."

"I would be very good for Debbie," Anna replied. "I'll call Mae's mother and arrange it. Thanks Rachel, you're a good sister."

"I wish Natalie could come too, but there's only one bed and besides, they won't like it if I bring two people at the same time. Natalie can come when Debbie goes home, if she wants to."

Rachel waited impatiently for Debbie to arrive and hugged and kissed her. She was ten years old, a beautiful little "black-haired chicken," as Rachel lovingly called her. Truly a little blue-eyed doll. "My sister," she said to herself proudly.

Rachel had been able to rent the bungalow at a very low rate since it was the end of the season. It was nicely furnished, with ample closets and windows and the interior was painted a cheerful coral. In the front there was a little garden with climbing roses and baby pine trees. There was a small kitchen sink and a two burner gas stove, shelves and a tiny bathroom. It was sunny and bright.

Anna was so glad when she read Rachel's letter: "We're a few minutes walk from Kiamesha Village and shop there. Also, they come around for food orders every day. We're ordering steak for tomorrow. Last night we had dairy. I cut a fresh tomato in half and put salt on it. Then we had a juicy piece of lox and pumpernickel bread with butter, and half a jar each of sour cream with a banana and two glasses of milk each, with chocolate doughnuts. Later we had chocolate ice cream frappes.

At last I am free for the first time this summer and I feel so good. It is a little paradise here. Let me know if Natalie can come. I wish you could get away to the country too. Maybe next summer, I hope."

Before Anna had a chance to reply to the letter, the weather turned cold and Rachel decided to go back home with Debbie. Natalie was susceptible to colds and it didn't seem advisable for her to come up to the mountains.

Rachel had been so busy all summer that she hardly had time to think of Kenny. She had missed him so much before she left and now that she was back, she took up where she had left off. She wondered how he was and what he was doing. She felt like telling him the reason that she had not gone to his parent's home for the Seder, but dared not. It would be too embarrassing. She was being frightened by a recurring dream. In it, Kenny's mother in anguish asked, "What did you do to my son?"

She resumed the job hunting. It was exhausting and frustrating. She applied at all the newspapers, magazines, publishing companies, advertising firms, anything that smacked of writing, but to no avail.

Cousin Dorothy Freeman said that her girlfriend had worked as secretary to a textile broker and had just quit and advised Rachel to apply for the job. She was hired. It was in the Pennsylvania Building at two hundred twenty-five West Twenty-Fourth Street in Manhattan.

She felt very uncomfortable about the way the boss, a man of about forty, looked at her. She was so ignorant about sex, but she noticed something was wrong. He kept touching his crotch. Then he started hanging over the back of her chair as she typed. He stood so close that she could hear his breath. She left the job.

Christmas was near and she was still unemployed. She was called back to work in the same department store where she had worked before.

It was temporary, for they hired extra help for the Christmas rush. The "Merry Girls" had disbanded. She got in touch with Fannie before new Years.

"You know, Rachel, sometime in November I happened to meet Kenny in the street. Remember we had a club party then? I forgot to tell you that I invited Kenny and he was there."

"I didn't go to the party because I had a misunderstanding with some of the girls."

Rachel was filled with remorse. If she had known he was going to be there, she would have gone. Was fate kind or cruel in not making her go? He must have wanted to see her or he wouldn't have gone. How did he feel about her now? He probably thought she had deliberately stayed away.

"Can you come over to my house tomorrow night? I'll call the other girls too. We have a lot to talk about, "Fannie said.

It was good getting together again. All the "Merry Girls" showed up. Dotty announced that she was marrying Eddie. Fannie broke the news that she was marrying Sammy, and Mary was hysterically happy for Fred had come back to her and they were also getting married.

They discussed "the first night."

"How will you know what to do?"

"My mother said that it will come naturally as long as you love each other."

"Nature will take its course."

"I can imagine how nervous I'll be, but I don't care what happens. If a fellow loves you enough to marry you and wants to spend his whole life with you, he deserves everything. He wants to take care of you and you want to take care of him, so you'd do anything to make him happy."

"You could never get close enough to the one you love. It's wonderful to know he'll always be with you, not just on dates."

They discussed the weddings, the bridal gowns, the thrills and hopes.

Rachel drank it all in. When would her time come to be happy as they were? Who would she marry? What would her life be like? She had always dreamed of glamour and wealth. Yet she knew her life would be empty unless she found a supreme love. To love and be loved, nothing could surpass that.

One day she walked into the St. Regis Hotel, just to look around. She observed the rich women in their costly furs and magnificent diamonds. Just one of those diamonds, she thought, could have bought Kenny and her a home and given them a start in some kind of business.

People were going into the Iridium Room of the hotel. Tears came into her eyes. What made these women better than she? They were just clever. You could be a beggar or queen depending upon whom you married.

When she worked in the wallet factory and went to the rest room, she had to pass the men who were hunched over their machines. They reminded her of busy spiders, spinning away day after day, only to have their fragile webs blown away by the wind. She hated the whirring machines and pitied the men who worked them, trying to eke out a meager living. The man of her dreams would have to create something more powerful than that.

CHAPTER 24

Maurice Schwartz was opening his Gramercy Arts Yiddish Theatre on Fifty-Seventh Street in Manhattan with "The Brothers Ashkenazai." Celia Lipson had a starring role in the show and her husband, Milton, played piano in the orchestra pit. She was helping them to improve their English skills. Rachel also visited Celia backstage and was enthralled with the activity and professionalism of the cast.

To Rachel's surprise and delight, Celia called her and told her she had talked to Maurice Schwartz about her and shown him her picture and he wanted her to join the group. Since she was pencil slim, he would put her into the chorus where the girls were all slim and wore frilly long gowns and delicate straw picture hats with satin ribbons.

Celia Lipson implored Anna and Jake to let Rachel go with them on their forthcoming performance tour of England and Israel. She said she and her husband would watch her carefully. They were going on a very fine steamship line. Anna and Jake berated Rachel, saying that "only bums are in show business," and steadfastly refused to give her their permission to go. With a heavy heart, Rachel thanked the Lipsons and stayed behind.

Heading home on a subway train after a miserable day of doing the rounds of the employment agencies, Rachel noticed the Help Wanted section of the New York Times on the floor near her seat. She picked it up and was attracted to an ad: "Lyric writer, to collaborate. Profit without investment." The train made a sudden jolt and the paper fell out of her hand and onto the lap of a woman sitting next to her.

"Oh, I'm sorry," Rachel apologized. The woman smiled and said, "That's all right. It's nothing."

"I'm so upset. I've been walking my feet off looking for a job. I want to write. I just picked this paper up and something caught my eye about a lyricist wanted. I'd love to put my poetry into music."

"Keep after your dream," the lady said. She seemed kind, intelligent and understanding. "You remind me of my daughter. She writes too. She works for a publishing company. Just keep writing and when you have something to show, call her." She wrote her daughter's name and business phone number down on the edge of the newspaper.

"Thank you so much. You never can tell. I won't forget."

They chatted all during the trip about half an hour and parted when Rachel reached her destination.

"Don't lose my daughter's phone number. She's very sweet. She'll advise you."

"She must be sweet if she's your daughter." Rachel left the train and as she looked back, the woman was waving goodbye to her, so she waved back.

"There are still good people in this world," Rachel thought. She tore the name and address off the edge of the newspaper and put it in her wallet.

When she got home, Danny and Tanya were there. They were also out of jobs, so they picked up the paper she had brought.

This again brought that ad to her mind and just for the heck of it; she sat down and penned a letter in a couple of minutes. Danny mailed it.

Two weeks passed and one morning a neighbor came in saying she had found a notice of "Telegram delivered," in the hall on the floor. It was for Rachel Blick. The Western Union boy probably had thought it was the wrong address because their name was Blickstein and she had not put "Blick" in the bell or letter box. In the confusion, he must have dropped the card on the floor. She called up Western Union and they read the telegram to her. "Would like to see you tonight in regard to ad in New York Times. Wire hotel Taft." It was signed J. Leman.

The fellow at Western Union suggested, "Why don't you call up the Taft." The telegram had been sent Saturday and this was Sunday morning, so she figured he might see her Sunday instead. She called the Taft and spoke with Mr. Leman. He said he was leaving right away for Albany, his permanent address, so he couldn't see her but would write all details from there.

A few days later she received his letter as promised. He had a music studio in Albany, was a music teacher and some publishers were going over his music. He needed a lyricist and would wire her when he came to New York again. He added that it was not necessary for her to answer, but she could if she so desired.

She answered him. He had also asked in his letter if she could read music. Although she could read music slightly, she replied that she could manage because she figured she might lose her chance if she said no. Besides, she could get someone to help her and he didn't have to know.

Another telegram came. Somehow they couldn't get together. When he could see her, she couldn't see him and vice versa. A few more telegrams came. She wrote him again. Then he sent her some of his music and some lyrics which another girl had made up. "See if you can improve on these and send them to me. Also write voice if you have any ideas on the subject."

The song was, "She's Just a Little Jitterbug." It was a nice tune and the other girl had written good lyrics, she thought. She doubted if she could beat those lyrics, but wrote three new sets with new ideas.

She wrote Mr. Leman saying that she had written three new sets of lyrics, but wanted to give them to him personally. It was a fast tune. She asked if he could write slow, sentimental tunes, the kind she was good at writing lyrics for.

"I'm enclosing two sets of such lyrics. Could you write music for them?" For better or for worse, she thought. Maybe he'd laugh at them and she'd never hear from his again. Her lyrics were: "Please Don't Kiss Me," and "My Heart Has a Feeling." She also sent him "voice" for his "jitterbug" tune.

She sealed the letter and met some of the "Merry Girls" as they were going to a dance at Sinai Temple where she gave the orchestra leader a copy of "She's Just a Little Jitterbug." The band played their own rendition of it and they got a big hand. Imagine how thrilled Rachel was, her chance at last!

A few weeks went by with no sign of Mr. Leman. Goodbye, she thought. He must be laughing at her. Then around Christmas time, another telegram came. She was so excited. Maybe she had talent after all. But maybe he was amused and wanted to see what kind of a sap she was. "Be in New York Wednesday, Taft."

She phoned Mr. Leman at the Taft Tuesday night telling him she would see him the next day as he had indicated in his telegram.

She said she'd meet him in the lobby. Luckily, Danny had come over that night. The family started warning her not to go, that she didn't know who Mr. Leman was and that she might suffer dire results. Danny defended her and said he would accompany her and see what's what.

The next day, Danny and Rachel went to the Taft Hotel to meet Mr. Leman. He had sent her a picture of himself with his orchestra, but it was small and she couldn't make out his face very well. When they got to the hotel, Danny asked a bell hop to page him. He did so and brought Mr. Leman back with him.

He was very nice, attractive. He wore a tan overcoat and carried a leather portfolio which contained his music. He seemed very energetic and distinguished. He tipped the bellhop and extended his hand to both Rachel and Danny, looking them up and down. Rachel was quite nervous. This is what she liked, people who were "alive," trying to accomplish something in life. He was probably wondering whether Danny was her boyfriend, she thought. "I'm Danny, Rachel's brother," Danny offered.

Mr. Leman glanced at his watch. "I've only got a few minutes. Have to rush down to W.O.R." Danny said, "Let's find a seat somewhere," and they went up to the balcony where they found a group of couches and armchairs. They took their coats off. Rachel felt better. Her new dress was very nice. They started to talk and Mr. Leman showed her some songs he had already completed, lyrics and all as well as some music which needed lyrics. She was thrilled beyond words at the thought of working with him.

"I'll go to W.O.R. tomorrow," Mr. Leman said looking at his watch again. "If we could get to a piano, I'd play the numbers for you. Maybe you could improve the lyrics and also write lyrics to the others. There was an organ on the balcony, but the organist was not due to play that day, or Mr. Leman said, he would have asked him to play the numbers for her. He also said that Enoch Light and his orchestra played in the Taft Grill, but not until nine p.m. and that maybe he'd play the songs.

"I have northing special to do today and I'm leaving for Albany tomorrow." He was business like, pleasant and sophisticated. She'd be proud to work with someone like him. His orchestra played over an Albany network. He also directed and taught U.S. marching bands, as well as music classes in an Albany college.

"Let's go downstairs and look up Rehearsal Halls in the phone book," he suggested. Danny had already left, saying that his wife, Tanya, was waiting for him. Before leaving, he had given Rachel the nod, indicating that he felt it was safe for her to continue with him.

Mr. Leman informed her, "There's the Haven Studios at Fifty-Fourth Street and Seventh Avenue. Let's try it."

The place was well furnished, but morbid looking. There were two queer looking men. One was an old man with glasses, lying on a couch. Both seemed to resent them. "We'll pay you for the time," Mr. Leman said.

They took Rachel and Mr. Leman to a studio, or living room, turned on the lights and they sat down at a piano which was in the room. Mr. Leman played two songs, a tango and a spooky type of tune. The place seemed a good background for the latter. She thought the music was great and he played beautifully.

They were there for about fifteen minutes. Mr. Leman paid them and they left and went back to the Taft Grill. He ordered a scotch and soda and she ordered a Tom Collins. Lucky that someone had once mentioned that a Tom Collins was a popular and mild drink or she would have felt like an idiot.

"I remember the tunes you played," she said, "but please write them down so I won't forget." He quickly whipped out a piece of lined music paper and wrote down the notes. She could see he was experienced.

"Oh, yes, there's another tune I didn't play," and he hummed it and wrote down the notes. Then he walked her to the station. She promised to write him in a few days. She was to arrange things such as plugging their songs here in New York. After all, he was out in Albany.

New York was where the action was. She'd see him when he came in from time to time to purchase supplies and material for his orchestra, classes and marching bands. He bought instruments, music paper, books and other necessities. "Any time you need me, I'll be there," he added.

When she got home, she tried the songs out on the piano. Thanks to Monroe, they had gotten the old upright piano for free. She interpreted the notes to a certain extent, partly because she remembered the tunes, but there were parts she couldn't figure out. Where could she get a pianist to help her? She had no money, for one thing.

She was coming home, the next day, wondering how and where she would find a pianist to help her, when a fellow from the next building stopped to flirt with her.

"Hello, Al," she greeted him, although she had avoided him before this. She knew he hung out on the corner with a group of fellows who harmonized and they sounded very good. "Do you know a good pianist?"

"As a matter of fact, I do," he replied. "Why?"

"I need some help. I'm doing lyrics for a song writer. He gave me some music and I have to hear it played so that I can write the words."

"Come down after supper and I'll introduce you to Jack Rubin."

Jack lived in the building next to hers. She explained the situation to him and he came upstairs with her and played the songs on the piano. He said his band was playing in a pretty big movie house and he might introduce the songs there. He told her there was a fellow down the block who sometimes vocalized with his band and that he would see that she met him. However, Rachel knew she would have trouble with Jack. He wanted to be paid for having played the songs. He was handsome, but he was very conceited. She said she couldn't pay him and he left. Later on, by coincidence, she met him at a New Year's Eve party and he wanted to kiss her, but she drew back.

The day after Jack had played the songs, Rachel wondered what she would do. She tried to decipher the notes, but couldn't get the tunes right. As she sat by the piano, an old school chum, Rosalyn Cream, walked in. It must have been fate, she thought, for she never expected her.

Rachel told Rosalyn about everything. Rosalyn said that a boyfriend of hers, Norman Jaslow, was a pianist and that he was a wonderful person. She phoned him and arranged that he go to her house as she had a piano, and they'd meet him there.

Norman met them and played the tunes beautifully and said generously that he'd be glad to be of help. He promised to come over to Rachel's house in a few days and kept the appointment on time. He said she could call on him whenever necessary and that furthermore he knew some friends who might be able to do something for her. He liked the songs very much and felt they held much promise.

Mr. Leman wrote and asked Rachel to find a rehearsal hall where they could practice the next time he came in. Of course, he would pay for everything. He would leave it to her to plug their songs and try to get them published.

Rachel took a day off from work and set out to find a rehearsal hall. She found out there were some in the Strand Building, so she walked into one of the offices there to find out if she could rent a piano and room in which to rehearse.

A very nice, courteous and obliging young fellow of about eighteen listened to what she had to say and told her his father, Dave Ringle, had written some very popular songs, and was a member of the American Society of Composers and Publishers (ASCAP). He had written "Wabash Moon" and other hits. He gave her some tips about the business and took her to a place where she might be able to arrange for a piano and rehearsal room. Then he walked her to the subway station, after advising her which publishing company might be interested in new talent and inviting her to call on him if she felt she needed further advice.

"I think the best place for beginners is E.B. Marks Publishing. It's at twelve-fifty or twelve-seventy Sixth Avenue. Also, let's walk over to Zane Grey's to inquire about renting a rehearsal room and piano there." What a nice guy, she thought.

"Don't forget to call me," he offered, as they parted. "I'll be happy if I can be of any help."

Before she went down the steps of the subway station, she stopped to look at the magazines on a newsstand. She noticed, "Metronome," "Cashbox," and "Orchestra World" magazine. The man who ran the stand told her that these were the top trade magazines for the popular music industry. If she could get her foot in the door by writing a column in one of these publications, she might meet someone who could do something about getting her songs plugged and published. You had to be careful. There were "song pluggers" around who promised results and were really charlatans, working scams to extort money from anxious songwriters. She would be cautious and seek out the legitimate people.

At night, she went down in front of the house with Natalie for some fresh air. As usual, Al, the baritone and Tim, the tenor and a couple of others were on the corner harmonizing, like a barber's quartet. Jack Rubin came out for a few minutes too.

Tim went into the candy store and phoned a friend of his, Hal Silvers, who played with his orchestra at the Pythian Temple, a very nice dance hall. It was a popular place in Brooklyn and Tim asked him to play some of Rachel's and Mr. Leman's numbers there. As for Jack, he seemed to get off his high horse a bit, probably because the girls ran after him and Rachel didn't. Fellows were funny that way. They didn't respond to any easy conquest, in most cases. Jack said he was playing Saturdays and Sundays at two Loew's Theatres and that he was thinking of giving her songs a shot.

CHAPTER 25

Rachel was working in the payroll department of the Works Progress Administration (WPA) as secretary to the head of payroll. The social worker, who helped them through the ordeal of moving when Rosie, the landlady, had sought to evict them, called and offered her the job.

Although Jake and Anna were too proud to accept welfare, they had to ask for help to avoid being put out on the street with their meager belongings. This made Rachel eligible for employment through them, even though they were not actually on welfare. She had no alternative but to accept the position. Jake had gone to Chicago again to try to get work or open a business with the help of his brother out there, and Rachel would have to help the family.

She kept where she was working a secret. Anyone who worked at the WPA had to be poor and she was ashamed of it. There was a group of men in the Payroll Department where she worked. Most were in their late thirties or forties and they treated her like a little sister.

One of the men was younger, in his early twenties. His name was Bob Kirsten. The first time she saw him and their eyes met, she felt an incredible bonding with him. It was as if she knew him, even though she had never spoken to him, as if he were hers. How could she feel so certain that he would respond in the same way? She had met so many men before and had been attracted to them, but this was different.

For the first few days, she watched him as he joked with the men, handled the big payroll sheets with efficiency and speed. When he passed her desk, she noticed he had deep dimples and green eyes, dark brown hair and a moustache. She liked fair haired men and disliked moustaches, yet what was it about him that made her so uneasy? Sometimes he smiled at her, sometimes he didn't seem to notice she was there. How could she even think twice about him, a WPA worker?

The thought of Kenny haunted her. She had spurned him because of his financial and social position. Once he had said, "It's the little things that count," when she spoke of wealth and prestige. Snob that she was, maybe he was right.

It was ironic that she could consider this fellow with the Clark Gable looks, probably poor as a church mouse. She knew if he gave her a tumble, she couldn't resist. She day dreamed that with his personality and her willingness to help him, they would get out of the WPA together. He would be a huge success and she would be a famous songwriter. They would start from scratch and conquer the world, hand in hand.

What was the matter with her? She was thinking these things and he hadn't even spoken to her, except for a few words about a payroll.

She busied herself with Mr. Leman, contacts with people who would help her in her quest to succeed with their music and wrote reams of lyrics to Mr. Leman's music.

Mr. Leman stayed at the Hotel Taft when he came in from Albany to buy music and instruments for his students at the college and for his orchestra and for the marching bands. As a poor girl from Brooklyn, she was excited by his confidence in her. He brought beautiful orchestrations of their songs, done by his friend, Archie

Bleyer, a famous arranger, and was purely business-like at all times. He dressed impeccably and was especially impressive when he wore his white suits in the summer.

Rachel succeeded in getting several well-known orchestras to perform their material, but it was always the same. A song could become famous if it was played on the air, but it could not be aired unless it was published first; a vicious circle. Then how could the publishers say they published songs heard on the air? What a run around.

And what about Bob at the office? She had been working there a few weeks when she found a note on her desk the day before Christmas.

"Would you like to go to a hockey game tomorrow at Madison Square Garden?" The Rangers, his favorite team, were playing. She accepted.

She attended a Christmas party that evening and got home very late. Snow was starting to fall. She was very tired as it was three a.m. when she got home.

She was supposed to meet Bob in front of Madison Square Garden at noon, but much to her horror, it was noon when she awoke. She hadn't even heard the alarm go off. She jumped out of bed, washed, got dressed and it was almost one p.m. when she left. It would take her almost an hour to get there from Brooklyn. The snow was quite thick too and it was freezing out. Would he still be waiting out there in the cold?

When she got to Madison Square Garden, her heart leaped. There he was, still waiting, his face red from the cold, walking up and down. They went in even though the game was almost over. They wound up going to dinner at Childs Far East Restaurant at

Columbus Circle, Fifty-Ninth Street, and then to see a movie and stage show at the Roxy.

All the while she felt she belonged with him. They talked about things as if they had known each other forever. Then he took her home. He would have to go home to the Bronx after taking her back to Brooklyn and it was very late. It had been a wonderful day. He leaned over to kiss her goodnight and she said instinctively, "I don't kiss anyone on the first date." He blushed profusely, said goodbye and left.

She could hardly wait to get back to the office the next day. Perhaps he would ask her out again. In any event, his actions or comments might indicate how he felt about her.

Business continued as usual. He said good morning and went on with his work, giving no indication of his thoughts. As the day wore on, she knew he would not say anything and she went home disappointed. It was not possible, she thought, to have such strong feelings about him and not to have them reciprocated. She still felt as if he were a part of her.

Two months passed by, with the situation being the same. Then on Valentine's Day, she received a Valentine from him. It read: "To a cruel damsel, the words you have spoken are cruel and tart. You have broken my slumber and also my heart." He signed it, "P.I.T.N. Bob." It meant, Pain in the Neck, which she had called him when he said something trivial on their first date. She said it in a casual way, not attaching too much importance to it and had in fact forgotten that she said it.

In the meantime, Mr. Leman communicated with her, saw her at the Taft whenever he came in to Manhattan and seemed to be pleased at the way she went about trying to promote their songs.

There were plenty of dates; she was always popular. For instance, Irving Marks; she told him about the songwriting. He was a nice fellow, but she felt he was immature since he took her to Madison Square Garden to a basketball game (NYU and Manhattan) and yelled every minute, jumping up and down in his seat. He called her after that and said he had a friend, Hal Gray, the orchestra leader, and that he would ask him to play some of her numbers.

Another fellow tried to date her and showed her a picture of himself with Xavier Kugat, the famous orchestra leader. His brother played in Kugat's orchestra. They specialized in rumba, tango and such and he'd try to get him to play our tango, "Tinkling Tambourines."

Mr. Leman was at the Taft again and she went to meet him. He brought some more orchestrations and said he liked the lyrics she had written. The Taft Organist was playing that day and he played their numbers.

She tried everything, followed every lead. Norman was a doll, so helpful. He came over often and went over the music with her. Jack Rubin came up too. His band was playing at movie theatres and he said he played their numbers and they always got a good hand. She went over to the Strand Building and saw that nice fellow whose father had songs published. He promised to show their stuff to his father.

On the way down in the elevator from the fellow, Dave Ringle, Jr's studio, a young man carrying a large instrument in a black case kept looking at Rachel so she ventured with a smile, "Have you got a good band?"

"Certainly, why?" he answered amiably.

"Well, it's a long story. I'm looking for a good band. But I'll try to cut it short." She told him all about herself, Mr. Leman and how they were hoping to get a break with perhaps a famous band to plug their material.

He walked with her to Forty-Second Street and it turned out that he played sax in Ray O'Hara's band at the Greenwich Village Casino and that they broadcast three times weekly. He gave her some advice, but said he couldn't do anything for her because she'd have to take that up with the leader and he wasn't the leader.

Irving Marks was a good kid, Rachel thought. He called and said he had an idea. Rachel wanted to go to the Patio Theatre to hear Jack Rubin's band so she asked if he would go with her and he could tell her about his idea. The band was quite good and Jack had them play two of her numbers. It was great hearing the audience applaud.

"I'd like to invite you to an affair at Manhattan Center given for refugees by City College Varsity. My cousin is well known at the college and he knows some officials there. Bunny Berrigan is to play at this affair and my cousin said he would put in a good word for you. Maybe Berrigan would introduce some of your numbers. If he does, you're practically "made.""

Irving took Rachel to the City College affair where Bunny Berrigan was playing. They found him in the lobby before he went on the bandstand. He was a real gentleman, very polite. He even helped Rachel on with her coat as it was chilly. He said he would have played the numbers if he had gotten them earlier, but didn't want to do it without rehearsing them first. He told her where to get in touch with him.

"I'm leaving for Boston on Wednesday. I could take the music with me and go over it."

"Thank you so much, but it's my only copy and it would be better to give it to you when you get back."

"Get in touch with me through MCA." He smiled and shook her hand.

Norman came over the next day. He brought a neighbor to the door.

"This is Bernie. Bernie, I'd like you to meet Rachel." It turned out that Bernie lived with his mother on the same floor as Rachel.

"Norman told me about you," Bernie said. "I know a lot of people. I could introduce you to some of them. Ring my bell after dinner and we can talk."

Bernie had a lovely mother. She was very friendly and so was he. He was having a "Jam Session" in his house that evening. He showed Rachel pictures of himself in "Orchestra World" magazine. Johnny Pals was his stage name and he played in an orchestra. He was usually vague about his career, but took her to the city to meet Clementi, the bandleader at the Hotel Edison. Clementi agreed to look her music over if she brought it to him.

Bernie would ring Rachel's bell and on the spur of the moment announce that he was going to the city to meet this or that famous musician and invited her to come along and she did. In most cases, he hardly knew the musicians, but was trying to break into their circles. She wondered how he had gotten the write-ups in "Orchestra World Magazine," one of the top three.

"I wish I could write a column for "Orchestra World Magazine," she said one day. "Then I could really meet the right people in order to further my song-writing career."

"Tell you what. Sy Berman is the Editor. Why not go up to see him. He might give you a break." As easy as that; that was Bernie.

He also told her that Sy knew everyone and that she should call him and ask him how to locate Bunny Berrigan.

She called Sy Bertel and he told her who Bunny Berrigan's manager was at MCA and she phoned him. He told her where to send the music. Mr. Berrigan would be at the Utica Hotel that Friday. "Send the music to me and I'll give it to him. I'm his Manager and my name is Harry Moss."

Mr. Leman came in to the Taft and Rachel met him. They went to see Clementi and later to meet Hal Grey who was playing at a dance at the Manhattan Plaza, Sixty-Six East Fourth Street.

Hal glanced at two of the numbers and briefed his band and they played the numbers right off. Mr. Leman had brought arrangements for various instruments and Hal distributed them.

People were dancing to their music. It was some thrill. When the music stopped, they applauded as Hal Grey said, "The composers of these new songs are here tonight and the spotlight fell on Rachel and Mr. Leman. Clementi had also promised to play some of the music if we would bring it to him in a week or so when he'd have more time to go over it. He would be playing at the Hotel Edison for an indefinite time.

At the Hotel Edison Rachel bumped into the first song shark. "I'm Freddie Vin, the songwriter. Everyone knows me. He showed her some songs that were published and promised her results for a small fee to cover his expenses. Having been forewarned, she didn't bite. It was amazing how convincing he was. The published songs were printed up professionally with photographs of popular singers on the cover.

Bernie said he had a girlfriend and that a friend of his had seen Rachel and wanted to date her. The foursome, which included Bernie's date, went to the Apollo to hear Fats Waller play.

Natalie was blossoming into a beautiful and charming young lady. She had natural blond hair, was slim and cute and danced unbelievably well. Her smile was like a Spring breeze. She had just turned sweet sixteen. As she had been ever since she was born, she was self-assured, no nonsense, cheerful and lovable. She never complained and came up with little thoughtful surprises. Everyone loved her.

Rachel was going to a dance and Natalie asked if she could come too. Rachel was so proud of Natalie and of course said she'd be happy to have her come.

One of the fellows who danced with Natalie came over to meet Rachel and announced that he was the pianist in a fourteen piece band and would be glad to introduce her numbers. Natalie had told him about her sister, Rachel's ambition. He said he was also an arranger and was arranging some of Cab Calloway's material. He was really talented for later on in the evening, he sat in with the orchestra and played terrifically well. He gave Rachel his card.

Everywhere Rachel went she met people in the music business, but she could see she was getting nowhere. It would either be the "big time" or nothing. In this business, you either made it big or were a disappointed failure. There were so many talented people around, each with hopes and dreams which were usually unfulfilled. She wasn't going to be a quitter. People did succeed. Those were the ones with stamina who persisted. It was a mixture of work and luck. As Anna said, "You don't get anything for nothing. You get what you pay for."

Rachel dropped into the Taft Grill to see Enoch Light who was the present orchestra leader. Mr. Leman had told him he was a frequent guest at the hotel and had given him some orchestrations of their songs. He had promised to look them over and possibly to play them in the Taft Grill.

Rachel phoned Mr. Light in his room at the hotel and asked about the music Mr. Leman had given him. He sounded very unassuming and pleasant. "I'm dressing for my radio broadcast. What is your name? I'll gladly see you after the broadcast. I'll expect you in the Grill."

She waited about two hours and went down to the Grill and walked up to the front where the orchestra was. She had never seen Enoch Light before so she didn't know who he was. A lovely girl in a silver lame gown, pretty face and dark hanging curls, sat at a table with a young man. She was Peggy Mann, Enoch Light's vocalist. She was sweet and friendly. "Mr. Light is in the telephone booth. I'll point out who he is."

Enoch Light came out of the telephone booth and approached her. "I'm going to look your songs over tonight. Please come back tomorrow night." Rachel felt funny about going back to "pester" Mr. Light so she wrote him a letter instead. If he were decent, he ought to answer. Whether he answered or not, Mr. Leman was coming in the following weekend and they would go to see Mr. Light together.

Another thing that bothered Rachel was Bob Kirsten. One minute he could pass her desk and beam at her and the next time he seemed to actually snub her. When she got his Valentine, she wrote a poem and put it on his desk. He didn't say a word about it, but she knew he had read it. It was a funny poem and referred to his Valentine. Why didn't he ask her out again, she thought? He blushed when he passed her desk. What was he thinking?

Rachel met Mr. Leman at the Taft and he took her to the Taft Grill for dinner. He gave the waiter a note for Enoch Light and asked him to join them at their table, which he did. They spoke for almost an hour and the result was that he returned the music with the envelope not even opened. He was more than nice.

"So many people come to me for the same purpose. Besides, we only have a fifteen minute radio broadcast, so I couldn't attempt to use it at the present time. Perhaps in the future if programs are given increased radio time." That was the end of the Enoch Light episode. Another disappointment; there were to be many other failed efforts.

For instance, she had left some of the music at Radio Station WNEW, but when she went back a few days later to see the results, they handed back the music, with an explanation of course.

A young man, Jimmy Rich, overheard the conversation and asked her to come into his office. He was one of the big shots up there; a wonderful young man. He seemed to pity her as he recalled, "I once did just as you are doing. It took the life out of me and it's doing the same to you." He said Rachel would have to try to win over Earl Pitt, the studio orchestra leader, and that all he could do was refer her to him. He looked the arrangements over and informed her that Mr. Pitt was broadcasting and if she waited a half hour, she could talk to him.

The broadcast was over and she talked to Mr. Pitt for a couple of seconds as he was in a hurry for something or other and he said she could show him the music any day at three o'clock in the afternoon. She went back and told Mr. Rich about it, thanked him and left, giving him her name and address.

In parting, Mr. Pitt had suggested that she see a friend of his, Bob Haring, at Shapiro & Bernstein, publishers.

Mt. Leman came in and they succeeded in getting some bands to play their songs, including the band that was playing at the Roseland Ballroom and another at the Hotel Astor.

Sometimes Rachel took a bus from where she worked on Astor Place to Forty-Sixth and Broadway. Having dinner at Childs was so nice, but she couldn't exactly afford it. The dinner was fifty cents and you had to leave a fifteen cents tip. Once in a while she splurged and bought herself a flower. She had better find herself a rich guy. She walked around drinking in the "high life," as she called it. She had had enough of poverty to despise it.

Natalie was not feeling well. She had pain in her legs. Perhaps if she had been brought up with adequate sleeping quarters and good food as well as peace and harmony, she and the rest of the family would be in better shape.

Just as well that Bob Kirsten hadn't asked her out again, the pauper. She checked herself at this thought. Something great would happen to him.

Rachel felt that Bob Kirsten was becoming a little more friendly. He sort of avoided her but whenever their gaze met, it seemed as if he liked her. Then why didn't he ask her out again? Sure enough, he wrote her another note: "Would you like to go out with me this evening to see "Sing for Your Supper," a play given by the Federal Theatre Project?" She accepted.

After that, they left the office together after work every day. The men in the office seemed to be glad about it. They kidded them and spoke words of encouragement. They meant well, but it was embarrassing. They took walks to Central Park, visited the zoo and rode atop Fifth Avenue buses. They went to a Chinese Restaurant and a radio broadcast.

Bob's brother was getting married and he had to go to rent a tuxedo as he was best man. She went with him and smoothed the shoulder of the jacket he was trying on and told the tailor it should be taken in. He felt uneasy at the way Rachel seemed to mother him for he was not used to such treatment, but it made her feel wonderful "taking care of him." She wished she could take care of him always, but he had not expressed his feelings towards her, even though his actions, including the notes he wrote her at the office, made her feel he might have fallen in love with her. She could only guess.

After they left the tuxedo rental place, they went rowing in Central park. As they walked, he said he "cared for her," but she wondered, did that mean love?

When they were in the rowboat, he asked, "Is there anyone you like more than me?"

She answered coyly, "Why?"

"I'd just like to know." Cat and mouse again, she thought.

"Why would you like to know?"

He got red. He stammered. It was hard to get it out. "Because I love you." There, she had gotten him to say it. She had felt it in her heart from the moment she saw him. She replied, "The answer to your question, is there anyone I like more than you, is no, because I love you too." She couldn't believe she had said it. Anna's words hit her again, "When you meet the right one, you'll know."

They embraced and kissed ecstatically. They turned the boat in and with his arm around her they ran out of the park, excited and laughing.

"Why didn't you ask me out after the first date?' she asked.

"Because you didn't let me kiss you and also you called me a Pain in the Neck. I thought you weren't interested in me."

Rachel and Bob's blossoming romance was a source of delight to the men in the Payroll Department. They were thrown together because of the depression, in the Federal WPA program. They were plain, good family men and were forced to work beneath their potential for the sake of their families.

At lunch time they amused themselves by playing cards in an anti-room. Bob occasionally joined them, but now that he had Rachel, he went out for a walk with her instead. They bought ice cream sandwiches and other goodies from the various vendors along the busy streets of lower Manhattan. With Bob beside her, she felt safe and optimistic. They talked about the future and the present suddenly seemed to brighten.

The days passed quickly. The men enjoyed teasing Rachel and Bob.

"Look at the lovebirds!"

"Kirsten, you're hooked."

"Rachel, you look ravishing in that dress."

"Kirsten, why don't you marry her?"

Bob showed his dimples as he quipped with the best of them in response to their taunting, knowing it was all in a spirit of affection. Rachel didn't mind at all. The two of them wrote notes back and forth.

Then it happened. Most of the people in the Payroll Department were laid off, including Bob and Rachel. The last day, they went to Central Park, sat down on the grass and looked up at the Essex House and she said, "Some day we'll live there. We are going to do something wonderful with our lives." He was so handsome and had such a wonderful personality. Failure did not even cross her mind.

The first day he went job hunting, he was hired by an employment agency, doing the office work and interviewing clients. She decided to do something about her music in between job hunting.

Rachel and Bob met at Horn and Hardart Automat as they had planned, had something to eat and then he accompanied her home to Brooklyn to meet her family for the first time. Anna, Danny, Monroe, Natalie and Debbie greeted him and he passed the test with flying colors. He looked so handsome in his dark, striped business suit.

After everyone had gone to sleep, he was still there. They were in the kitchen having tea, when suddenly he said, "Look up at the ceiling in the right-hand corner." She couldn't imagine why, but she looked up anyway and saw nothing there.

"Don't look at me," he said as she turned to question him. "Look up again and you'll see." While she was looking there, he asked, "Not now but as soon as I'm able to, will you marry me?"

She heard herself saying, "Most likely." Was this her, giving up her dream so easily? But not really; how could he fail? They would have a wonderful life together, everything she had dreamed about.

He was headstrong and stubborn, but nobody could get him to melt as she could. "You have to get down on your knees to propose," she ordered. Without a qualm he got down on his knees at her feet and proposed formally. He wiped the sweat from his brow, then got up and kissed her. As long as they were together, nothing else mattered to her. Hand in hand, they would conquer the world.

CHAPTER 26

It was damp and slushy and a wet snow was falling. A group of songwriters stood in front of the Brill Building. It was a hangout for songwriters who compared their material and talked about the possibilities of having their songs published.

The Brill Building was the headquarters of most of the prominent publishers in New York City. Every songwriter hopeful tried to pass through their star-studded portals. If they were lucky, someone would try their numbers out, usually on an old upright piano in one of the publishers' offices.

It was a business fraught with tension and anxiety, frustration and usually failure. Rachel walked right up to a small group of people who were gathered in front of the entrance to the building. Everyone thought they had a sure hit. She knew what she was up against.

It was exhausting, running around following every lead in her search for employment, practically penniless and worried about the family. In addition, she was trying to become a famous songwriter.

Then, there were some misgivings about Bob. Could it be that her guilt in the outcome of her affair with Kenny had subconsciously led her to want to be supportive of Bob? She had openly shown her disdain for Kenny's "lowly" status and her fear of the future with him. Why then did she settle for Bob who was really in the same, if not worse, position than Kenny? Was she so in love with him that she was throwing all caution to the wind in her desire to help him?

Kenny had been so gentle, so sweet, so caring, while Bob was romantic in a more manly way. Yet he seemed so dependent upon her. He needed her and perhaps that brought out her mothering instinct. He had eyes for no one but her, took the long trip on the subway to Brooklyn every single day and stayed very late before heading for the Bronx. He couldn't get enough of her. He kissed her incessantly, but never made other demands upon her. She was worried about his lack of sleep. To make him leave, Anna would finally come out of her room and jokingly take a broomstick and tell him to go or risk her using it on him.

Rachel decided that while she was still unemployed she would see if she could write a column for "Orchestra World" magazine. She bought a copy and looked it over and went up to the magazine's office. Perhaps they would give her a chance to write a column and thus she would get to meet people who could help her get her music published.

She entered the office of "Orchestra World" magazine. The editor, Syd Berman, was seated at a cluttered desk looking over scripts, proofs and photographs which were to be part of the next issue of the magazine. He looked up.

"Can I help you?" he asked, pipe in mouth.

"I'd like to talk to you, please."

He motioned her to sit down on a chair next to his desk. She got to the point. "I'd like to write a column for your magazine. I'm not asking for salary to start, but if you like what I do, we'll see."

He took a few short puffs on his pipe and eyed her casually. It was easier than she thought. "I could use someone to write a column about arrangers for the big bands and also the publishing companies. As you meet them and write about them in your column you could try to get ads from them.

For instance, our Christmas and Easter issues feature a lot of ads. There are other greetings too. You'll get twenty-five percent of the amount of each ad you get. The front cover entire page with their photograph could net you a good sum."

"Thank you very much. You won't be sorry."

"Study the columns. Here is a card. What's your name? I'll put it on the card so that you'll be able to get in to see those you want to."

"Rachel Blick." He gave her the card. "I'll call you in a couple of days," she said. He switched his pipe from one corner of his mouth to the other without any emotion. "Fine," he said without looking up from his desk. She left the office, elated, but a little dubious. "Where do I start?" she asked herself.

She met Bob at the Automat and told him everything. Then they took the subway to Brooklyn. He pulled her towards him as they sat on the train. He put his arm around her and held the collar of her coat together, protectively to keep her warm.

CHAPTER 27

Dorothy Kilgallen was the most widely read of the Broadway gossip columnists. She wrote "The Voice of Broadway— Broadway Bulletin Board." Rachel read the column excitedly:

> Artie Shaw, the swing king, may make the rival bandleaders very happy in a few months by abdicating and retiring to write serious jazz symphonies . . . Tommy Dorsey split up with his brother, Jimmy and formed his own band. Some of his hits are "Night and Day," "Stardust" and others . . .
>
> Ingrid Bergman, Selznick's new sweet-dish sensation, hasn't gone to Germany to make another picture as rumors stated. She cancelled her UFA contract and is in Sweden . . .
>
> Upon her arrival from Europe, Merle Oberon walked into her hotel carrying a gas mask in a tiny red velvet case . . .
>
> George Raft suffered a serious eye injury this week; four stitches taken.

There was Dorothy Kilgallen in New York, Louella Parsons in Hollywood; plenty of room for another columnist. Rachel could broaden her "Arranger's Spotlight" column by meeting the big band leaders and asking them if they'd give her some information, perhaps including themselves. Then she would meet the arrangers in person, either interview them or at least get some news morsels from them. She loved Tommy Dorsey's band so she would see him first.

After arrangements were made to meet Tommy Dorsey, she told Bob about it. He accompanied her. They took the elevator to the penthouse of the Hotel Pennsylvania. Because of his conservative nature, rather timid in situations like this, Bob seemed in complete disbelief at Rachel's confidence and daring. She opened the double doors to the ballroom a bit and a man asked why she was there.

"Mr. Dorsey is expecting me. I'm from "Orchestra World" magazine.

"Come in, please." He showed them to a table and went up to the bandstand. During the next intermission, Tommy came over to their table and sat down.

"What would you like to drink?" he offered amiably.

Neither Rachel nor Bob drank. "Thank you, some ginger ale, please," she replied.

"The same, please," said Bob.

As he listened to Rachel telling Tommy Dorsey about her column and getting the name and phone number of his chief arranger, Paul Wetstein telling him how she loved his music and that she was writing music herself, which she wished he would hear some day, Bob absolutely cringed in his chair.

The first hurdle was over. Tommy Dorsey, one of the greatest bandleaders of the day, respected and listened to her. Far cry from the Rachel Blick of Brooklyn, ignored and heckled by her unhappy family, the penniless, lost Rachel. Sitting at the table with Tommy Dorsey, amidst the impressive guests, alive with music and lights, Rachel knew that she would be a big success some day and Bob would be at her side, supporting her and being equally successful in some way. He would find something wonderful to do.

Rachel called Paul Wetstein. She had to turn in her first column in two weeks so she wasted no time in meeting him as he agreed to the interview. She told him that Tommy Dorsey agreed to it and he readily met with her.

It was great, in fact, easy, for she was genuinely interested in people. He was friendly and "regular," remarking that he was telling her things he had never told anyone before. He was twenty-seven years old, had worked for Rudy Vallee and Phil Harris. The first arrangement he did for Dorsey was "You are My Lucky Star," four years ago and worked only for him the last four years. He told her how his ambition was to write for movies, motion picture scoring, and that he played the piano, his hobbies, etc.

Bob had not gone with her as there was no reason to. She met Wetstein in the daytime. Bob said he'd go with her at night, sort of as a protection. Rachel informed Bob that she was going to see Gene Krupa next. He joined her.

She arranged to see Krupa backstage at the Paramount Theatre where he was appearing. She showed her card and the guard let them in. Two girls were waiting to see him. They said they were his friends. There was also a man named Willie (The Lion) Smith.

Willie (The Lion) Smith was a black man, who possessed a mouthful of totally gold teeth. He was very friendly and fairly shouted when he spoke. "My philosophy is that no matter how big you are, always remain the same sweet way." When he heard of her ambition as a songwriter, he immediately offered, without being asked, that he would help her. He was most generous.

1939
Ray Eberle and Marion Hutton, Glenn Miller vocalists

1939
Buddy Rich, Drummer with Artie Shaw

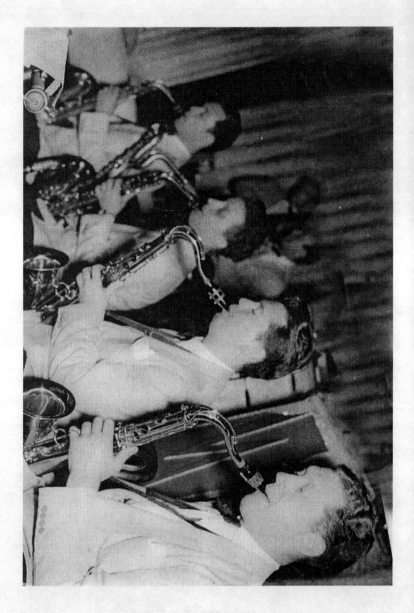

1939
Ozzie Nelson's Orchestra
Saxes: Bill Nelson, Charles Bubeck, Jimmy Murphy, Bill
Stone

1939
Glenn Miller

Just then, the other black man came in. He said not one word. He was the opposite of Willie Smith. He was shy and wore an old gray felt hat.

"He's the brother of Clarence Williams, the publisher," Willie said. "Can we be at the publishing office tomorrow at four o'clock so that the songs Miss Blick here has written can be tried out?"

"Sure," said the shy one.

Willie continued, "I'll meet you there and after that, Rachel, I'll give you a tour of the territory and talk to you about arrangers."

With that, Gene Krupa came backstage from his dressing room. He wore a flannel bathrobe and a beautiful smile. He greeted the two girls and also Willie Smith, warmly. Then he turned to Rachel and Bob.

"I'm from 'Orchestra World' magazine," she said. I'd like to write about your arranger in my column. Where can I reach him?"

"His name is Milt Raskin. He's my pianist and arranger."

She had brought some of the arrangements of their numbers that Mr. Leman had made and thought this was a great opportunity to tell Gene Krupa about them.

"Okay, I'll try them out, but I can't say when. In fact, Milt and I are leaving, so I'd better not carry them around. Bring them to me at the end of the week."

"Thank you, I will," she said. I'll do a write-up on Mr. Raskin in another column when he's in town."

Rachel and Bob met Willie (The Lion) Smith the next day at Clarence Williams Publishing Company. Then Willie took them places and introduced Rachel to many people in the music business. As they walked in the street, Maxine Sullivan stopped to talk with Willie as well as the female press agent for Glen Gray's Casaloma Orchestra. Willie seemed to be well known and popular, a great jazz pianist.

Fifty-Second Street abounded with night clubs. The "Famous Door" was one of the most popular ones. Rachel decided to go down there and meet Fats Waller, who was playing there. He was a fabulous jazz pianist. She would interview his arranger for her column. Bob accompanied her.

After showing her card and stating her business, Rachel and Bob were escorted to a table. "Fats" joined them.

"I'll bring Don Donaldson over," he said. "He's the one playing the second piano. Don and I have this duo piano act. Don is also the arranger for the band."

Rachel was becoming a real pro and enjoying every minute of it, while Bob couldn't believe this was real. He couldn't imagine how she had the nerve to talk to these celebrities as if they were casual acquaintances. It came so naturally to her.

Don Donaldson came over to the table and sat down. "Good evening," he said warmly.

"I'm from "Orchestra World" magazine and would appreciate interviewing you for my column. Can we make an appointment? By the way, you and Mr. Waller are great artists, remarkable."

"Thank you," he beamed. "Just name the day and time and I'll try to meet you."

"How about tomorrow at three?"

"Fine. How about our rehearsal hall?"

"Please give me the address and I'll be there." As easy as that.

When Rachel went to the rehearsal hall, all the fellows seemed to look at her in amazement. For a lark, she pretended to lead the band and did it so well that the fellows laughed and said she ought to be in their band.

Rachel told Don all about her music and asked him if he would record the numbers for her so she could try to promote them. As usual, she had the music with her. Mr. Leman had given her arrangements for all the instrumentalists and Don handed out the arrangements and the musicians played the numbers outright without rehearsing them. They responded positively.

"Tell you what," Donaldson said. "Get a band and a vocalist and call me and we'll all meet at the Nola recording studio.

She wasted no time. There was a young band leader who had a fourteen piece orchestra. She knew he was looking for publicity. She called him and put the proposition before him. When he learned who would be soloing on the piano, he accepted the opportunity.

That night, Rachel went down to the Bal Tabarin night club to ask a singer she had heard and liked whether he would do the vocal on the recordings. To her amazement he said yes.

Everything worked out perfectly. Everyone agreed to do the recordings without remuneration if she gave them ample publicity which they needed. Mr. Leman wired her the money to pay the recording studio. Now that she had the recordings, she would tackle the publishers and whomever, especially the disc jockeys.

Rachel met every band leader of note and consequently their arrangers, Louis Prima, Teddy Wilson, Fred Waring, Count Bassie, Ozzie Nelson, Guy Lombardo, Horace Heidt and the rest.

When the Christmas issue came out she had gotten ads from most of them. When she walked down Broadway, celebrities greeted her by name. Maybe it was because she was the good little girl in a business which sometimes got rough. Maybe it was because they sensed her love and adoration of music and the people who gave it to the world.

She wrote a column about publishing company arrangers. The real biggies were Shapiro Bernstein, Chappel's, Robbins and many others. She loved to go up to Irving Berlin's office and visit Helmy Kresa, his arranger. As the others did, he would give her the latest bits of news concerning his organization. There was more to it. He was a wonderful gentleman who went over her lyrics graciously and pointed out the good and bad points. She learned so much from him. He kept a photograph of his lovely daughter on his desk and Rachel thought that perhaps he was treating her like another daughter.

The wheel of fortune was turning fast and she wondered where it would wind up. One day she went home and visited a neighbor's daughter who lived on the same floor as the Blicks. They were listening to the radio when lightening struck. President Franklin Delano Roosevelt was speaking in a terse voice, "We are at war. The Japanese have attacked Pearl Harbor."

"Oh, my God," she gasped and ran into her apartment. Her first thought was of Bob. "What if he's killed!" The President announced that single men would be called first. Danny and

Monroe were married. Most of her friends were married. It was bad enough seeing her father leave all the time, watching her mother and the rest of the family suffer. She couldn't bear the thought of being without Bob. She would be lost. She ran out of her friend's apartment into hers. The phone rang. It was Bob.

She gasped, "Did you hear the news about us being at war?"

"Yes," he said simply.

"When I see you tomorrow, we've got to talk," she said anxiously.

CHAPTER 28

"We are at war," flashed the newspaper headlines, and the radio echoed the ominous news. It was announced that all eligible single men would be drafted first, then married men and lastly married men with children.

Bob had taken the day off and he came over around noon time. She was very distraught and had hardly slept that night. She said she thought that they should get married right away since the war was declared the day before, December 7, 1941, and she had heard that anyone married before the end of the year would still be classified as a married man and it would give them some more time together.

He told her that he wanted to enlist in the Signal Corps so that he would have more of an opportunity to become an officer rather than a private in the Infantry. He had found out that morning that he could do that. They would send him for training to the Radio and Television Institute for six months before inducting him.

Bob told Rachel that he loved her very much and would be happy to have her as his wife. However, there was a complication.

"I've always dreamed of having a beautiful wedding," Rachel said. I'd be dressed in a long white gown with a beautiful long train and a headpiece and you would be wearing a tuxedo and top hat. There would be a glorious reception with flowers and orchestra and I would carry a bridal bouquet of white gardenias."

But your parents don't have the means, and neither do we."

"I've got it all planned. We'll figure out whom to invite and calculate the amount of cash presents we'll get. We'll need a deposit for the flowers, the musicians, the caterers and money to get invitations printed. When the wedding is over, we'll use the cash presents to pay the caterers and musicians. We've been saving a little so we can make it."

He looked skeptical and visibly uncertain. "That's taking a big chance."

"Don't worry, be positive. We'll make it, you'll see."

"Rachel, I've got to tell you this. I'm quitting my job. It's not for me. Instead, I'm going to Washington, D.C. until I'm reached on the waiting list for the Signal Corps training."

Upon Rachel's recommendation, they both sent in applications for federal jobs and Bob had received a telegram that morning. He showed it to Rachel:

> Report for work on January 5th, 1942 at the General
>
> Accounting Office; salary $1440 per annum as Clerk
>
> Grade 1.

"I received a telegram yesterday too," Rachel exclaimed. "I'm to report on January 5th also as Clerk Grade 1, $1440 per annum at the Board of Economic Warfare."

"Let's get married New Year's Eve," she said excitedly and we can go to Washington together and start working. We'll get married in a Rabbi's study. Monroe and Blanche will be our witnesses.

Then we'll look for a hall for our real wedding and get back to work in Washington by Monday."

He marveled at her sureness, her "nerve." He could never be as positive as she was. He loved her and needed her and trusted her intelligence.

"Whatever you say," he replied.

"Then it's all set," she said. "But I want you to know something." In the Jewish religion you're not supposed to get married in a white bridal gown unless you're a virgin. So until the "real" wedding, we'll be married legally, but will not consummate the marriage."

"Whatever you say," he replied, "even though it's foolish."

"Let's go out and find a Rabbi for New Year's Eve. We'll tell our families. We'll also find a caterer for the "real" wedding. Oh, yes, and we'll also call Monroe and Blanche and ask if they'll be our witnesses when the Rabbi marries us on New Year's Eve."

It was a hectic day, but Rachel plowed on with Bob at her side and everything was accomplished. The Rabbi said he would marry them in his study on New Year's Eve.

They made arrangements with a caterer for the "real" wedding on February 15th, the first date available. They hired an orchestra and made an appointment with a photographer. Monroe and Blanche were thrilled to be the witnesses and Blanche told Rachel she knew someone in the flower market who would give them the bridal bouquet and all the other flowers at an incredibly low price. They ordered the flowers and the invitations. Then they made plans for going to Washington, D.C.

When New Year's Eve came, Rachel, Bob, Monroe and Blanche arrived at the Rabbi's house. A party was in progress with a houseful of guests, a small orchestra and buffet dinner.

Bob requested that the musicians play "I Love You Truly," as he and Rachel walked down the aisle in the Rabbi's study while all the guests came in for the ceremony.

They were pronounced man and wife right about the stroke of midnight, with everyone kissing and hugging and saying "congratulations" and "Happy New Year" at the same time.

Rachel was happy, but sort of worried as well. She could imagine Kenny's surprise if he knew this. For a fleeting moment, she gave way to doubts, but when they left kissing, arm in arm, the full realization of what had happened hit her. He was hers. She loved him and he loved her. She had nothing to fear. Hand in hand they would succeed and build a wonderful life together.

Bob took Rachel home. Monroe and Blanche were with them. When Anna answered the bell, Jake, Natalie and Debbie came behind her. They let out a scream of delight and clapped their hands. "Here comes the bride and groom—good luck!"

Everyone kissed and wished each other a happy New Year. It was very late and after a few minutes, Monroe and Blanche, who lived in the Bronx, said they'd better be going. Bob went with them as he too lived in the Bronx.

As usual, Monroe tried to hide his emotions. "good night everyone and good luck Rachel and Bob," he said through clenched jaws, trying to seem casual.

"I'll be back tomorrow, as soon as possible," Bob told Rachel as he kissed her cheek.

"Be good to each other," Anna said, looking at Rachel and Bob with misty eyes.

When they had left and the others had gone to bed, Rachel tried to organize her multitude of thoughts about her forthcoming "real" wedding on February 15th, their new jobs in Washington, and the fact that she and Bob had just been married, the ceremony at the Rabbi's house and all.

She would have to go for a fitting for the wedding gown. It was white satin, luxurious, with a lavish train and lace above the bodice trimmed with tulle and small white satin buttons. The headpiece was stunning with a high crown, inlaid with pearls and a long lace veil hanging down the back, all rented, of course.

Bob looked like Clark Gable in a beautiful tuxedo and top hat, also rented. His dimples were deep like Gable's and she loved the way he blushed when she dabbed them lovingly with her finger and called him Clark.

When Rachel awoke in the morning, Anna was ironing Rachel's things. Everyone else was still asleep. Rachel wanted to hug and kiss her mother, but said instead, "Thanks, Mom." She felt flustered standing there, loving her mother, knowing she wouldn't be seeing her for a while, but yet afraid to show her feelings. She wanted to grab the iron and tell her mother to rest and to do the ironing herself, but she knew her mother wouldn't want that. She felt wanted and loved when she did things for her children. It would be better to let her be.

"You washed, ironed and packed for me when I went on that vacation with Dotty and also when I went away to work in the Catskills. I really appreciate it."

Bob came and after talking it over, they decided to leave for Washington the next morning. This was New Year's Day and they were scheduled to report for work on January 5th. They might as well get there and find a place to live and explore the town.

Rachel was torn between anticipation, doubts, sadness at leaving her family and happiness about her marriage to Bob, the new jobs, being in the Capitol of the United States and worried of course about the war and its consequences.

It seemed to be happening so fast. Anna had finished packing the worn out, beaten valise and Bob had gone home and come back with a small satchel in which he had one change of underwear, two shirts, a tie, a toothbrush, toothpaste, talcum powder, shaving items and a few handkerchiefs.

It was time to say goodbye. Jake was going to work and they kissed him. "I hope you make it all right," he said with a quiver in his voice, and he was gone. Oh how she loved him and pitied him.

Leaving her mother was the hardest. They kissed and hugged. She noticed her mother's worn but immaculate housedress, her bright blue eyes, her defeated look. She had called Danny. Of course, Tanya didn't even come to the phone. Sweet Danny, married to that woman who was older than he was, so unfriendly, so demanding. She also called Monroe and Blanche with a twinge in her heart. She hugged Natalie, beautiful, uncomplaining, self-sufficient Natalie and then the final coup, her youngest sibling, Debbie, her "little black chicken," with her jet black hair and blue eyes. "I'll write soon. Take care of yourselves."

Bob carried her valise downstairs and she followed him, turning back to throw a kiss to them all as they waved from the staircase. As they opened the door and went out into the street, Rachel felt a surge of pain go through her for a moment. They walked to the subway and went to Manhattan where they boarded the train to Washington.

When the train pulled out, her eyes filled with tears. "Take it easy," Bob said and he pulled her towards him. She was scared, her new husband beside her and everything else. "Till death do us part," went through her head.

The trip took five hours. She calmed down. It was so exciting, just married, going to work in Washington during the war; World War II.

Too bad World War I didn't fix everything.

"Washington," roared the conductor. They got off the train and bought a newspaper. "Furnished rooms for rent on northwest Thirteenth Street." They phoned and were told there were still vacancies. They took a cab since they didn't know where any place was.

"Let's take a room with two beds," Bob said. "I don't know how we'll be able to afford two rooms."

"We'll be working in a few days. We'll show the landlord the telegram and maybe he'll let us move in with deposits on the two rooms, without paying the whole rent in advance."

"Impossible," Bob said, but he agreed that they could try. They arrived at a three story house. The entrance foyer was nicely furnished, carpeted with a table and lamp and a couple of upholstered chairs.

"Washington is bustling because of the war," the landlady, a refined, well-dressed woman, commented. "You can't get anything lower than this price anywhere. My rooms are nicely furnished, comfortable beds, good heat, clean, fine tenants and in the heart of everything. We have mostly Government employees." She showed them two rooms, right next to each other, after Rachel told her they were to be married on February 15th.

"Rent is paid weekly in advance. That will be one week for each of you in advance, please."

"Please look at our telegrams showing where we'll be working. We'll be getting our first pay checks in two weeks. We'll pay part of it now, but don't worry, my sister-in-law is Senator Carr's secretary. You can call her for references."

Bob couldn't believe what he heard. "You folks look very respectable and I love newlyweds, so okay. Please remember, no electric stoves, no cooking in the rooms. Good luck. I'll bring up some linens."

"Thank you so much. You won't be sorry," added Rachel. When the landlady left, Bob said, with a sigh of relief, "I've got to hand it to you, Rachel." He pulled her down on his bed. "Now I've got you," he teased. She laughed, also relieved. He kissed her passionately as he had never kissed her before.

Exhausted, they both fell asleep on Bob's bed, arms around each other.

It was still light when they awoke and they went out to get something to eat.

Washington was thrilling. It was the first time they had been there. For the next few days they went sight-seeing. They saw the Lincoln Memorial (a huge statue of Abraham Lincoln sitting on a chair), the tall Washington Monument facing the Potomac River and the White

House. They saw the Capitol Building with young armed soldiers standing guard on the steep steps leading to the entrance. After all, we were at war, which made the United States more vulnerable to attack by dangerous enemies. There was the Soldiers' Home on huge grounds, all fenced in, for veterans. Inscribed statues were all over Washington for heroes who had served our country well.

On January 5th, Rachel and Bob awoke early and went to their respective jobs. Rachel's office was at Dupont Circle. It was housed in a luxurious suite of rooms, having once been a hotel. There was a beautiful bathroom, including a shower.

Her supervisor, Mr. Castle, welcomed her and showed her around. There were not too many employees, comparatively speaking. He took her to a huge room which had thousands of folders, each coded and containing important and secret information. She was to get familiar with them so that she could produce them rapidly when called for. It was also her duty to code and file new documents as they arrived.

"You have been very carefully investigated from the time of your birth until the present because your work is highly confidential. Do not speak with anyone regarding our operations," Mr. Castle instructed. He showed her a teletype machine which constantly spewed out news and information from all parts of the world, including the war zones.

Every day after work, Bob met Rachel outside the building where she worked. They exchanged events of their work day. He liked his job at the General Accounting Office. Since he was adept at figures, his job was very gratifying. She was intrigued with her job at the Board of Economic Warfare.

They walked quite a distance to their favorite restaurant, had dinner, and sometimes went to the movies. On weekends they explored Washington and the neighboring Alexandria, Virginia and Silver Springs, Maryland. They took lots of pictures.

They were so happy and content just being together. Rachel had always felt so alone, so unloved. Bob's warmth, his manliness, encompassed her. She felt secure and safe as she had never felt before.

February 15th was approaching. She now understood the importance of her job. One day during the height of military operations, a group of top brass military men came in the office and sat around a table. They were decorated with loads of medals on their jackets. Rachel was the only other person in the room where they sat with the documents they ordered her to bring in.

They asked for a German munitions folder and she brought it out to them. They spread a diagram and map on the table and she saw it. Shortly after, the newspaper headlines read, "German munitions factory destroyed." She couldn't believe it, but it was the place they had targeted right before her eyes. It was awesome. She had a part in her country's destiny, perhaps in the destiny of the world.

Then there was the teletype machine which brought in amazing pieces of news and information. "People in France are so hungry they're eating cats and rodents." So horrible, so disgusting. What was the crazy world coming to? Or rather, the people, the bad ones, she thought. Wouldn't good people like to live in peace, as Jake always said, "live and let live."

To be trusted with information about spies and other subversive elements, she found out they had investigated her so thoroughly that they even went to the house on Dumont Avenue near Pennsylvania Avenue in Brooklyn where she was born. Someone told Anna about this, someone she still was in touch with.

Rachel and Bob volunteered to be Air Raid Wardens. They were given helmets. It was eerie when the sirens sounded. They would go out into the darkness to make sure no one had lights on in their houses. After all, this was Washington, D.C., the capitol of the United States. It might be bombed and they would be out there. It was scary, but they wanted to do it.

They left for New York and their "real" wedding a few days before February 15th. According to Jewish tradition, Rachel and Bob could not see each other on the day of the wedding before the actual wedding, so he stayed at his parents' house and she at hers.

Then came the big event. She looked gorgeous in her white satin gown with its long train and its lace bodice trimmed with two rows of tiny white satin buttons. Her headpiece had a standup brim, satin and tulle with a long lace veil. Rachel still weighed ninety-six pounds and her tiny waist was incredible. She carried a large bouquet of gardenias.

Monroe and Blanche's little daughter was the flower girl and she did her part adorably, strewing rose petals down the aisle as she walked. Bob looked handsome in his tuxedo and top hat, especially when he smiled and showed his dimples. His brother was Best Man. Blanche was Maid of Honor.

Anna looked lovely in her beige lace gown and Jake was at his best. Danny was exuberant, but Tanya's face was as stern as ever. Poor Danny, he didn't deserve this.

Everything went so fast. The food was luscious, but Bob and Rachel were too excited and busy, greeting everyone, going around to each table, so they hardly ate.

After the last guest had left, Rachel went to the ladies room and started counting the checks and cash gifts. She had enough to pay the caterers and musicians. Whew, what a load off her chest. There was just one hundred fifty dollars left over.

Then bride and groom changed into street clothes and left to spend the night in a hotel on Forty-Second Street, the Times Square Hotel. When they got to the city it was about two a.m. Rachel was wearing a gardenia corsage with a white satin ribbon. They passed the Hotel Astor. People were coming out and shouted, "good luck to the bride and groom."

The first night of their honeymoon was like a movie love story. She was his now, body and soul. "How beautiful you are," he said. Finally she fell asleep on his chest like a child, trusting him and feeling safe and happy that he was hers.

In the morning they went to Hector's restaurant on Broadway for breakfast and she showed him the cards from the guests and gave him the one hundred fifty dollars that was left over.

"You amaze me. You had your wedding, even though there was no money anywhere to start with."

She laughed. "It takes nerve and determination."

They went back to the hotel room, picked up their things and took the train back to Washington.

1942 Brooklyn
Rachel and Bob's Wedding

CHAPTER 29

1942
Rachel, Washington D.C.
Capitol Bldg. in backround

1942
Rachel, Washington D.C.
In front of the Washington Monument

Washington, D.C. was brimming with activity. The war had reached heightened proportions. Letters from back home in Brooklyn spoke of hopes and fears, food rationing, departure of young men for the various armed services, the shortage of men at home, the despair of girls whose boyfriends had left, the anguish of married women, especially those with children to care for and raise, the casualty lists and so on.

Rachel had heard that Eleanor Roosevelt was working with Melvyn Douglas, the actor, in the Office of Public Information, which was one floor below where Rachel worked. Rachel was returning from lunch, when she encountered a small crowd of people waiting for the elevator in the lobby.

"I'll take you right up to your floor first, Mrs. Roosevelt," the elevator operator exclaimed.

"Oh, no," Mrs. Roosevelt protested. "Please proceed as always. I wouldn't think of it." Mrs. Roosevelt seemed to catch Rachel's gaze and smiled at her. Rachel smiled back.

After that, there were a few chance meetings and Rachel felt she had found a wonderful friend. She told Mrs. Roosevelt about her recent marriage, her job, and her ambition of becoming a songwriter.

When Rachel and Bob returned to Brooklyn, Mrs. Roosevelt wrote to her:

> I'm not a great judge of music, but I have a friend, Sylvia Fine, Danny Kaye's wife, who can advise you as to the merits of your music. Send some of your material and I'll show it to her.

Rachel was elated, not only for having met her heroine, but being befriended by her. The truly great have time for everyone, she thought, regardless of how busy they are.

A few weeks after sending Mrs. Roosevelt some of her music, Rachel received a letter. It was from Sylvia Fine's secretary saying she had gone to Europe but before she left she asked her to write. She mentioned that Mrs. Roosevelt had sent her the music, but since Mrs. Fine would be in Europe for quite a while, she could not do anything about it and that she wished Rachel good luck. She also expressed the fact that she thought the lyrics were very good.

Bob and Rachel savored each moment they spent together. Before they knew it, Bob was called into service. First of course, he had to go to New York City to take the Signal Corps training courses at the Television and Radio Institute. This would take six months. At least they would have six more months to be together.

They rented a small renovated apartment in a two-family house just a block from Rachel's family's apartment. Anna gave them an old dresser and kitchen table with four chairs and some dishes, pots and pans. They bought a spring and mattress, some curtains and other items. It was like heaven to them.

Six months passed by too quickly and Bob received his orders to go to the processing center at Camp Upton in Long Island. Army pay was fifty dollars a month so Rachel worked while Bob was in training. He had orders to leave, just on her birthday, and it was the worst birthday of her life. They went out in front of their house, kissed and embraced.

"I won't look back," he said as he started to walk away. She watched him go until he turned a corner and was out of sight. Then, she went upstairs and went wild. She ran out to some neighbors and managed to sell practically everything in the small apartment. Then she went to her family's apartment to stay there until she heard from Bob and could possibly join him.

About a week later, Bob sent a telegram informing her that he was at Camp Crowder in the Ozark Mountain region of Missouri. Long letters came between them daily. He wrote fifteen pages, saying how much he loved and missed her. He was away many times, on bivouac, training out in the fields, crawling under barbed wires and what not.

"If you come out here," he wrote, "you would not be seeing much of me. Besides, men are being shipped out to the battlefronts every day. I don't know when my turn will come. You may come here and I'll be on my way somewhere else. I don't want you to suffer out here all by yourself."

"I don't care. I can't stay here, sleeping on the couch, waiting for the mailman, longing to be with you."

In the meantime, Jake had formed a solid friendship with a Mr. Spacker, a wealthy businessman in Bayonne, New Jersey. Mr. Spacker said he would help Jake financially so that he could open a fur store in town. He loved Jake and believed in him. Jake found a store right off the main street so the rent wasn't too high.

"Anna darling," he said, "Mr. Spacker is lending me money to get started and I'm opening a store in Bayonne, New Jersey. There's a big Army base and also a Naval Base out there and hundreds, if not thousands of people are working there, so they have money to spend. I know I'll make out well."

They were still living in Brooklyn and Jake couldn't cover expenses at first, so it was arranged that Natalie who was nineteen, would go to the store every day from Brooklyn and take care of it while Jake got a job in the fur market in Manhattan.

It was a long haul for her. People started coming to buy coats, jackets, scarves and other furs. Natalie won them over with her beautiful smile and cheerful personality. She took in repair orders and had Jake call them in the evening with the estimates.

After working in the city all day, Jake went to the store in Bayonne and worked late into the night, then went back to Brooklyn. He hardly slept. Also, he returned to the store early in the morning on Saturdays and Sundays to do the actual fur work.

Since the business was doing well, Jake made Danny a partner in the business and taught him everything. Tanya put herself on the payroll even though she only came in for a couple of hours. Little by little she took over.

The workers stiffened when she came in. They were afraid of her. Poor Jake, he didn't say anything, but he almost burst with pain when he said good morning to her and she just passed him by as if he weren't there. He shook his head sadly when the family spoke about her behavior. "I don't want to make trouble for Danny," he would say.

Danny and Tanya had moved to Bayonne and Jake was still commuting from Brooklyn. Jake was a good soul and never confronted Tanya for Danny's sake. She never asked Jake to spend one night at their apartment to spare him the trip when he worked late into the night and had to return in the morning.

"Pop, "Danny said one day, "Tanya and I are going away for a few days. I'm giving you the key to our apartment in case you want to sleep over. But, be careful, don't leave any evidence that you were there."

As it happened, one night it rained so hard that it would be a pity for man or beast to be out. Jake slept over. He was very careful to leave everything as it was, but one thing went wrong. He left a window slightly open.

When Tanya came home, she saw it and the truth came out that Jake had slept there. Danny paid for it. For a solid month she gave him the silent treatment. He told Jake, who felt miserable knowing he could never expect any kindness from Tanya, his son's wife, and still worse, neither would Danny. She was mean through and through.

Danny became one of the most loved proprietors in town. He was completely honest and never let anyone buy a garment that didn't fit right. He wrote excellent advertisements for the local papers and before long, his efficient management, plus Jake's superb craftsmanship paid off. They added a better class line of dresses, fur trimmed coats, suits and general sportswear to their fur business.

After Danny came in to the business, Natalie left and got a job at the Army Base in Bayonne. She worked in Personnel, testing job applicants and processing new employees. She was a Grade two employee, as most of the girls were. She advised Rachel to come to see her in Personnel and gave her a typing and steno test, which she passed with flying colors. Then she called Captain Reisler who needed a secretary.

"Natalie, I'm not going to be a Grade two," Rachel announced.

"Listen, Rachel, they're not hiring anyone above Grade two."

"I don't care. You'll see, I'll get it."

Natalie, so darling, so beautiful, so efficient, was Grade two and here was Rachel saying this to her. Natalie had been there a few months doing a good job. Everyone admired and loved her as usual. She had a certain quality, hard to explain, which drew people to her. Perhaps it was her non-judgmental, self-assured, laissez-fair character.

Natalie told Rachel where to find Captain Reisler. In her level-headed way she didn't mention how handsome he was and how all the girls were going ga-ga over him.

Captain Reisler was deep into a pile of paperwork and telephones, and people were waiting to see him. He looked up at Rachel.

"Did you just come up from Personnel?" he asked. "I was expecting you." He interviewed her and said, "Fine, can you start tomorrow?"

"I can start right now," she said. "You look like you could use some help."

"That's for certain," he smiled.

He was blond, blue-eyed, tall and square shouldered. He wore his Army uniform exceptionally well. She could see that he was strictly business. After all, this was war and he was running the Priorities Department.

"The only thing," she said, "is that I couldn't work below Grade three. My husband is in the service and I have to support myself."

"Okay" he said. "I'll call Personnel."

"Thank you so much. Should I report for work tomorrow morning?"

"Nine o'clock, please."

"I'll be there."

When she went downstairs to tell Natalie the good news, Natalie was flabbergasted.

"How do you like that; here I am, Grade two and you come in and get Grade three." But dear Natalie, she was glad albeit surprised and Rachel kissed and hugged her lovingly. "My beautiful sister," she said to herself. "How I wish her happiness."

Shortly before Bob left for Camp Crowder, Natalie married Ralph. Like Bob, Ralph left for military service after having enlisted in the Air Force. It was surprising that she married a furrier as she often said she'd never marry one.

Ralph was handsome, also daring and before long he was a Captain, a bomber squadron leader. He was constantly sent to different locations for training, never staying in any one place for long. Natalie followed, enduring such hardship that she paid for it with her health.

When Ralph left for the service, Natalie rented a furnished room in Bayonne and started working at the Army base there. Then when Rachel started working there too, she moved in with Natalie. They shared a double bed in an old grey shingled house, which looked like a haunted house. They had to eat all their meals out, and being on Army pay, they ate cheaply and sparingly.

Danny and Tanya lived in a nice apartment house a block away from there, but Tanya never invited them over. It wasn't fair; Bob and Ralph were out there sacrificing for people like her. Danny would have gladly done his share, but he had been rejected for military service because he had rheumatic heart disease. However, she still had her husband with her. She should have been at least a bit grateful.

Business was very good. Jake and Anna were moving to Bayonne. Natalie left to join Ralph in Biloxi, Mississippi. Rachel was going to join Bob in Missouri, but she waited until her mother and father moved to Bayonne so that she could help them get set. It only took two weeks, but it seemed like a year. She was leaving the next morning.

"Debbie, I'm going to miss you so. I hate to leave you to look after Mom, but I have to go. Papa means well, but he's lost. The only thing he knows is the store. Danny is so good, but he has Tanya to account to." Her heart was torn in two. She knew there was no one on earth who loved a sister more, but she loved Bob too.

CHAPTER 30

Rachel dragged her valise into the train as Anna, Jake, Natalie and Debbie waved to her from the platform. The train was crammed full with uniformed soldiers. The rancid smell of cigarettes pervaded the air and the car was smoky and uncomfortable.

A few women, including Rachel, sat in the rear. It was to be a thirty-six hour ride to St. Louis, Missouri and then they were to be transferred to a cattle car and continue on for twelve more hours, a forty-eight hour trip.

Rachel was frightened, but glad that she would be with Bob soon. When the train arrived in St. Louis, they were informed that there would be a two hour interval until they boarded the cattle train.

Rachel was eager to see everything so she got into a cab and asked the driver to show her the town. He took her to the Famous Barr Department Store, where she quickly bought a hat and walked to the "Belcher Baths." She could smell the sulphur from the baths way down the block. She drank in all the sights and met the train on time.

They arrived in Neosho, Missouri at three-thirty a.m. It was quiet and dark on the station and no one was there but a young soldier in his uniform, Bob. They embraced and he said that they'd have to hurry, that he had a pass but had to be back in his barracks by four a.m.

He had reserved a room for her at the Capitol Hotel. He had a cab waiting and they reached the hotel in about ten minutes. She was exhausted. They walked through the lobby where a bunch of cowboys were huddled around a fireplace. Rachel noticed their boots, spurs and cowboy hats, just like in the movies, also a couple of spittoons.

The men eyed Bob and Rachel as they passed. Bob took her to a room nearby, on the same floor right past the shabby front desk, kissed her hastily and left immediately.

"Get the bus to the camp in the morning and look for me in the camp cafeteria about noon."

Rachel was scared. The door had a broken lock on it. She took the rope off of her tattered valise and tied one end of it to the door knob and the other to a chair which she tilted against the door so that she would hear if anybody tried to get in the room. Then she fell across the bed with all her clothes on.

When she awoke it was daylight. She took her valise and went outside. The air was gloriously clear and her adventure began. She found out that a bus to the Army base stopped at the door and when it came, she entered it. There were huge mountains all around, such as she had never seen before, the Ozark Mountains.

"Camp Crowder," announced the bus driver. The place was buzzing with activity, soldiers, and women alone or with babies everywhere. There was a reception center where the women were seeking help in finding a place to stay. They were crowded into a waiting room. It was awful to watch young girls nursing their babies. She was lucky she didn't have a baby under these circumstances. It would be difficult enough fending for herself.

She ran around trying to find out about everything. All she had was a few dollars in her pocket and a broken valise. She found out that if you worked on the Base you could live in the Women's Dormitories, otherwise you had to find a room in a private place. She was warned that the people of Neosho did not take kindly to folk from the eastern part of the United States and referred to them as "foreigners."

Rachel met a young woman, Mary Ellen, who was a newlywed. Her husband was also at Camp Crowder. She and Rachel looked for a room together. They found one to share in a Minister's home.

The minister's wife was very suspicious of them. They dared not say they were from New York. Rachel took advantage of having lived in Chicago and told her she lived there, so they got the room.

The room was in an attic, but homey and spotless. There was a big double bed and on it was a beautiful hand-made patchwork quilt. The polished wooden floor had a hand-woven round rag rug in the center of it.

That night the two girls got into bed. It was very quiet and the moon shone through the attic window. They had been whispering for a little while when they heard someone running wildly up the stairs. They opened the door slightly. It was the minister's wife. She was carrying a shotgun.

"What are you all talking about? You must be Easterners," she yelled angrily. Mary Ellen froze. She looked at Rachel in terror. Rachel was quick with an answer. "We were just saying how beautiful your quilt and rug are and how clean everything is. We're from Chicago." She smiled and said good night and closed the door gently.

The woman turned and went downstairs, apparently to bed. The girls didn't dare move or talk, but Rachel said almost without sound, "We'd better run for it. Leave everything here and our husbands will get it for us tomorrow.

They waited until everything was quiet and then tip-toed down the stairs and out the door as stealthily as possible and began running. It was cold and there were a million stars in the sky above the mountains. They ran all the way to a house where Mary Ellen had met an elderly lady. She had shown the woman how to sew and she had said, "If ever you need me, consider me your grandmother and come any time."

They were real hillbilly folk. Everybody was asleep, but "grandma" answered their frantic knocking at the door and let them in. After she heard their story she led them into an unheated room where they buried themselves under the quilt in the antiquated bedstead and clung together for warmth until their chattering teeth finally quieted down.

In the morning they were given a fine breakfast and went into the living room. It was a large room filled with members of the family, including many barefooted children, some chickens and pigs all running around.

After properly thanking "grandma," they set out for the Camp. They waited for hours until their husbands showed up in the cafeteria as they had arranged. They told them about their experience and both men went to reclaim the valises.

When they came back, the girls separated. Rachel was on her own again. Rachel linked up with another girl who was also looking for a place to stay. She was attractive, but rather stocky and sexy looking. She told Rachel about some cabins which were for rent. They went there and rented one.

The cabin was at the edge of the woods, near a bar and grill. It had a gas heater for warmth, but no cooking facilities. Rachel was afraid to be in the cabin alone at night and the girl promised to return at night to sleep there. But when night came, she did not return.

Rachel put the heater on and fell asleep exhausted. Her bed was close to the wall under the window. She was awakened early in the morning by a loud sound, and horrors, there was a cow with his head inside the partially open window, looking down at Rachel!

The next night the girl still did not return. Rachel could not sleep, especially because she had heard that wolves roamed around in the woods and she actually heard them howling.

In the middle of the night, Rachel walked into the Bar and Grill. The waitress, tough but human, welcomed her and invited her to sit down, which she did for the rest of the night. Cowboys frequented the place all night and drank heartily at the bar while a nickelodeon blared. Better than being in that cabin alone.

In the morning she returned to the Camp and found out that her absent roommate had the reputation of sleeping with soldiers and had been banned from the Camp. What should she do now? Rachel pondered.

The only way out was to get a room in the Women's Dormitories at the Camp. The catch to it was that you had to be employed at the Camp to live there. After much inquiring, she found out that there was only one job in the whole place and that interviews were being held at that moment. It didn't matter that it was in the Tailor Shop, taking in and giving out soldiers' clothing.

She had to get into the Dormitories. She got the job. After getting the necessary approval, she moved into the Dormitories. It was heaven compared with what she had been through. The rooms were nice and properly heated and the toilet facilities were very good with ample sinks and lavatories and mirrors, and companionship of the other young women who were in the same boat as she was.

The biggest surprise was that Bob's barracks were right across from her window. In the morning she looked out the window and saw Bob marching in line with his buddies. He waved up at her as they marched by. Sometimes he yelled, "Rachel," and before long all the fellow soldiers waved along with him and shouted, "Rachel," as well. It was hilarious, embarrassing, but heartwarming.

She could hardly wait for the weekends when Bob got a pass to the "Guest House," reserved for husbands and wives if you applied in advance and were lucky enough to get it.

It was wonderful being together. They hugged and made love and held on to each other as if each time was the last time. There were weeks that he went on bivouac when she spent the evenings in the U.S.O. trying to be distracted from her loneliness by watching the shows and dancing with the soldiers.

She was no longer working at the Tailor Shop for she had gotten a job selling jewelry at the Post Exchange. The night before shipping out the young soldiers would ask her to visit their mothers or girlfriends when she got back to New York and convey their love. It was heartbreaking.

The war was in full swing. President Franklin Delano Roosevelt, Commander-in-Chief, briefed and encouraged the public. The headlines read: "The Allied Forces landed in North Africa; Britain began heavy raids on German cities; Japanese forces moved into the Philippines, Manila and Singapore; U.S. B-17's bombed Rouen, France and B'24's bombed Naples, Italy. Major General

Doolittle led a bombing group over Tokyo. Roosevelt asked Congress for fifty-three billion dollars for the war effort."

"War was inhuman. God had created man in His image and had given him his own free will. Maybe God was crying when he saw what was happening," mused Rachel. "But couldn't He stop what was happening?"

The news: "100,000 Japanese Americans sent to camps; four hundred and eighty-eight ships built in one year; gasoline rationing goes into effect; draft age lowered to eighteen."

Phyllis's kid brother was eighteen and was oversees just a few weeks when he was killed. His mother went into such shock at the news that a lock of hair in front of her head turned white overnight.

The people back home were making money working in defense plants and as civilian Army and Navy employees, and were able to spend. Jake's business flourished.

"Anna, darling," Jake said. "I found an empty lot on Broadway right near the Post Office. Thousands of people pass there. What do you think of my buying it? I'm going to get a very big rent increase when my next lease is up. If I own my own place, I won't have a landlord and the location is great."

"Where will you get the money to build on it? You'll have a place for cats to piss on."

"Mr. Spacker said he'll help me."

Anna changed the subject. "I'm worried about Natalie and Rachel, and Debbie should be out seeing young men instead of having to keep me company at night when you're in the store. I tell her to go, but she doesn't want to leave me."

"I'm going to build a fur storage warehouse under the store," Jake declared. We'll put in air conditioned vaults and people will all store their fur garments there in the summer. Also, tailors will take in furs for storage too and bring them to us. We'll make lots of money."

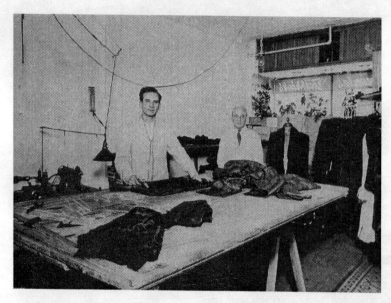

Jake and Danny in their workshop at the new "Brownies."

Jake and Danny in their enlarged and
modernized store "Brownies."

CHAPTER 31

Bob's Company was preparing to ship out to a War Zone when he became ill. He was confined to the Army hospital with influenza, followed by post-influenza neuralgia and an acute sinus infection. When he was nineteen, before he and Rachel had even met, Bob had a double Caldwell sinus operation. The rigid outdoor training had done him no good. He received an honorable discharge and he and Rachel went back to New York together.

"Let's go to Texas as long as we're way out here," she pleaded.

"That would be wasting time," he said. "We've got to get back to New York and find jobs and a place to live."

"We could do that a week or two later. I've always wanted to see Texas. If we don't go now, who knows if we'll ever go."

They left for New York, his duffle bag thrown over his shoulder and she toting her old worn out valise, again reinforced with a piece of rope.

They found there was a housing shortage in New York. With no possibility of finding an apartment, they rented a miserable small room in a middle aged couples' apartment in the Bronx. The place was kept filthy. There were roaches and even mice. Rachel and Bob stayed in their room reluctant to so much as come out and take a shower in the dirty bathroom with its dirty shower curtains.

As a returning veteran, Bob was reinstated in his former Government job in Manhattan. They searched and found a furnished studio efficiency apartment there. It was heaven, by comparison. The furniture was Swedish Modern, light wood and the rent included housekeeping service. It had a Murphy bed which they pulled down out of the wall at night.

When Bob left for work, Rachel went out to Gristedes, bought some food, and put it in the small refrigerator and cabinet. When she returned, she found the bed had been made and pulled back into the wall, the carpet vacuumed and everything dusted. However, they could not afford the rent so they hunted for an apartment in the Bronx.

They found one on Olinville Avenue near Burke Avenue. It was in a nice brick six-story apartment house. It had a kitchenette (sink, stove, refrigerator and cabinets behind folding doors in the living room).

Rachel found a job as a secretary in a Manhattan office. "Orchestra World" magazine had folded since the big bands had mostly given up and the "big band era" was over. Most of the "Merry Girls" had gotten married and moved away.

Natalie and Ralph also returned. Ralph had been a Captain, a bomber squadron leader in the Air Force. His group moved constantly and Natalie followed wherever they went. She was so charming, so pretty and so good. Rachel and Bob greeted them lovingly.

"Bob and I want you to stay with us until you find an apartment," Rachel offered.

Natalie did not look well. She explained that when they were in a town near the Mexican border, she had gotten malaria. She told stories of the terrible hardships she had gone through while Ralph was in rigid training; so rigid and prolonged in fact that he never went overseas before he was finally discharged since married men were being let go.

Sometimes, like in Biloxi, Mississippi, Natalie got a job teaching (a license was not required there and she was very good with the children). The officers were given a house to live in. Ralph's buddies came there almost every evening and Natalie cooked nice meals for them.

Ralph was grounded because his eyesight did not meet requirements and he was put on carrots (for vitamin A) for a couple of weeks to improve his sight. Natalie and Ralph waved to the fellows as they took off, when shockingly, the plane exploded and crashed before their eyes. Natalie said she could never forget this incident.

Another bad experience was when she had to move in with a man and his wife in Biloxi, Mississippi. No cooking was the rule. She couldn't even have a cup of coffee there in the morning.

One day, Natalie said, she set out through the wooded area as usual to a diner for some breakfast when a fierce tornado hit. She crawled on her hands and knees all alone to avoid being hit by lightening. There were large hailstones falling all around her which were unbelievable.

Poor Natalie; she was not well. All this had taken its toll upon her health. The bad part was that Ralph took all this for granted. Bob, on the other hand, had warned Rachel of certain hardships and said that as much as he wanted her to be with him, perhaps she shouldn't come. In his own selfish way, Ralph instead had urged Natalie to join him.

Rachel could not bear to hear Natalie's hacking cough all night, but when she knocked on the door and asked if there was anything she could do, Natalie, as well as Ralph, resented her interference so she stopped showing her feelings.

Bob helped them in their search for an apartment and he found one for them further up on Olinville Avenue in a similar apartment building as theirs. It was also a six-story brick building, fifty-two apartments, right near a lovely park. It had a large bedroom, living room, kitchen and bathroom and a nice sized foyer which they made into a dining room.

They all eased back into civilian life. Ralph knew his craft very well and the fur market welcomed him back as a mink cutter. Natalie got a job as a bookkeeper but the marks of her years of hardship as a Camp follower during the time of Ralph's military service were most evident.

Jake put his words into action. With Mr. Spacker's help, he and Danny bought the lot and built a new store on it. They also built a modern fur storage warehouse underneath it with air conditioned vaults, exactly as Jake had planned. Danny took care of the advertising and they had a very successful opening.

Debbie came to the Bronx to visit her sisters. She squirmed as she sat on the couch in Rachel's and Bob's apartment. "I have something to tell you. When I went on my vacation last week, I met a wonderful fellow. I took some pictures of him with my camera. Should I send them to him?"

"Of course," Rachel advised her.

"Will you help me write a note to include with the pictures?"

"Sure." Rachel was used to that. Everyone asked her to help them write letters. She dashed them right off. It came easy to her.

Paul called Debbie and thanked her for the pictures. He started dating her and within six weeks asked her to marry him and she accepted. It was a spontaneous love affair. Paul was decent, good looking and wealthy besides. "Thank you, God," Rachel said to herself. "My darling little Debbie will be all right."

Jake could now afford to make a beautiful wedding for Debbie. It was a lavish affair in the Belmont Plaza Hotel in Manhattan. Her in-laws provided the flowers, which were unbelievable.

CHAPTER 32

Jake's words came back to Rachel, "A worker will never be rich. The only way is to have your own business." These words rang in her ears, especially when she was discouraged.

There was a big world out there and she wanted to be part of it. How could she do much for others if she didn't first do something for herself? If the war hadn't come, she would have written more songs, maybe even the lyrics for a Broadway show. Then she would have had the power to go on to do the things she longed for like opening an orphan home, feeding poor people, etc. Dreams, dreams; but things usually happen as a result of dreams.

Talking about dreams, Rachel had an upsetting and recurring dream. It was Kenny's mother, whom she had never met. "You didn't come to the Seder. Look what you did to my son. He loved you so." That dream besieged her so many times. She would awake with her heart pounding.

Rachel never held things back from Bob. She would tell him and he just turned over and went back to sleep, saying, "It's only a dream." This dream had even followed her to the Army, far away from home. So many times she was possessed with the desire to find Kenny and tell him she didn't come to the Seder because she had nothing to wear. It would console him to a certain extent. But although she found his name in the Brooklyn phone book, she couldn't bring herself to call him, perhaps out of loyalty to Bob or fear that Kenny might be married and it would be inappropriate. Maybe he even had forgotten of their "young love."

She would have to resume her songwriting and other writing, perhaps a novel, telling all that was in her heart. In the meantime though, she would have to be more practical. She had had enough of being poor.

She'd have to sidetrack her dreams and make money through business. She had an idea; since buying an established business would require a lot of cash and she didn't have any cash at all, she would start a store from scratch.

Bob, as usual, thought the whole idea was impossible since he was a very negative person, afraid to take chances. For instance, he was incredibly efficient in his office job, as well as neurotically prompt and time conscious. Yet, he hesitated asking for an increase for fear of being fired. In the Civil Service bulletin, they mentioned him as having "an eagle eye" and "that no error can escape him." They lauded his accomplishments with small monetary awards from time to time.

Rachel was undaunted. She knew that Bob would actually offer no opposition and that he would help her in any way possible. She would find an empty store and open a stationery business. The main item would be greeting cards as they reaped one hundred percent profit. She would purchase the cards carefully, studying their verses. She was good at that. In addition, she would carry toys, "best seller" books, commercial stationery to a limited extent, school supplies, party supplies and whatever else.

Bob went along with her. His love, his loyalty would carry her through. He was always there for her, called her many times during the day and was just happy to come home to her each night.

They walked along a busy Bronx avenue and almost immediately spotted a prospect. It could easily have been bypassed, but she recognized its potential. The place had evidently once been a store, but its long front window had been removed and the place was being used as a Charlotte Russe stand. A Charlotte Russe was a delicious concoction. It was served in a cardboard base. It was made of sponge cake and topped with whipped cream and a cherry. It was very popular.

The place had been closed and upon inquiry, Rachel found the landlord who said the fellows who operated it had gone out of business because of the way they handled things. Rachel asked if the landlord would replace the window and rent the store to her.

She could just picture the long front window with a display of greeting cards, best seller books, an array of plush cuddly toys such as teddy bears and other little animals, an assortment of dolls, games, party hats and favors and more. She would try to get a franchise from the Womrath Rental Libraries and that would be a good way to build up the business by discussing the books with the customers. The better greeting card companies had franchises too and she would try to link up with them.

"How do you expect to do all this?" Bob inquired.

She had a notebook in hand. "Will you go with me to various stores and find out where they buy their merchandise, compare prices and get any other advice possible?" she asked.

"Okay, if you think so. What about money?"

"First I'll get all the details and then ask my father to lend me one thousand dollars. The rent is only fifty dollars a month and although the place is small, it's near the subway station and the cross-town bus stops right in front of the store. The display window is large and will be noticed."

"Woolworth's is right across the street from the place. Do you think you can compete?"

"That will be very good." Woolworth's closes early and people who want things will go there but come to our store if they find Woolworth is closed. They'll also come to us for items they can't find there."

"I'm not quitting my job. I'm not good for business."

"You can keep on working, but you can help in the evenings and on Saturday. We can go to the jobbers and buy merchandise on Sunday. It won't be easy, but we'll be able to make some money."

Rachel always had to start things, but there was no question that Bob would tag along and help. He was so handsome, so efficient and had a good sense of humor. The customers would love him, she thought. But, the enterprise would be hers and she would be free to wield her imaginative mind and be successful. Then one day she would be able to do all the things she wanted to like write her music, her novel and reach out to people who needed help, community work and philanthropic work.

Her dreams, her dreams; they pervaded her soul. She couldn't just settle back and miss all the beauty and excitement of the world and its people and things or she would reach the end and leave nothing for posterity, nothing much to be remembered for. A wasted life; she would be buried and forgotten.

Everything went along beautifully. She walked into similar stores, notebook in hand, explaining that she was not opening a store in their area, and would therefore not be a competitor.

Bob stood by hardly able to believe how these strangers shared their knowledge and good wishes, telling her of the best wholesalers and jobbers, giving her the benefit of their experience. Rachel even got the name of an inexpensive but creative window dresser who would set up the front show window.

Rachel wanted to have a neon sign put up with the name of the store, "Sincerely Yours," as she would name it. She got an electrician and carpenter very reasonably and had a neon sign put up. It was red and easily seen from quite a distance. Jake lent her the one thousand dollars which she promised to pay back as soon as possible.

She started on a shoestring and had to be very careful. A carpenter built some shelves on which she propped up soft, new plush teddy bears and the like, and a few dolls which she purchased on credit with her father's help. Natalie came over and helped her paint the shelves pink and they put up blue and silver wallpaper. The greeting card jobbers furnished the greeting card racks which ran down the length of the store.

"I have an idea," Rachel told Bob. "You've got to look big or people won't buy. I'm going to get stacks of empty boxes and pile them way up to the ceiling. Only the top two or three boxes will have merchandise in them so it will look as if we have plenty of merchandise. As soon as we sell, we'll replenish. In that way, we'll have more and more merchandise as we'll use the profits to buy more." She was excited at the prospect.

Bob merely looked on in disbelief. "Good luck," he said.

Rachel had flyers printed which were handed out all over the neighborhood announcing the grand opening. She bought a small toy movie projector, a little doll carriage and a doll and mentioned in the flyer that if you made a two dollar purchase, you would be eligible to win one of these prizes.

When the doors opened for the first time, she was astonished to find that a line of people had formed down the block and people came in and started to buy. The small store was crammed. Bob got into the action.

"Don't forget to be back at six o'clock for the raffle," he said. "Hope you win."

It was a great day. After closing the store at night, they took all the proceeds out of the drawer under the counter, put the money in a cloth bag and were glad when Natalie and Ralph suddenly rapped on the glass window of the door.

"We figured you'd be tired, and besides you'll be safer in our car with the money," Natalie said cheerfully. They had bought an inexpensive used car.

When they got home, Rachel pulled down the Venetian blind in the living room and they counted the money. They had made a pretty profit. Rachel was elated. Bob, in his usually efficient way, was more concerned with the accuracy of counting.

"Isn't this wonderful," Rachel beamed.

"Of course," he replied, as he continued counting and writing numbers.

CHAPTER 33

1945
Rachel outside her store "Sincerely Yours" Shop. Bronx, N.Y.

The store was doing very well. As soon as the merchandise in the top boxes was sold, Rachel rushed out to the jobber and bought some more. She and Bob didn't drive so they didn't have a car. She hailed a cab and came back breathless, lugging the merchandise. She had to hang a sign on the door, "Will be back soon."

Before long, all the boxes were filled with stock. The lending library was a drawing card. Rachel read every book so that she was able to recommend and discuss them with customers who came into borrow books and consequently made purchases.

Rachel was an excellent buyer and never misjudged the potentiality of an item. Furthermore, if someone asked for an item which she didn't have, she would say, "We're getting it in tomorrow," and she made sure it would be there for them. The volume and variety of items thus grew.

She hated violence and although she knew a jobber who would have supplied her with metal toy guns, despite the metal shortage because of the war, she refused to sell them. Every little boy expected a "Cowboy gun." "I think it's terrible to give a child a gun. How old is your child? Why don't you give him this instead?" Invariably they would purchase a more appropriate toy and commend her. Fathers would stop by after coming out of the subway from work and actually ask her what to buy for their children. They trusted her sincerity.

The business was thriving to such an extent that there wasn't enough room for the added merchandise and greeting card racks and Rachel knew something would have to be done. She made an appointment with the landlord. He was a shrewd man, a lawyer.

"The place is too small. I want to add sleds, doll carriages and other larger items. I have an idea. If you enlarge the store by extending it into the backyard, I'll pay you triple the rent, one hundred fifty dollars a month instead of fifty, and I'll sign a five year lease."

The landlord deliberated for a moment and then he replied, "Tell you what. If you do the enlarging yourself, I'll let you continue to pay fifty dollars a month with a ten year lease." He knew as well as she did, that because of the war it was difficult to get building supplies and that they were therefore very costly.

"I don't have the money," Rachel said. The deal was off.

It was rough going. The heat in the store was inadequate and there was an awful coldness coming up from the floor. Bob came in after work and opened on Saturdays so that she could come in a little later. On Sundays they went to the city to buy merchandise. When they got back, they put the prices on each item.

Rachel drank in the books all around her, the best sellers, the lending library books and the children's books. Lyrics came into her thoughts and she jotted them down. She wanted to make some money, but there was no question where her heart was. Songs, books, someday she would write, she must, otherwise she would burst with all her thoughts bulging within her brain. She had to express herself in song, in book, in poetry, in anything that would be seen or heard. In addition, it would earn her the money and the power to do some good in the world. Maybe it was the loneliness, the humiliation, the poverty of her childhood which drove her in this direction, the helplessness of her illness and the years of fighting rheumatic fever.

Another thing, she found herself peering into baby carriages to admire the babies. At such times, she would have a deep yearning to have a child, to be a mother, to be the best mother that ever lived. Her child would have everything she never had. She would raise him or her according to her way and see that he or she would be molded into a beautiful human being. It would be a miracle come true, her very own child to love and to be loved by and hopefully to revel in her child's happiness and accomplishments.

Wonder of wonders, the doctor confirmed the fact that Rachel was pregnant.

"Nobody but we will take care of our child," she informed Bob. "I'm putting an ad in the newspaper and selling the store as quickly as possible." Bob couldn't care less. He looked at her with love in his eyes and slight bewilderment at the news.

"Mommy," he teased and kissed her. She knew he'd be there for her and their child.

The store was sold within a week and they were off on a two week vacation to a Catskill Hotel with Anna and Jake. With the store out of the way and the baby coming, Rachel was very happy. She sat on the lawn with Anna and Bob and couldn't believe it when Jake came riding up on the lawn on a horse." "My father," she beamed. "What a guy. Live and let live," was his motto. And what about her mother who worried, struggled and sacrificed for her children? It was good spending time with them each priceless moment.

CHAPTER 34

Rachel and Bob eagerly awaited the birth of their first child. Bob treated her like a princess during her pregnancy. They would sit together and wonder at the movements of her abdomen as their developing son or daughter stirred within her.

Jason was born at about the expected date. He was a beautiful eight pound baby. It was amazing to see what a beautiful head of dark brown hair he had. It fell down his neck. The doctor had given her calcium pills and ordered her to drink a lot of milk, which she did.

When Rachel came home from the hospital with the baby, she found that Bob had printed a huge sign which spanned the length of the living room wall. "Welcome home mother and baby!" He was the most wonderful husband and father in the world. He insisted on making the formula in his own efficient way. Everything had to be measured exactly and the bottles had to be boiled in a sterilizing rack.

Those were glorious days. Rachel sat outside in front of the apartment house with other young mothers, their baby carriages before them. She knitted matching sweater and hat sets for her baby. He was a good, beautiful baby with a happy smile and she adored the way his face would light up when she cooed at him.

When Jason was about ten months old, she put him in a playpen in the living room near the kitchenette where she could watch him and do her work. She noticed that when she would turn the radio on and he heard music, he would stand up, hold on to the rails and jump up and down keeping perfect time to the music. No matter how occupied he was, his response to music was unbelievable. His two precious little teeth would appear as he smiled and cavorted to the music. It was a delight to behold.

At five, Jason was taking singing lessons in a local studio. The group of children, singers and dancers entertained at hospitals, nursing homes and community functions. He was a big hit wherever they performed.

There was a woman and her husband in the building where they lived. Marie and Rachel became friends and Marie told her all about her husband, Carmine. He was a piano teacher and a composer who had many numbers published, but they never went anywhere. He was the Assistant Director of the Newark Opera Company. A famous baritone, Guiseppe Valdengo, sang one of Carmine's numbers when he performed at La Scala and a recording company recorded it. Marie said he lacked ambition and drive and encouraged Rachel to collaborate with him, which she did.

Marie and Carmine had a son Jason's age and they became friends. They were both eight years old. One day Carmine asked Rachel to come upstairs as he had to show her something. As they approached his door, she heard someone playing the piano. She thought it was one of his advanced students. The rendition was beautiful. They went into the apartment and there was Jason playing the piano. He had never taken one piano lesson. He had been playing with Carmine's son and had sat down at the piano.

"I thought you should be aware of this," Carmine said in awe.

"Once in a great while a musical prodigy appears," Carmine continued. "Your son displays that rare talent."

Rachel wasted no time. She called the Julliard School of Music and related the whole story. They asked her to bring Jason in. After hearing him play, they said they would like to enroll him in their Preparatory Division.

"I can't afford it," Rachel said remorsefully.

"Don't worry, he'll be on a scholarship basis."

Carmine knew somebody who wanted to get rid of an old upright piano. "They're moving out of state. The husband happens to be in the moving business and he said he would bring the piano to you without charge."

When the piano arrived, Rachel found it very unattractive. It had been painted a dark brown and the paint was peeling. Rachel, Bob and Jason worked on it for weeks until they had sanded it down to the bare wood and then shellacked it into a light wood. On Saturdays she took Jason to the Julliard School for theory and harmony training and piano instruction. On Sunday, they went to his teacher's home for additional piano instruction.

Rachel also became active in the PTA at school. She wrote articles for the school paper and became Publicity Chairman for the school. As a result of her articles in the local newspapers, and bringing the plight of the school to politicians, the school received a one million dollar grant from the Board of Education to build an auditorium and lunchroom which were sorely needed. "You ought to write a book," people told her, as usual.

Carmine and Rachel continued writing songs. She wrote the lyrics and sometimes she gave him ideas for melodies. He would write the notes out and his friend, an arranger, would help him with the arrangements.

Rachel was the aggressive one who tried to promote their numbers, but she expected another child. She bore a beautiful baby daughter. Since her children came first and Bob worked on most weekends and holidays, all her time was given to the children.

Then Natalie, Debbie and Monroe moved to Queens and since she wanted to be near them, she and Bob decided to move there too. Since they didn't have a car, and neither did Carmine, they rarely saw Carmine and Marie after that.

Caryn was three and Jason ten when Jake had a stroke. Anna was very sick too with congestive heart failure. Since Natalie, Debbie Monroe and Rachel lived in Queens, they moved Anna and Jake to an apartment near them.

Danny ran the business in New Jersey, and although Monroe wanted to join him, Tanya, as usual, got her way and succeeded in getting her sister's husband into the business instead. Monroe became very bitter since he was a son and a top-notch furrier, whereas Tanya's sister's husband knew nothing about furs.

The fur market was very slow so Monroe spent most of his days with his sick parents. It was very sad, Jake in his wheelchair barely able to talk or move, and Anna choking on her own body fluids because of the congestive heart failure.

It was turmoil. It was very difficult trying to get proper help in the house. Rachel was there all day. She would drop Caryn off at Debbie's house and pick her up late at night. Debbie took care of her two children and Caryn. Jason came home from school, did his homework, practiced his piano and ate the dinner Rachel had prepared for him.

Natalie did her share, although her heart condition became worse. Danny would eat his heart out when he came once a week from

New Jersey to check on things and to bring the necessary money for the week.

Jake and Anna never reaped the fruit of their labors. Doctors, nurse's aides, physical therapists and medicines ate up their money and they were too sick to go anywhere or do anything.

The strain was too much. Four years had passed since Anna and Jake had moved to Queens. Monroe had a heart attack. Natalie was told she would have to have open heart surgery. Finally, Jake had to be taken to the hospital where he died.

Anna was now in such serious condition that they decided not to tell her about Jake's death. She died a week later. Neither knew of each other's deaths. According to Jewish custom, the family sat Shiva, the traditional way of mourning, for one week, and then again for another week, first for their father, and then for their mother.

Natalie's open heart surgery was scheduled. Rachel and Bob went to her house to see her every day. She hardly complained, although it was plain to see how ill she was. Everyone loved her because she was so warm and giving. She never lost her wonderful sense of humor. Her artistic touches pervaded their small apartment. There were shelves filled with her extraordinary ceramic creations and an abundance of beautiful plants hung from the dining room ceiling. Ralph's uncle was an artist and he had bequeathed a number of his paintings to them and they also adorned the walls.

Rachel sobbed broken heartedly when she heard the bad news. Natalie's operation, wherein they had replaced two valves, had lasted fourteen hours, but she died in the recovery room an hour after the operation.

Not long after Natalie's death, Danny developed a cough. He was informed by the doctor that it was the result of his bout with rheumatic fever in his youth. Rachel longed to go to his home to see him, but was afraid that it would cause a confrontation with Tanya since only Tanya's sisters were welcome.

Horror of horrors, Rachel got a call from Monroe, who had been informed that Danny had a massive heart attack and died before they could even get him to a hospital. What made it even more ghastly, was that there was a cemetery strike and they held his body in a plastic bag in the funeral parlor for two weeks until he could be buried.

Monroe was so distraught that he had to be restrained from going to the cemetery to bury Danny himself. It was winter and the ground was frozen and it would have been a grueling, if at all possible, ordeal. Monroe's physical and emotional condition would have made this a dangerous thing for him to do, so everyone restrained him.

The strike was finally ended and Danny was buried. Monroe was a vessel filled with anger, remorse and sorrow.

"Poor Mom, poor Papa, poor Natalie and now, poor Danny," Rachel remarked sadly to Bob as her eyes filled with tears. "There's just Debbie and me left, and whatever shell of a man Monroe has become. It's unbelievable what can become of a family."

"You'll have to accept it and go on," Bob said in his usual way of dealing with reality. She knew he cared. He had helped her so much with Mama, Papa and Natalie and he loved them all, but he always avoided unpleasant truths. She, on the other hand, mulled things over and over until she was weary.

Before Danny died, he told Monroe that if anything happened to him, he should run the business. He had hidden ten thousand dollars behind a certain radiator in case he needed it for expenses.

Jake was president and founder of the business and had taken Danny in. Anna had warned him to consult a lawyer and have everything put in writing, but Jake trusted Danny and let things go for fear of having a confrontation with Tanya and setting up arguments between her and Danny. He never thought that Danny would die so suddenly at the age of fifty-six.

After Jake and Anna died, Danny ran the business, but when Danny died, Tanya refused to let Monroe take over. She hired an unscrupulous lawyer and absconded with everything, the building with its fur storage vaults, all of the merchandise, money and other assets. She even found and took the ten thousand dollars which Danny had put behind the radiator for Monroe. She had a new will drawn to replace the old one. Thus, as Anna predicted, Jake and Annie's children were cheated out of their inheritances.

"The best thing to do is keep busy," Bob advised Rachel. "Write songs; write a book. You've always wanted to do that and everyone tells you they think you can do it."

"I'll try," she promised, but first I have to get a job. Jason will be going to college next year and we'll need money. I'd love to be able to stay home and do something about my music and write a book, but we're so much in debt and have no savings."

"I'll keep my extra jobs." He had his full time job, worked as a salesman after his regular work day, in an apparel shop and was a Maitre'D on weekends. He never complained and was just happy to spend whatever time he could with Rachel and the children. They adored him. He was content to have a picnic in the park whenever possible. He didn't drive because they didn't have a car.

"I'm going to take driving lessons," Rachel said."

"We don't have a car; what's the use?"

Debbie and Paul are letting me practice on their old Buick, which they rarely use."

"Uh, huh, good luck." Then he went to the kitchen. He came back with an apple and started eating it as he walked to his chair.

"Want an apple?" he asked her.

"No thanks. You eat too much. You're getting too heavy and so am I."

I was a size four until after Jason was born," she continued," now I'm a size twelve."

He put the TV on. "I'm watching this show," he said impatiently. He finished the apple and started eating a caramel which he had tucked in his fist. He laughed, "So all we do is eat. What else is there to do? Work, work, work, no money, no car."

"I wonder when we'll be able to go on a vacation," she asked, wearily. "We've got to borrow some money again, you know. Caryn has to have orthodontia. There's a space between her two upper front teeth. She's so beautiful; I don't want that to ruin it for her."

"How about some coffee and toasted English," he offered.

She sat there watching TV while he went into the kitchen to prepare the snack. A gorgeous female vocalist was singing about love. It was so romantic that she cried. She thought about herself in high heels, dancing with fellow after fellow, size three or four, how they raved about her flawless skin, her vibrant personality. She thought about Kenny, breaking up because of the Seder that she didn't, couldn't, attend, the dreams about his mother crying, "What did you do to my son?"

Where was the rich, distinguished man she was going to marry, the luxurious home, the cars, the vacations? She had always been afraid to marry Kenny because he had little education and questionable prospects for the future. She remembered how terrible poverty was. Why was it that although her future with Bob was also risky, that she married him? Was it on the rebound after the breakup with Kenny? She had felt very guilty about the Seder incident and how badly Kenny felt and the effect it had on his family, especially his mother. Could it be that she repented by marrying Bob?

"Here it is," said Bob as he put the coffee and muffins on two snack tables. "Do you want me to pick up a birthday cake for Jason's birthday tomorrow?"

"I'd appreciate that. Get one with chocolate frosting and white cake inside. Tell them to write, "Happy Birthday, Jason on it in blue icing."

"How about not cooking tomorrow? I could pick up some Chinese food. Jason and Caryn would love that."

"Okay, once in a while on a birthday, why not."

After they finished having the coffee and muffins, they watched some more TV. Rachel cleared the snack tables and washed the dishes. Caryn and Jason had already gone to bed.

Rachel and Bob went to bed too. The minute Bob's head touched his pillow, he was sound asleep. She lay there for a long time thinking, planning, reminiscing. They had put their bed in a corner of the living room and given the children the bedroom, after putting up a partition, thus giving each child their privacy.

Rachel thought of the past, the celebrities she had interviewed in their lavish homes, the summers she spent in the Catskill hotels, writing and producing children's shows, her office in Steinway Hall on Fifty-Seventh Street in Manhattan where she did rewriting, ghost-writing and public relations. The office was magnificent and she didn't even pay rent. She had been working as secretary to a famous beauty editor who let her share the office instead of getting a salary.

On and on her thoughts ran, the songwriting and how her numbers were being performed in various hotels and nightclubs only to be stilled by the war and her marriage to Bob and going to join him in Missouri at Camp Crowder. Everyone told her Jason was slated for stardom and she hoped he would fulfill his dreams better than she had.

She finally fell asleep. She awoke to see a glimmer of light entering the room. She stole a look at Bob sleeping there beside her in the early dawn. He would soon be up and rushing to his office. His office was his predominant interest. He was possessed with promptness and "efficiency." He always carried a few pens, some cards, clips, rubber bands, a thick address book and what not in his bulging pockets. He had no hobbies and hardly any interest in anything other than his office, his wife and children.

"I'll call you from the office," he said as he kissed her quickly on the cheek.

"Have a good day."

"You too."

Then he was off, briefcase in hand. He called her when he had arrived at the office, then about five or six more times during the day to see what she was doing, to ask if he should bring something on the way home.

After he had gone, Rachel looked out of the window. Winter was past, the earth was alive. It amazed her how the bushes and trees, covered with heavy snow, dry and dead as they seemed, had now budded, greened and bloomed. Could people be like that, she wondered? Or do we just cease to be?

She threw some bread crumbs out the window and a little bird pecked at them. It was uncanny how he appeared so swiftly, then saw her at the open window and flew away, a crumb in his beak. Enough of that; Today was Jason's birthday. There were things to do.

"Happy Birthday," Rachel, Bob and eight year old Caryn sang in unison to Jason. "I can't believe you're fifteen," Rachel exclaimed after Jason had blown out the candles on his birthday cake.

Jason smiled s they all embraced and kissed. Then he sat down at the piano and started to play. "Play my favorite," Rachel requested, and without hesitation, he played Chopin's beautiful "Prelude in A Major, OP 28, No. 7." She gripped the edge of her chair; his playing was awesome.

From the age of eight, when his talent first became apparent, he spent every possible moment at the piano, even in the morning, before he washed, brushed his teeth or had his breakfast. In inclement weather, when he stayed in, he would practice ten or more hours. She would hear him play a phrase over and over, dozens of times, until he got it exactly right. Rarely she would warn him that if he didn't do a certain thing which had to be done, she wouldn't let him open the piano that day. However, she could never keep this threat, for she knew it would have been his ultimate punishment.

A few days after his birthday, Rachel accompanied him to Radio Station WNYC. He had been chosen by Juilliard to represent them on "Young America Plays." He played Haydn's Sonata, Schumann and Poulenc's Toccata. It was beautiful and unbelievable.

A television scout heard him and asked him to play on a popular talent show, The Sonny Fox Show. He did his own rendition of Leonard Bernstein's music from "West Side Story." The audience applauded enthusiastically.

"Where do you live?" Sonny Fox asked him.

"In Queens," he replied.

He came across gorgeous on the screen. You could fall in love with him when he smiled.

"How old are you?"

"Fifteen."

"Where do you study music?"

"At the Juilliard Preparatory Division."

"Was that your own arrangement?"

"Yes."

"Did you write it down, or did you remember it?"

"Remember."

"Wow! Fantastic! Will you play again later in the show?"

"Thank you; I will."

He came on later, playing Toccata by Poulenc and then the "Gravy Waltz," which he had heard on the Steve Allen show, "Peter Gunn," "Kitten on the Keys." It was terrific.

"America has come up with some fine young pianists and here is another one on his way," exclaimed the host of the show.

Rachel kissed him when he came out of the studio. "You were wonderful. I'm so proud of you."

She had a lot to be thankful for. She had the most beautiful children in the world. They excelled in school, always bringing home honors. Jason won the Spanish medal and the Science Project award, not to mention his accomplishments with his musical talent.

Caryn studied ballet and was outstanding. She always had top grades at school and was given leading parts in school plays. Both she and Jason were always in intellectually gifted classes.

Bob could not be at the performances. He was working at the caterer's and there were important weddings taking place. He couldn't disappoint them or perhaps they wouldn't use him anymore, and Bob needed to earn the extra money. Jason said he understood. Rachel had them make a record of the programs so that she could play them for Bob and also keep them as remembrances.

CHAPTER 35

Jason graduated from college earning a Bachelor of Arts Degree. He had majored in Music.

"I'd like to take some time off before I go for my Masters Degree and possibly a PHD."

"What would you do in the meantime?" Rachel asked.

"Play club dates, or 'gigs' as they call them; also study with a great jazz teacher at Juilliard. I'll make some money. Most classical pianists are starving."

Caryn was taking this all in. She was twelve now and getting more beautiful each day. She was like a curly haired blue-eyed doll. In addition, she acted ladylike and grown up and was extremely intelligent.

She loved her brother and he loved her. One Easter, he brought her a live bunny. He always did nice things for her. He was seven years older than she was, his little sister.

Jason was very much in demand. He was always booked for jobs. He played at weddings and Bar Mitzvahs at first, but then he was engaged to play at nightclubs, hotels, restaurants and private parties. After a while he said, "I can't stand most of these places. In the clubs, they drink and smoke and laugh and talk so loud that they don't even hear what I'm playing. They prostitute my art."

"It must be awful," Caryn sympathized.

"I heard Oscar Peterson play a few times. He's unbelievable. I asked him to recommend his teacher. I want to get into jazz. I love it. And another famous jazz pianist wants to teach me free. I'm going to look into it. Another thing, I've accepted a job with a hotel in the Catskills as a pianist in the band. I'm earning room, board and salary. I'll have good accommodations and will eat with the guests."

For the next four years, Jason played at all the best Catskill hotels. He played for the shows at night, then late into the night at the hotel nightclubs. In the afternoon, he taught music at a high school.

When Rachel, Bob and Caryn visited him he would reserve a table for them near the stage and announce on the microphone, "We have some special guests here tonight, my Mom, Dad and sister. The orchestra is dedicating their first number to them." People would remark that he was too good to be playing there.

"Bob, I feel terrible. I don't think Jason is happy. He doesn't look well. He hasn't found himself."

"You can't do anything about it," Bob answered.

"Maybe you should try to talk with him."

"You know how he is. He likes to work things out himself."

You never knew what Jason would do. "Mom," he told her when he came home to visit, "I got my Master's Degree."

"What, why didn't you tell me you were working on it?"

"I wanted to surprise you. I attended a college up where I was, during the daytime when I wasn't teaching at the high school."

She hugged him tightly. Dad and Caryn will be so glad. We've got to celebrate.

"I'm coming home. I'll get a teaching job and my own apartment." He seemed relieved.

"I hope you're not disappointed, Mom. I know you thought I'd be rich and famous as a performer."

In her heart she was. All the years of sacrifice, all the years of work and practicing and trying, but when she looked at the peace he had finally found, she said to herself, "thank you, God. Bless him and forgive me if I tried to influence him to go into something he didn't want or need; but he was so good at it. Maybe he was trying to please me. He could have made it "big" but he did make it big. He found peace. "What could be bigger than that?" she consoled herself.

Rachel, on the other hand, could never forget her dreams. Many times at night, when she couldn't sleep, she thought about life, people and things. Sometimes she would write these thoughts down to perhaps be used in her future songs or a novel.

When she wanted to share thoughts with Bob, he had no comments. Yet, he was always there for her and the children. He insisted on doing all the food shopping. He carried his efficiency home. There was never any item lacking, including light bulbs, toilet paper and anything else that was needed. He was the most reliable garbage taker outer that ever existed.

They had been married twenty-five years. It was their silver wedding anniversary. Debbie and Paul made a beautiful surprise party for them at their home. Rachel was flattered by the fact that Bob came home on their anniversary wearing a gold wedding band. He hadn't told her anything about it. After twenty-five years of marriage, she thought. I'll bet some husbands harbor secret thoughts of hiding their wedding bands. In addition, he gave her a lovely wedding band with small diamond chips and rubies. When they were married, she had picked up a thin gold wedding band for five dollars and when she lost it while in the Army Camp in Missouri, she felt terrible.

How could Kenny compare with this long-term relationship between Bob and herself? Their years together had proven their love, their loyalty and devotion. Yet, she could never stop wondering about Kenny, whether indeed he was still alive. She had told Bob all about it and he made nothing of it, not so much as a comment. The dreams about Kenny's mother saying, "What did you do to my son?" skimmed off him like water off a duck's back. She knew he trusted her implicitly, that she would never betray him.

"I've been promoted to Office Services Manager," Bob informed her. She was elated. "How wonderful. You deserve it. Congratulations, and she hugged and kissed him. "Are you getting a raise?"

"Yes, it's about time."

"Caryn and Jason will be happy. They really are crazy about you."

With Bob's salary increase and Rachel's working too, they managed to buy a home. It was a glorious thing, the privacy, the space. Jason had come back from the Catskills and he loved the house, but he would be moving out as soon as he got a teaching job. Caryn would be going away to college. That was the irony of it. If only they had grown up in a house like this instead of a crowded apartment.

Soon Jason got a teaching job and found his own apartment and
Caryn was away at college. "The empty nest syndrome," hit
Rachel and Bob but they felt it was best for their children, who
would learn how to function by themselves in the world. They
were adults now.

It was Spring. A soft breeze blew and the air was swathed in the
sweetest perfume that wafted from the garden in back of the
house across the front lawn where she stood looking at the assorted
colors of tulips, the purple and pink azaleas, the lush green lawn
and hedges. "All this just for the two of us. I wish Caryn and
Jason were here to share it with us," she thought regretfully.

Bob called from the open window, "I made the salad."

"Thanks, I'll be right in to make the rest of the dinner."

The phone rang just as she stepped inside the door. It was Monroe.
He was extremely agitated. "Blanche left me. She's in Florida
and wants a divorce."

"What happened?"

"After thirty-two years, supporting her and raising two children,
she sneaks out on me."

"How awful. If there's anything we can do, let us know," she
said, as she tried to console her brother.

This would be his finishing touch, Rachel knew. Monroe had been
a good husband and father. He had met Blanche and married her
within a few weeks, "love at first sight." She never had to work a day
in all the thirty-two years they were married. They had one thing in
common, they loved their children and would do anything for them.
Who but they could know about the rest? Why?

Bob tried to change the subject. "Your retirement dinner is less than a week away, Rachel. Let's get there early for the occasion." That was Bob, always early, always efficient, but too anxious, Rachel thought.

About seventy-five of Rachel's colleagues, also Bob, Caryn, Jason and a few close relatives and friends, came to her retirement party.

Rachel felt very honored by the wonderful tribute paid her. The speeches, the excellent menu, the smiling faces of those who attended, were all so gratifying to her. Now she would have a new life. She looked forward to it. She would do community work and help those less fortunate than she was, and of course she would finally write that book. No rocking chair for her.

She did not waste time. In a matter of weeks, she joined the National Council of Jewish Women. They needed a Bulletin Editor and she accepted the position. She enlarged the Bulletin and with her experience of interviewing people for her column in "Orchestra World" magazine, she interviewed outstanding NCJW Executive Board members in their homes and wrote about them in the Bulletin. She was Bulletin Editor for two years and the reaction was inspiring.

"We love to read what you write."

In addition to being Editor, she was Publicity Chairman and committee member of many community projects. "It is better to give than receive" was so true. It was gratifying to serve on the Executive Board.

She wanted Bob to retire, but he kept putting it off. His years of working were so ingrained that he was afraid to leave. He had finally had a series of promotions and at present he was Property Management Director for the entire eastern territory.

Reluctantly, he retired. After his wonderful retirement dinner, he proudly wore the solid gold engraved wrist watch they had given him. The trouble was that he was not just admiring the watch; he was watching the hours slip away each time he looked at it. Rachel could see how restless he was and she knew he was not happy.

It was no surprise to her when he started reading the want ads. "Maybe I can get a part-time job," he would say. He became irritable, saying he never should have retired and blamed Rachel for urging him to do so.

"Most seventy-seven year old men are happy if they can afford to retire. Look at Debbie and Paul. He's ten years younger than you are. He's happy to be retired. He and Debbie play Bridge with friends, go to ceramics classes where they make beautiful ceramic items, to museums, shows, concerts and now they spend their winters in Florida. He even learned how to cook and loves to do most of the cooking."

"That's Paul. Everyone's different."

"We worked hard and now we ought to relax and enjoy the fruits of our labor. You're your own boss. You can sleep later."

He cut her off. "I don't like to sleep later. Work is the best thing for anyone. It keeps you young." He was getting angry. "Don't tell me what to do."

She was afraid of the future. Bob's brother was eighty-three and still working "Best thing in the world," he would say to Bob and Bob would agree. What was there to look forward to? She started to think about Kenny again. He always listened to her and also shared his thoughts with her; he probably would have loved to be retired.

How and where was he? She wished that she could tell him at last that the reason she didn't go to the Seder at his house was because she had nothing to wear. She wouldn't be ashamed to tell him now. She was a mature woman, not a child any more.

What if she called and he was annoyed or what if he had a wife and she answered the phone? Bob knew about Kenny and he wouldn't be angry if she called, but would it hurt him? He never talked about his feelings. So she fought the impulse as she had so many other times.

She had better get started on that book. Everyone expected it of her. She had taken so many writing courses throughout the years and had read so many books and articles about writing, that by now she ought to be able to do it. Surely, she would succeed, yet she was afraid that everyone would ridicule her if she didn't.

The diaries! It would be painful, but she would have to go down to the basement and bring up the metal box in which she had stored them and see if they were still legible. From the age of fifteen to twenty-four, they had been her friends every night as she wrote in secret all the events and yearnings of her heart.

It was both exciting and frightening to go down to the basement and start reading them. She had written them in ink and they were very legible and the pages seemed well preserved, but when she picked them up, they began to fall apart at the edges. She decided to type everything before they fell completely apart and was beyond deciphering. Once that was done, she would begin her book, writing about those years. Then she would go ahead and continue on to the present.

For two years, whenever possible, she typed what was in her diaries. Reliving the past was very painful. She wondered more than ever about what had happened to everyone and among others, she tried to locate the "Merry Girls." The only one she could find was Dottie. Dottie and her husband, Eddie, had visited her ten years previously, right before they moved to Florida. Fanny and Sammy were supposed to come for dinner that night too, but at the last minute their son came in from college unexpectedly and they cancelled out. That was the last time she spoke to Fannie.

"Hello, Dottie. You'll never guess who this is. Remember Rachel, the Merry Girls?"

"Oh, I can't believe this. I think of you many times. How are you and your family and everything?"

Dottie remembered everything, the dates, the parties, the time they went to the camp together, the fellows from West Point, etc.

"Do you remember when we were on that vacation together, you got poison ivy and I was afraid I'd catch it because we slept together?" Dottie asked.

Rachel told her about the book she was writing and how she was going through the diaries.

"I even found the pressed corsage Kenny gave me when he took me to my Prom.

"We all thought you would marry him."

"You wouldn't believe all the souvenirs I found between the diary pages: the program from your high school graduation party on the boat, menus from restaurants. The prices are really something, like a whole dinner for fifty cents."

"Fannie and Sammy and some of the others also moved to Florida," Dottie said. "I wanted to find them, but Eddie is in a nursing home with a neurological problem. He's in a wheelchair. I spend most of my days there, so I don't have much time to think about anything else."

"I'm so sorry. I can just see him, young and handsome; so many years have passed."

I heard from Helen a few years ago. She married a fellow named Stanley. He's a high school principal and they have two children and live somewhere in New Jersey," Dottie continued.

"I knew it. She was always into books, just like her father. She liked intellectuals and educated fellows. I'd love to see Helen. We were so close," Rachel responded wistfully.

"I don't know her name by marriage, so I don't know how we could locate her."

They exchanged information about who had died and other things and promised to keep in touch.

Rachel continued typing from the diaries. She came to the day that she met a lovely woman on the subway who had encouraged her to write. She said her daughter was a writer and to tell her that her mother gave you her phone number and knew she would help you. The phone number was there. How could she think of calling? She must be crazy. She dialed the number.

"Paramount Publishing."

"Can I speak with Sylvia Roth?"

"This is Sylvia Roth."

"I don't know how to start. So many years have passed, but I never forgot your mother. I met her when I was a very young woman. She encouraged me to continue writing. She said her daughter was a writer and that if I called her, she knew she would help me. I wrote the phone number in my diary.

"My mother was a wonderful person."

"Is she still alive?"

"No, she's been gone a long time."

"God Bless her soul. I still remember her goodness, her caring for a young girl she didn't even know. I met her as I was going home on the subway, miserable, after a fruitless search for employment. I told her how I had walked my feet off, going to newspapers, advertising companies and what not, to no avail."

"Send me your manuscript after you finish it and I promise to read it." She turned out to be an Editor and said something about her involvement with screen adaptations. "Like mother, like daughter," Rachel thought. "I know she'll help me." When they finally met for lunch, Rachel found her to be more than middle aged. How time had flown.

Now that the diaries were typed out and with the prospect of having the manuscript read, Rachel at last started writing the book. She was at the typewriter every spare moment. Bob was very supportive and queried her from time to time as to what page she was up to. Caryn and Jason were enthusiastic too. Her NCJW sisters asked her how the book was going and wished her good luck asking her to let them know when it would be published so that they could buy a copy.

Bob was getting more and more restless. Retirement was not for him. He went out for coffee and a roll each morning, then went food shopping whether anything was really needed or not, went to the post office to mail things or buy stamps, went to the tailor shop with an item to clean, went, went, went. He went out for the newspaper so that he could search the want ads for a job.

The worse part was his becoming angry, introverted and depressed. She stopped telling him about other men who enjoyed their retirement and instead called some friends who were in business and asked if they could use him in their office. She fantasized about what her life might have been if she had married Kenny. She looked through old photo albums to try to look back into the past. Finally, she could stand it no longer.

Hy was the one who knew about her and Kenny. He had dated Fanny. He had come over after the Seder incident. She had to find out what had happened to Kenny and his family. Berman, she remembered, Hy Berman. Maybe he was still living in Brooklyn. It was luck at first try. It was a common name and might not be him. She felt her face get hot and her heart beating fast as she dialed the number and a man answered.

"Is this Hy Berman?"

"Yes," he said. The voice was somewhat familiar.

"This is going to be strange, but over fifty years ago, I knew a Hy Berman and I found your name in the phone book. Did you have a friend named Kenny way back then?"

"I did. Who are you?"

"Do you remember the girl he dated, Rachel Blickstein?"

"Yes."

"I'm Rachel Blickstein."

"I remember everything, how you broke up and all."

"Do you remember how I was invited to go to his house for a Seder and I called him the last minute and said I couldn't be there? He and his family must have thought I was terrible, but the truth was that we were so poor that I didn't have anything to wear and was ashamed to tell him."

"I remember everything. You wouldn't tell me why either."

She could hardly wait to hear. "We and a few of our friends played cards together until he died thirteen years ago."

"He's dead, he's dead," she sobbed. "Now he'll never know the truth. "Was he married? Was he happy?"

She was shocked when Hy told her, "He was married and divorced three times. You did good not to marry him. Tell me about yourself."

"I married a very fine man. We are very devoted to each other. We have two beautiful children, a son and a daughter. We have a lovely home. Now, tell me about yourself."

"I married someone a few years older than myself. I am seventy-eight years old and my wife is eighty-one. We have one son."

"It is incredible how the years go by. I can see you now at one of our parties, Hy, always the life of the party, telling jokes. You were so happy-go-lucky. You wanted to be a writer too. I still have a manuscript you gave me to read, it was about how to make the world a better place to live in."

"I know you used to write too."

"It's been a lifetime, but I'm finally writing a book. That's why I'm calling, trying to put the pieces together for my book. I can't believe Kenny is dead. What about his parents and his beautiful sister, Dolly, and his brother Sammy's wife, Beattie?"

"Dolly died a year ago. As a matter of fact, Beattie died only a few months ago. His mother and father died many years ago. They're all buried in a cemetery on Long Island."

"Kenny was so sweet and gentle and loved me so much. I can't believe he was divorced three times. Maybe he loved me so much that no one could take my place," she sobbed.

"I know someone who never married after parting from his girlfriend. You did good. You probably would have been a divorcee. "By the way, how is Fanny?" His voice softened. "You know, I liked her very much."

"I'm going to keep trying to locate her. I haven't seen or talked to her in years. You know, she married Sammy, don't you?"

"Yes." There was a pause. "I'll be in touch with you."

"Thank you so much, Hy. You are very kind."

Regardless of what Hy told her about Kenny, she felt lost knowing he was dead. It left a void in her heart that she could not explain.

CHAPTER 36

Rachel lay in bed listening to the beautiful music on the small radio on the night table beside her bed. Songs of unrequited love, in haunting rich tones, were emanating from an electric guitar, violin and piano. A young woman was singing her heart out about her lost love, or was it love? She was just a teenager then and so was Kenny.

Bob's side of the bed was empty. She turned the radio off and looked at the clock on her night table. It was nine a.m., Sunday. She got out of bed, put her slippers and robe on and went downstairs. He heard her coming down the stairs. "Good morning," he called from the kitchen.

"Good morning," she responded, as she went into the kitchen. Bob was drinking prune juice. He was losing his hair and what was left of it was turning gray. He had been so young and handsome when she married him and she had been so pretty. The years had crept up on them, little by little. So much time wasted by the bare necessities of survival.

"One more week to go," Rachel reminded him and we'll be getting remarried at our Golden Wedding Anniversary celebration."

"Fifty years," he exclaimed, "and I still love you, you son of a gun."

"Through thick and thin, we've worked together and there's never been a question of loyalty. God has been good to us, even though we've had to struggle," she said.

She went on. "Leave it to Caryn and Jason. They didn't overlook a thing. The invitations are out of the ordinary, the décor and menu are terrific and almost everyone invited is coming, about seventy-five people. Jason says the orchestra he hired is tops. After all he knows so many musicians and bands."

"By the way, Caryn said everything will be video-taped."

"A real wedding, I'm so excited. We'll walk down the aisle and Rabbi Melman is going to do the ceremony. Can you imagine, our children will be giving us away! Jason is married, so that's okay, but I feel funny about Caryn. We should be giving her away. She's so beautiful and so intelligent with a wonderful career and all and yet with so many boyfriends she's thirty-six and still not married. She loves children. If she waits too long, she won't be able to have any."

"There's nothing you can do about it."

She might as well have talked to the wall, she thought. Yet wasn't it true that there was nothing she could do about it? Caryn was extremely independent. She would finally do the right thing.

The week went by and Rachel and Bob entered the catering hall to celebrate their Golden Wedding Anniversary. Caryn and Jason had picked them up and driven them there. Everything was magnificent. It was truly a glamorous affair, meticulously planned from start to finish. The motif was black and gold. The tablecloths were black with gold satin ribbons adorning them. There were tall slim vases on each table, reaching up almost to the ceiling, each containing white orchids. Place cards, napkins in the dining room and restroom had RKB engraved on them. Matchboxes on the table, containing both matches and after dinner mints, were all shiny black and gold engraved with RKB too.

The food was international, served by chefs in high white caps, Chinese, Italian, American style, unbelievable desserts, a huge wedding cake, a fantastic bar. The greatest joy though was the speeches made by Caryn and Jason extolling their parents' virtues and thanking them for everything, which was mentioned in detail from the time they were born to the present.

As they sat at their table, too thrilled for words, Jason made an announcement. "My mother is a very talented woman, as you will hear when the orchestra plays a medley of all the songs she wrote."

Jason sat down at the piano and joined in with the orchestra. It was too much. This was the pay-off, her children's tribute to her and the man she had married, who was their father. It was worth all the years of sacrifice. And now they were remarried. The last stretch was coming. When Anna and Jake died, at least neither knew of the other's passing. Please, God, keep Bob well. I need him.

Rachel took the bride and groom figurines off the top of the wedding cake to keep forever. The affair was over. The guests said their goodbyes. Rachel and Bob's wedding picture had been placed in the lobby on the table with the place cards for the dinner and Rachel packed it up to bring it home. It was a day never to forget, all videotaped.

Going home in Jason's car, Bob laughed. "Wasn't that something, when the Rabbi put the glass down on the floor and I had to break it, how he said, "How is your foot, Bob?" But I broke the glass in one shot. Not so bad, eh?" The breaking of the glass was a Jewish custom, depicting the destruction of the Temple in Jerusalem, as the Rabbi explained during the ceremony, which was held in a large chapel on the premises, bedecked with dozens of flowers.

"You're okay," Jason beamed. He was driving and he glanced sideways for a second and patted Bob on the arm.

"And how," Caryn echoed. Then as an afterthought, so as not to slight her mother, she added, "And you look so beautiful, Mom; at least ten years younger than you are." "Thank you, dear God," Rachel said silently. Please take care of my dear children."

How many years were left? Months, weeks, days, or less? Every moment would be more precious now. How could Bob want to spend these priceless hours working in some office? They should be doing more important things together. It was no use; she would have to help him, as usual. He had to work in an office. She would try to get him some sort of a job.

The next morning she called a dear friend whom she had already spoken with regarding Bob's desire to be occupied, preferably in an office. Luck was with her. She and her husband ran a rather small funding office, dealing with mortgages. It was about five minutes away by car.

"I was going to call you," she said. The girl who works in the office is in the hospital and won't be back for a couple of months. Bob would have to answer the phone and use the computer. With his experience, it would be easy for him and at least we'll be glad to have someone dependable."

Bob went down there the same day. He phoned and said he had already started working there. When he came home, he was almost his old self again. Rachel pitied him. How could he waste those last precious days?

And what about her? She knew what she had to do. She would try to finish her book as soon as possible. She could use the money to carry out her plans to further her many community projects. There were so many people and causes she could help. The following books would come easy. There was so much material piled up inside her head and cartons of manuscripts she had written and put aside through the years.

CHAPTER 37

The weather was terrible. With the wind chill factor, it had been much below zero for most of the last ten days. Snow and ice kept covering the front steps of the house way down to the curb. The driveway was impassable so the car stood in the garage. It was difficult finding anyone to shovel the snow or apply sodium chloride, or try to chop the ice.

Throughout all this, Bob insisted on going in to the office. He made very little money, yet he called a cab and went despite Rachel's pleadings. "You shouldn't be going out with angina. It's too slippery and you could fall." The radio kept blaring the weather report, but he wouldn't listen. He left saying, "Don't tell me what to do."

She would lie in bed, thankful for the warmth, the opportunity to rest, to read or listen to the television until he called to say that he had arrived safely. During the day, he called her repeatedly, "What are you doing?" Do you need anything from the store?" Rachel could not figure him out. Where were the "Golden Years?"

She had not known the serious side of Hy Berman. He had seemed like a comedian way back then. Now he wrote her about his life, his family, in letters and poems. "You cannot write or call me. My wife doesn't want me to contact you. I don't know why, but I don't want to aggravate her, so it will have to be that way. I will call or write perhaps, but infrequently."

It was good when Hy called or wrote to talk about old ties. He helped her to sort out the past. He sent her pictures of Kenny while he was in the Army. He told her something about Kenny's marriages. Bob spoke with Hy several times and thanked him for his sincerity. It would have been so wonderful if he and his wife could have visited them, but that was impossible because of his wife's stance, foolish as it was. He was a good husband. His wife was in her eighties. Could it be that she was a jealous person, or was she ill or what? He would not say.

While Bob was away during the day, Rachel worked on her book, but found she had to get up often and walk around to try to ease the numbness she was having in her left leg. She went to her internist who sent her to an orthopedist, who sent her to a neurologist. The neurologist said she would have to get an MRI of her thoracic spine. When he got the report, he called her.

"You have a tumor which is compressing the spinal cord, which in turn is causing the numbness."

She was shocked and couldn't believe it.

"What should I do?" she agonized.

"Get it out as soon as possible or you'll be paralyzed."

"Where shall I go?"

"To a neurosurgeon."

She got the pictures and report of the MRI and took them to three prominent neurosurgeons. They all confirmed what the neurologist had said. She decided to go along with Dr. Cantor who was chief of Neurosurgery at one of the best hospitals in New York City. She was surprised to see how young he was, probably in his early forties, but he had already proven himself. His reputation was impeccable and his skill was miraculous. He cared about his patients and treated them as individuals.

Caryn had accompanied her mother when she went to all three neurosurgeons. "I get nervous when I go to doctors," Rachel had told her. "It would be good to have you there with me."

Caryn asked Dr. Cantor the pertinent questions. He was very polite and explicit. He assured them that she would be getting the best care.

"Could she have a private room? My father wants to stay with her and he could sleep over if she had a private room."

"Don't worry, it will be arranged."

"How long will the operation take?"

"About eight hours; that includes preparation for the surgery."

"Do you think I have a chance?" Rachel asked.

It was a stupid question, but he answered with a smile, "You'll be fine." He got up and took her hand in his. "I'll schedule the surgery for two weeks from now. I'll be away for a week. I'm going to Brazil to do some lecturing." He shook Caryn's hand and said, "If you have any questions, be free to call me."

"By the way, how long does it usually take to recuperate from this kind of surgery?" Rachel asked as they were walking out of the office.

"Naturally, every case is different, but I would say about six months."

Rachel knew this was a very serious operation. She would have to psyche herself up to face it. *I can't die. I want to be here when and if Caryn gets married. I want to know my grandchildren. I want to be with Bob. He needs me.*

She walked around the house and prayed to God to spare her. Bob and she had worked so hard to acquire this lovely home. Nothing had come easy. She looked out of the back picture window in the den, at the trees, shrubs, the sky. How could she leave all this? She shuddered at the thought of being buried in a dark and lonely cemetery. In winter the ground would be frozen. In summer the sun would beat down brutally. *Please God,* she prayed, *if I've done anything wrong, it was unintentional. I only want to do good things. Spare me so that I can be even better.*

To lighten the burden of her loved ones, she pretended that she was fine. She bought some nightgowns, two lovely robes, slippers and some makeup to take to the hospital. She made sure that everything was in order, her will, her insurance policy, and paid all the bills.

Despite all the tension, she called the publisher and was lucky that Sylvia Roth was in and spoke with her:

"This is Rachel Kirsten. Do you remember me? I'm the one who . . ."

"Of course, how are you?"

"Something awful has happened. I'm going to the hospital in a couple of days. My leg was numb and they found out that I have a spinal cord tumor. They have to operate and remove it."

"Oh, I'm so sorry to hear that."

"I've written one hundred and seventy-eight pages since I spoke with you. Would it be all right if my daughter brings it over to you tomorrow? I am so anxious to hear your opinion of it."

"That would be fine. Please get well. I wish you luck."

"Could she come after work, about five thirty?"

"I usually leave before that, but I will wait for her."

"Thank you so much. You are so kind, like your mother."

"I hope so. Let me hear how you are."

Caryn took the manuscript there the next day. "I can't believe how sweet and friendly she was. She was so sorry about your going for the operation as if you were an old friend."

"I told you about her mother. It probably means a lot to her that she was following her mother's wishes to help me after so many years. It almost seems unreal. Fifty years ago and I can still see myself on the subway talking to her mother. My memory is uncanny."

"I know, it's amazing."

It was getting close. Soon she would be in the hospital. For the sake of her loved ones, she would have to appear brave and cheerful. She went to the beauty parlor and had her hair done. She urged everyone not to worry that it would soon all be over and they would go out and celebrate.

Bob, Caryn and Jason were there as they wheeled her in the direction of the operating room. Dr. Cantor and the anesthesiologist were there too. She tried to be brave and told them not to worry, that she'd be fine. That was all.

She awoke in the recovery room. Bob, Caryn and Jason took turns coming in for a few minutes each. She was groggy, but lucid, they told her later. They were so proud of her, being in great pain but enduring it stoically.

She was finally out of the recovery room and in her private room, where she remained for eleven days, Bob at her side. How loyal he was. He slept on a cot beside her bed and only went out to eat in the hospital cafeteria or for a short walk to buy something in the vicinity.

She was sorry he had to sleep on the uncomfortable cot and had to be awakened during the night when interns and residents came in to see her. When a nurse was too busy to respond to her call for help, he was there for her.

Dr. Cantor came in every day. "How do you feel?" he asked. "I'm in excruciating pain. It feels like an Indian threw a tomahawk into my upper left back." He laughed. "That's quite a description. You should write a book."

There it was again, I should write a book. Always people saying that. "As a matter of fact, I am writing a book. As soon as I'm able to, I'll finish it. I'll dedicate it to you, I promise, so that your wonderful work can go on. You saved my life. I'll donate the money for a wing to be built, the Cantor Wing for Neurosurgery."

"No, please. But I do wish money could be allocated for neurosurgery research."

"I won't forget."

"About your pain, when I removed the tumor, I had to remove the nerve that was in the tumor as well. That's why you have all that pain. I'll prescribe a more effective pain killer. In due time the pain will subside."

CHAPTER 38

One of the first things Rachel did when she came home from the hospital was to call Susan Roth who was very happy to hear that the operation was successful. She said she liked the way Rachel wrote, but couldn't say any more until she got the rest of the manuscript.

Rachel was unable to write for the next four months because she could only sit up for small periods of time and certainly could not type. It was only now, after five months, that she was starting to have less pain. She was beginning to walk without relying on the cane that the physical therapist at the hospital had given her.

Bob started taking her out, to a restaurant, a department store, the beauty parlor and for short walks. It was wonderful being alive and starting to go out. She cherished everyone and everything even more because she almost had lost it all.

She had received so many flowers, cards and phone calls while at the hospital and after coming home. It made her feel so loved and needed. She started writing again and vowed to repay everyone for their thoughtfulness and kindness if the book was published.

She thought of the time when she had written and directed children's shows in the Catskills so many years ago. If the book ever became a movie, she could assist in directing it, since she had lived it all. "Dreamer," she stopped herself, but she remembered Frank Sinatra as a very young man with a dream, who followed that dream. The scene at the Roseland Ballroom where she met him and how he inspired her came before her eyes. Why was she so haunted by the past?

Again, she thought of Kenny. He died and never knew why she didn't go to the Seder, nor did his mother ever know. Why not forget all this? Why did she even dream about it?

She felt she couldn't have pulled through this terrible time without Bob's loyalty and help, but he was becoming more and more irritable. Well, who wouldn't be, she reasoned; eleven nights and days in the hospital with her and now home most of the time.

They had a part-time nurse's aide for the first two months, but now he had taken over. That wasn't the whole thing. He ached to go back to work in an office again. That had been his life for the last more than fifty years.

She told Bob she would manage and that he should call the office where he had been working to see if he could return. They told him they didn't need anyone else right then. He started looking through the want ads again. He just didn't seem to be interested in much any more. His lack of enthusiasm and communication saddened her.

She kept thinking of the past, her Prom, Kenny, the "Merry Girls." She even remembered the black dress with the net sleeves (to hide her thin arms) that she wore over and over again on dates and the rose colored satin blouse she had loved.

When Bob took her to a department store, she saw a dress like that black one and a blouse just like the one she had loved and she almost bought them. She pictured herself back again in Brooklyn in the precious days of her youth, dancing with a fellow's arm around her waist as he looked admiringly into her eyes.

When she saw a young, pretty girl looking through the racks of clothes, tears came into her eyes. Then she would look at size four or six for Caryn and buy something for her instead. She couldn't wait to see Caryn try it on and see how beautiful she looked. Many times she found herself buying something for Caryn rather than for herself, even though Caryn could well afford to buy things for herself and had closets full of clothes.

It was incredible that so many years had slipped by. Most of the great musicians of the Big Band Era had passed on. Many theatres, hotels and nightclubs were no longer in existence. Most of family and friends were gone, including most of the "Merry Girls," whom she finally tracked down. Brooklyn, although greatly changed, was still there and would remain in her heart forever.

It hurt her to see how Bob had aged. She tried to encourage him to renew his interest in life, people and things. He had been a very handsome young man whom everyone thought looked like Clark Gable, dimples, smile and all. Now he was just a shadow of himself. The only thing that brightened him was reminiscing about his former career.

"Will you help me rewrite my resume?" Bob asked. "Of course," she said, and dropped what she was doing and typed the resume for him. In the meantime, it satisfied him.

"You did a great job, thanks."

It was at times like this that she thought of Kenny and the past, when she was young. Regardless of what Hy had said, she couldn't let go of her beautiful dream. Had she really loved Kenny? Why did it bother her so much? After all, Bob had been her mate all these years.

They had shared so much together. Wasn't he her true love? Was there only one great love in a person's life or could there be other loves equally as great? In the days of her youth, everyone, including the "Merry Girls," used to refer to their love as "the one and only." That was a different era.

Today there were so many divorces and many "relationships." Of course there was this new thing, "Women's Lib." If things didn't suit a woman, it was so much easier to change the situation by switching to another man. After all, today's women were better educated and held high paying jobs and could support themselves. They could be independent.

The phone rang. It was Jason.

"Hello, Mom, how are you?"

"Better."

"That's great."

"Did you teach at school today?"

"Yes. I'm on my way home. You know I finish teaching at three."

"How was it today? The newspapers and radio and TV keep reporting all the violence at the public schools. Your school was mentioned as being one of the worse as far as crime is concerned."

"Everything's fine, Mom. Don't worry so much." He laughed. "Here's a good title for a book, "The Book of Fears." She laughed too. She loved his sense of humor. Once when the family all talked at one time, arguing a point, he had said, "Here's a good way to make some money. We could put up a small booth and call it the "Arguing Booth" and charge fifty cents a couple for admission." It was really funny. Couldn't you just see those angry couples going in there to let off steam and coming out smiling? It wasn't just the idea, but the way he told it that was ridiculously incredible.

Rachel combed her hair and dabbed on a little makeup. She felt awake now that Jason said he'd be over soon for a short visit. She had been sort of droopy, but he always had a positive effect on her. Bob seemed to come alive too. He stood by the window, ready to run to the door when Jason's car pulled into the driveway.

"Hi Mom and Dad," he greeted them, with a hug and kiss for each. Then in his usual way of surprising them, like when he announced that he had earned his M.A. degree, he said, "I told you that I was studying arranging and that I was doing some composing. Well, I've just made a CD. I've included some of the songs you wrote, Mom. The band and vocalist are great, and I'm featured on keyboard."

"How wonderful," Rachel exclaimed almost in disbelief. So he hadn't given up performing after all! His years of work and sacrifice weren't wasted. He played the CD for her. He was more than ever a master of the keyboard.

"Do you know what made me do it?" he asked. "You know I always loved that song you wrote for Dad on your twenty-fifth wedding anniversary, "You're Still My Love." When the guests at your fiftieth Golden Anniversary heard it, they had tears in their eyes. Although you wrote it for Dad, it hits everyone who's been married for all those years. It could even be played at wedding ceremonies. I put that number in the CD and added two more that you wrote."

Then, before he left, he didn't forget to play her favorite, Chopin Prelude in A Major, Opus 28, No. 7. So beautiful, she could cry; so loving and thoughtful for him to remember.

CHAPTER 39

Rachel and Bob entered the cemetery. They were going to visit the graves of Anna, Jake, Danny and Natalie. They drove through the gates, parked on a road near the gravesites and walked uphill on a narrow dirt path between the tombstones. There at the top of the hill were the graves of Rachel's beloved departed members of her family.

In accordance with Jewish custom, Bob said a prayer and placed a small stone on top of each monument, then he stepped a short distance away so that Rachel could stay awhile in privacy. She always spoke to each of the deceased individually as if they could actually hear her. Then she also placed a stone on each tombstone as Bob had done so that if anyone should visit the graves, they would know someone had been there. Her eyes red from crying, she then turned away, walked over to Bob and held on to his arm. They got into the car and were leaving the cemetery when they passed the cemetery office.

"Bob, please wait here a minute. I know you'll think this is ridiculous, but Hy said Kenny and his family are buried in a Long Island cemetery. I want to go into the office and find out if this is the cemetery." Bob knew all about Kenny, the Seder, Hy, the whole thing.

"Okay, if that's what you want. I'll wait."

She ran up the steps to the office and approached the clerk. "Do you have a record of a Kenny Miller being buried here about thirteen years ago?"

The clerk looked through the files. "Yes, I'll give you a cemetery map which will show the location of the plot." She thanked him, went into the car and showed the map to Bob.

"I want to visit their graves," she said tersely. "At last I'll tell Kenny and his mother the secret I've been carrying all these years, that I didn't go to the Seder because I didn't have anything to wear."

"That's a good idea," Bob said. "You've kept this secret in your system too long."

They found Kenny's grave and she felt strange seeing his name on the tombstone. There to the left and slightly in front of his grave was another tall tombstone. Dolly Rubin, evidently her name by marriage, was written on it, and to the right were Kenny's mother and father. Bob had walked enough of a distance away to give Rachel the freedom to vent her emotions, but near enough to be in view in case she needed him.

It was desolate, eerie and hopeless standing there in front of his grave, facing the irrevocable. She broke down and cried, tears streaming down her cheeks as she sobbed bitterly, blurting out, "I'm sorry I couldn't tell you why I didn't go to the Seder. I was ashamed because I had nothing to wear and you thought I did it on purpose. All those years I kept the secret that I couldn't come because I didn't have a dress, coat, shoes or anything, just my winter clothes. I have suffered so much because of how it ended between us. I was young and it would have been the first time your family met me and I wanted to make a nice impression on them." She tried to choke back her tears. "Thank you for making me feel wanted and loved."

Then she moved in front of his mother's tombstone and spoke as she continued to cry. "I am Rachel, Kenny's first girlfriend. I wanted so badly to come to the Seder so many years ago, but I had nothing to wear and I was ashamed to admit it, so I didn't come. I didn't want to hurt your son. He was so good and sweet. I've never forgotten what happened and it's been over fifty years. Please forgive me. It wasn't my fault. I was young and immature and didn't know what to do."

Then she turned and walked quickly away, without looking back. Silently she took Bob's hand and they left. When they got in the car, she whispered, "Thank you, Bob. Now that I've told Kenny and his mother the truth I can have peace."

"I'm glad," he said simply.

She wanted so much to tell Hy what had happened, but she dared not call or write him. I would not be right to ignore his wife's wishes and perhaps cause trouble. She tried to guess why his wife didn't want him to speak with anyone from the past. Perhaps she knew of his feelings for Fannie and she didn't want old feelings to be stirred up again, or was it something else? She would just have to wait until she heard from Hy again.

Sure enough, Hy called a week later. "I've been thinking of you. How have you and your family been?" She told him about her operation, the cemetery, her family and asked about his.

"The years have gone by slowly but surely, Rachel. We're old now, in body if not in mind. Like an old car, we start to break down. I too had an operation recently." He told her about the operation.

Hy continued, "I think of our youth too, but let me tell you, it's no use. I'll quote you from a poem I read: "Why trade today's perfume for a flower that has lost its bloom?"

"You're right, Hy. I'm going to try to spend less time living in the past and pay more attention to the present. I kept my faith in God even though I needed such a serious operation and He pulled me through."

He changed the subject. "By the way, how is your book coming along?"

"I've been working on it again. I'm almost finished."

"You said you'd be writing about Kenny. May I give you my opinion? I've given it much thought and I think I know what's bothering you. I don't think you loved Kenny. You needed the attention he gave you. You didn't even know what love was then. As long as you didn't tell him and his mother the so-called "secret," you could still hold on to your youth. Kenny represented your youth, the high school Prom, the parties, the dancing. It's over now, except for some memories which you can always keep."

Then it all poured out of her, from her heart, her gut. Tearfully, she spoke. "You've helped me so much, Hy. It's true, he was my youth, but my real love is Bob, the father of my children. I know now that real love has to be nurtured by time, by sharing experiences, by helping each other, even forgiving each other. I wrote a poem, "Love Comes Softly." I feel that's the truth."

"You're free now, Rachel; free to love Bob. You can recapture your youth through your children. At the same time, you must go on with your own life in the present. You don't have to fantasize anymore. Now you have a good ending for your book. Please send me a copy if and as soon as it's published."

"I will, I will; you'll be the first one if it's published. Thank you so much for everything. God bless you and your loved ones."

She wrote well into the night and couldn't believe it, but she finished the book. The next day she called Susan Roth.

"This is Rachel Blick."

"I'm glad you called. How are you feeling?"

"Recuperating, but still a little way to go. I called to tell you I finished the book."

"Remarkable. Many people try to write a book but give up."

"Can my daughter bring the manuscript over?"

"Of course, when?"

"How about tomorrow at five o'clock?"

"Very well. I'm glad you're feeling better."

"Thank you so much. I'll wait to hear from you."

Two weeks later, Susan Roth called. "No quarrel about your writing. You write beautifully. You'll have to find an agent. That's the first thing. Keep trying and good luck."

Rachel was determined to see this thing through. She had good reason. She wanted to keep her promise to Dr. Cantor to help support further research in neurosurgery. She wanted to help in the fight against cancer. Also, she would get involved in seeing to it that no poor child would ever know the feeling of hunger as she had. If she were successful, she might be in a position to accomplish these things.

She put a tape into the tape recorder and played the song she had written for Bob on their twenty-fifth wedding anniversary. "You're

Still My Love." As the music played, she went into the bedroom, lifted their wedding picture from the dresser, gazed at it for a few moments, and then pressed it to her heart.

After that, she pulled out a list of current literary agents, went to the phone and started dialing.

GB